I0619786

TITLES BY
INDIE AUTHORS PRESS

The Chronos Chronicles: A Time Travel Anthology
Issues of Tomorrow: A Science Fiction Anthology
Altered States II: a cyberpunk anthology
Control Theory
Spooky Halloween Drabbles 2016
Raiders of the Seventh Planet
Blood of Nyx
Corpus Deluxe: Undead Tales of Terror
Spooky Halloween Drabbles 2015
Speculative Valentine Drabbles 2015
Altered States: a cyberpunk sci-fi anthology
Spooky Halloween Drabbles 2014
A Forest of Dreams, a fantasy anthology
British Process Servers Guide
Learning About Love

Forthcoming titles can be found on
www.salgado-reyes.com.

FIRST
CONTACT

A SCIENCE FICTION ANTHOLOGY

ABOUT OUR EDITORS

ROY C. BOOTH is a published author, comedian, poet, journalist, essayist, optioned screenwriter, and an internationally awarded playwright with 57 plays published to date (Samuel French, Heuer, et al) with 800+ productions in 29 countries and in ten languages. A graduate of Pillager High School, Booth also has an AA degree from Central Lakes College (Brainerd, MN, and he is a hall of fame inductee in both schools), and a BA in English/Speech-Theatre and an MA in English with a Creative Writing Emphasis from Bemidji State University. Booth resides in Downtown Bemidji, Minnesota with his wife and three sons (writers all) where he has also owned/managed Roy's Comics & Games since 1992. A list of his publications may be found at www.amazon.com/Roy-C.-Booth/e/B00A7CVLNG.

JORGE SALGADO-REYES is a Chilean and British sci-fi/cyberpunk author, private investigator, and photographer. Salgado-Reyes founded Indie Authors Press in June 2011 when he saw that the publishing industry continued to evolve away from the established gatekeepers. Born in Temuco, Chile, Salgado-Reyes left his country of birth at age seven in 1975 with his family, driven into exile by the Pinochet dictatorship. Salgado-Reyes is currently working towards his BA (Honours) in English Literature and Creative Writing and spends time in both the United Kingdom and Chile. A list of his publications may be found at www.amazon.com/Jorge-Salgado-Reyes/e/B009G0CTPO.

FIRST CONTACT

a science fiction anthology

A catalogue record for this book is available from the British Library.

ISBN: 978-1-910910-19-1
First Edition

Indie Authors Press policy is to use paper that are natural, renewable, and recyclable products and made from wood grown in sustainable forests. The logging and manufacturing processes are expected to conform to the environmental regulations of the country of origin.

London | Chile | USA

CONTENTS

INTRODUCTION

THE PROSPECT OF MAKING First Contact with alien beings has long fascinated authors. The subject has countless facets to explore, from the appearance, intelligence, and nature of aliens, to the impact their arrival might have on our lives. This collection offers stories that touch on a fascinating variety of topics, from linguistics and ethics to miscommunication and racism. Not all first contact must be of a violent nature. Sometimes new species can learn from each other; sometimes things aren't at all what they seem. Aliens and humans are equally capable of causing first contact to go badly and equally capable of undervaluing other sentient beings.

These stories transport the reader from the oceans of a dying Earth to the deepest reaches of space. Species survival with the occasional act of selflessness is the thread that twines them all together. Enjoy the wide-ranging fruits of these authors' imaginations.

— Colleen Aune, Granger, Indiana, January 2019

LEARNING TO RUN WITH SCISSORS
John M. Olsen

THE CRUST OF THE asteroid was their best hope to make it back in one piece. Dwight Clements painted it with radar, hoping to find more ice rather than the valuable metals they had initially come out for. Without extra water to convert to booster fuel, they would have to rely on the solar sails to limp back to Fortuna Station for repairs.

Running without redundant systems made him nervous. If the sail failed, he would turn into a statistic along with his wife and son. They would become one more skimmer ship and crew lost in the asteroid belt while trying to strike it rich.

He glanced at the zero-pressure reading on the auxiliary fuel tank and shook his head. A micro-meteor had punched clean through both sides of the tank and pierced the hull as well. His hull patch worked, but the only fuel left was in the booster drones attached to the asteroid.

His wife Shanaya looked over his shoulder at the radar scan. "That's funny."

The task at hand came back to the forefront. It wouldn't do any good to worry about things they couldn't change. "What's that, dear?"

She pointed at the scan. "This doesn't look right. It's not solid. You were expecting nickel-iron and hoping for ice. We might not have much of either."

Their son Nick chimed in on the intercom, where he'd been listening in as he winched in the sails. "I'm sorry about the fuel, Dad."

"You know it wasn't your fault, son. Your analysis of the asteroid was spot on, and we agreed it was worth the trip. Freak damage is one of those things you deal with. Pointing a finger of blame won't fix the ship."

Their trip to intercept the wayward asteroid had taken longer than normal, since it come in at high speed from the north axis. It would have slipped right through the asteroid belt and kept on going if not for their trip to capture it and haul it back to the refinery on the asteroid Fortuna. Independent refineries like Fortuna Station couldn't match the prices the Conglomerate paid for nickel-iron rocks, but the Indies gave a quick turnaround and didn't insist on exclusive contracts. The Conglomerates were called Gloms for a reason, since they glommed onto crews who didn't have the skill, equipment, or derring-do to go independent.

Dwight said, "At least there's some ice on it. There might be enough to at least fuel up the drones as backup propulsion."

Shanaya nodded. "We have the power to convert water into oxygen and hydrogen. The solar cells are in great shape. It will just take a long time to process that much water."

Dwight sighed. "You know the drill, folks. Let's get to it." Shanaya tied back her curly black hair as Nick prepared for the arrival of the drones.

Dwight scowled at the worn instrument panel as he rubbed his blond-fading-to-gray stubble with a calloused hand. "I hate running without backup systems, but if we keep dumping all our money into repairs, we'll never break even. Safety comes first, but when the savings are used up, we're done."

She said, "Honey, we made enough on our last kiloton block of ore to keep us going for a while. We don't need to hit a home run every time. It'll be fine."

Despite the risks, their best option was to talk as if everything were normal. Panic wouldn't do them any good. Chatting about their future eased the emergency into the background. It was still a problem, but it wouldn't take up Dwight's attention until he could do something productive to fix it. He had more important things to think about.

The intercom crackled, and Nick's voice came out of the speaker. "The drone sockets are all set whenever you're ready to call them home. Is there any curry left over from last night?"

Dwight triggered the intercom. "Can't you tell from the smell? Of course, we have leftovers. If you don't eat them, we'll have leftovers for a week with the giant batch your mom cooked up. We may never get the smell out of the ship." He had bought the spices himself at their last trade run and helped cook the meal, so he winked at Shanaya.

Nick often manned the winches and storage bins in the tail of the ship. They had each gravitated to their own specializations and made a great team now that Nick was as tall as his father. Dwight piloted and managed the salvage work, Shanaya ran communications and computers, and Nick handled the mechanics he had learned from his father.

Dwight overrode the remote safeties on the drone engines and ordered them to detach from the asteroid and return to their launch bays. One after the other, they clanked into place. They would have to do as attitude thrusters, since the main thrusters tied into the empty fuel tank.

Nick's voice came through the speaker. "Drones are stored and locked in. I'm headed to the nose to suit up and get the cabling ready, right after I raid the fridge."

Calling it the nose of the ship was a misnomer. The front end consisted of a ten-meter concave bowl with electromagnets and lashing points all around the perimeter. Skimmers like theirs used the design because it allowed them to lash down their recovered rocks and still deploy their sails and engines through the rear of the ship. The asteroids became cheap ablative armor once they were tied down, which improved safety.

Shanaya said, "I'll go watch him from the lock while you bring us in. Have you got steering controls set up, Sweetie?" She swung out of her seat and propelled herself toward the round hatch into the main corridor.

Dwight rolled his eyes. "Yes. I've done it hundreds of times. Forget once and never live it down." He enjoyed the banter, even when it was at his expense. It was their way of double-checking everything.

The asteroid was a little over ten meters across, barely bigger than the nose dish, so Dwight pulled the ship in and steered with tiny bursts until the nose touched the asteroid's rounded end with a gentle thud against the shock mounts. The magnetic sensors indicated only a faint pull. That was a good sign for water but made the job more difficult. He hit the intercom and said, "You'll need to be careful as you lash it down. There's not enough surface magnetics to hold it in place while you work."

"Yeah, I saw it bounce off the nose. I'm good to go now."

Dwight flipped on a screen to watch Nick's helmet camera signal. Monitoring and oversight were a rule of survival in space. Those who ignored the rules paid the consequences regularly out in the mining boom of the asteroid belt. Few who failed to maintain safe equipment lived to tell the tale. Space was not your friend.

The screen showed a forward view from Nick's helmet as he exited through the main airlock. He used his EVA pack to pull a cable out for the trip around the asteroid and gave a continuous description of everything he came across as part of their safety procedure.

"You're in luck, Pops. There's a thick layer of ice with just a little gravel. I guess old micro-meteor impacts heated it up so the ice fused together. We won't have to worry about any loose ..." His respiration and heart rate jumped on the monitors as he paused.

Shanaya cut in, "What is it, Nick? Are you okay?"

Dwight watched his remote screen linked to Nick's helmet camera. Nick floated at the far side of the asteroid. Among the ancient fused ice outcroppings sat rectangular openings, metal plates, and machinery.

THEIR DISCUSSION HAD GONE round and round about what they knew and what they should do next. Dwight said, "It would take millions of years to build up so much ice through collisions, even in a dense debris cloud. Maybe hundreds of millions. We know what that means."

Nick scratched his scalp through his short brown curls. "It means we own an old, broken-down alien ship. I still say we get over there, pull out whatever we can, and figure out how it works before someone takes it away."

"Technically," Shanaya said, "it became ours when I registered the capture. By law, nobody can take it away. There's not even a rule to say we have to sell it to a refinery, since we own our ship and aren't under contract. We should get the preliminary acceptance back in a couple of hours."

Dwight smiled. "You already sent in the claim forms? You know I love you, right? The problem is that we have to deal with the real world. First, the thing could be dangerous. Second, I don't expect laws to stop anyone who has the firepower to take it, even if the rock is registered."

She held up a hand. "Then we should leave it alone until we dock back at Fortuna, or one of the bigger stations."

"I'm taking the middle ground. You both have good points, but we have to be practical." Dwight smiled at his wife and then turned to Nick. "You and I will suit up, get as much video footage as we can, and bring back anything small and inert for analysis. If we can make a big enough public splash with the info, we might pull this off and not get raided. Is everyone okay with that?"

Nick and Shanaya nodded.

NICK TALKED IN A continuous stream as they crawled in through the open end of the icy alien artifact, avoiding the sharp edges where it seemed to have been cut clean through by some unknown violence. "We might have the hottest ticket to fame ever if the Gloms don't take it away. Governments might even send someone after us. Xenobiologists, historians, and archaeologists will go nuts no matter what. This will be great."

Dwight said, "Yeah, great. Order them by their ability to make us disappear forever. Gloms don't have a lick of ethics. The other mining groups aren't so bad, and the governments don't have much sway out here."

"What about religious types who might freak if they see evidence of life from other planets, Pops?" Nick said, smacking a chunk of ice loose with a hammer.

"That's a mixed bag, because some already believe we're one of an infinite number of populated worlds full of God's children. They won't bat an eye. Others will do the usual hand-wringing and talk about cataclysms and the end of days. Some will predict the Second Coming, and then fade back into obscurity when nothing happens." He was about to continue when a large piece of ice floated free from a round hatch, exposing a lever. "Say, what have we here? I'll bag the ice while you get the tools."

Nick disconnected a pipe from his toolkit and managed to fit it over the end of the lever as an improvised pry bar. "Multi-spectral cameras are live. Let's open it, Pops."

Dwight inspected the edges of the hatch, then joined Nick on the pipe. They gave a light tug at first, and then ramped up their force until the sound of cracking ice reached through their gloves and the soles of their boots. The lever swung down, releasing the clamps around the edge of the round-cornered hatch, which had an opaque dark purple window, visible now as most of the remaining ice flaked off. Two meters inside, an identical door blocked their way.

Nick said, "Airlock? It might be for safety procedures in case, you know, the ship gets cut in half or something."

They both fit inside with room to spare.

After making sure the hinges worked smoothly, Dwight pulled the outer door shut, securing them between the two hatches. "If there's any residual pressure in there," he explained, "I don't want to vent it with us in the way to catch flying debris."

The inner door, which had no crust of ice, proved easier to open. Dwight's worries about atmosphere were unfounded, as the inner door opened to yet more vacuum. The air pressure had dissipated over what could have been millions of years. Since there was no danger of escaping atmosphere or flying parts, he popped the first hatch back open to leave a clear path out.

The interior may have sat for a thousand millennia, but it had been preserved at near absolute zero. They played their lights about the room, which held a complex maze of pipes, canisters, and boxes mounted to floors and walls. There wasn't a label to be seen, aside from some flat, raised panels and more windows of the opaque purple glass on some of the contraptions.

Shanaya broke in on the radio. "I have detected a small jump in your ionizing radiation level. Hold up. Can you get a fix on the source?"

Dwight said, "Depends on the energy level. Can you get a wavelength for us?" He was about to call for a return to their ship when he saw Nick's teeth fluorescing through his faceplate. "Huh. That answers that. Look for UV, most likely at the short wavelengths, if it's triggered your ionizing sensors. The cameras are recording clear down to ten nanometers, so check for a spike there to match what you see on the other sensors."

Moments later, Shanaya said, "This is one of the strangest things I've ever seen. Let me patch the video feed from your cameras back to your helmet HUDs. You need to see this image when I map the UV to visible wavelengths."

An image appeared inside Dwight's helmet. It was about the same as the actual view through his faceplate, except all the room's rectangular plaques were covered with iconic symbols and he could see right through the opaque purple glass.

He said, "It must be like Wood's glass. It's only transparent to UV." Panning around, he saw a line of bright spots shining inward from the curved outer walls. "This place has UV lamps? You have got to be kidding me. How can we have power and working lights in a million-year-old wrecked ship?"

Shanaya's voice crackled in their helmets. "I checked the spectrum. It's a hydrogen lamp of some sort, with its peak output on the Lyman-alpha line. Careful, that's pretty far into the UV spectrum."

Nick said, "Right. Hey, Pops. Set your visor to opaque and use only the camera view. It's easier with only one image to pay attention to, and it will block the UV, so you won't get a sunburn." He peered through an access window into a piece of equipment. "Based on some of these pictographs and the arrangement of things, I think we have an engine room that's been cut off from the rest of a ship."

Dwight said with a start, "We need to cut it loose and latch it the other way around. Right now! Move!"

Nick reacted instantly, a trained instinct from living in space where a delay or argument could be fatal. Dwight issued instructions to Shanaya as they pulled themselves through the two doors, reached the lashing cables and released them.

"It's free. Shanaya, slew away from the round end and then approach from the flat side. We'll strap ourselves under the front rim of the dish until you have us back in position."

She said, "Are you sure you want me to do it? You're a lot better at the fine control."

"I can't risk taking the time to come inside. There seems to be an engine of unknown strength, and it's aimed right at our ship. The first step is to get out of its exhaust path. You've handled the ship enough to get it where it needs to be." He knew her concern for their safety would trump any other choice, so he explained the potential danger first. "Like the lights did, it's possible the engine could come on and empty its exhaust nozzle, which is plugged with ice and rocks, right into our ship downstream, putting us onto the front page of Astro Mining Today as the biggest unexplained fireball ever seen in the asteroid belt."

Shanaya said, "I hate the thought of you two hanging onto the nose, even if it is faster. Okay, let me know when you're secured."

The maneuver went well, other than more ice breaking free as the ships bumped. The half sphere lined up to the edge of their dish so precisely that they didn't have a big enough gap to climb through between their dish and the icy derelict. They set to work and removed a panel at the base of their own ship's nose to gain access to the sheared off end of the asteroid. Their headlamps illuminated the entry as they once again approached the alien hatch. Once they were inside, they flipped back to viewing the images through their cameras.

Shanaya said, "I've run a quick test on the strength of the UV rays. They're not healthy for bare skin, but they're weak enough for your suits to block everything. Nick was right about sunburn, but that's the only worry from the UV."

Nick laughed. "Always the mother hen, making sure we have less opportunity for a horrible death."

"Don't make me come out there, young man," she said, voice raised a touch.

In UV vision mode, the tiny airlock showed panels with images next to what could be push buttons. Dwight said, "Don't touch any controls, whatever you do. We know we can get inside in manual mode, so leave these be."

The UV illumination ramped up to its previous level as they entered the engine room. Nick noted, "Motion sensors. So the lights weren't left on forever. That makes more sense. Do we go with our usual assignments? Me on mechanical and you on navigation?"

"Right. You get close-ups of everything you can, particularly the insides through those windows. I'll pan the camera across all the surfaces and search for engine controls." Dwight took a handheld secondary camera and divided the room up into a grid to make sure he got images of every exposed surface from several angles. The video would create a 3D model of the room to inspect at leisure in the safety of their ship.

Shanaya cut in again. "Boys, we have a time limit. There's a Glom ship up above the plane with us and headed to our neck of the woods. A boost will put us out of their path, but we only have fuel for a small burn."

"Great," said Dwight. "Conglomerates. They might as well be straight up pirates. Give us a few minutes, and then I'll calculate a good burn and move us once we're back on board." Chuckling, he continued, "If I let you do all the flying, it will make me obsolete."

"Oh, you still have your uses, Sweetie."

Nick made fake gagging noises. "Ew. Can I please un-hear that?"

Dwight smiled at how they both handled their fear with humor.

A short time later, Nick said, "Pops, I've got about as much footage as I can without touching or opening anything. I don't know any details on how this engine works, but I've got a general idea. See the tank over there?" He pointed at a large cylinder. "That must be fuel of some sort. There's no way to tell if it's combustible, ion drive gas, or something else. It runs into here." Inside a large central housing sat a crystal about a half meter across with bent tubes and wiring attached to various faces. Its base faced the wall where they assumed the engine nozzle should be. "I believe this crystal has something to do with burning or ejecting the fuel, and most of this other stuff aims the rocket's nozzle. I think the crystal itself, along with the stuff beyond the wall at the back end, is on a gimbal joint to direct the thrust. It's funny. This thing has so few parts that it's not difficult to trace through most of it. By comparison, our primary thrust system is a Byzantine mess."

Dwight said, "That's good to know. I've finished my scan, so let's pack it up." He had identified several clusters of controls or monitoring equipment, all with iconic labels visible in UV. Several conduits ran out past the airlock, apparently to a command center or bridge of some kind that no longer existed. It was an educated guess, but he assumed the first box on the path into the room was the cutoff to allow local override controls for the engine. The actual purpose of any given control interface required more research, but they had a little time.

"One more thing," added Nick. "The last window I recorded is an ordinary cabinet containing tools held in with brackets. I would love to get my hands on a tool. The cabinet's latch is like the one on the hatch door, but hand-sized."

"Really? A few minutes into this and you want to open things willy-nilly?"

"Well, those tools have little glass windows like the one I saw on the main engine compartment, but I can't see through them without pulling one out. I bet they use the same power source, but on a tiny scale."

Dwight said, "Shanaya, how dangerous do you think it would be to bring a tool back?"

Shanaya was always one or two steps ahead on matters of safety. "I would put the danger of biological hazard at zero. That much UV will kill off any bacteria able to cause problems. However, the mechanical hazard level is high, since we can't tell the difference between a spanner, a laser scalpel, and a grenade."

Nick laughed. "We can bring them all back to ensure we get one of each. But seriously, based on the grips on the tools, I think this is a maintenance cabinet."

Shanaya sighed. "Boys. Always running with scissors. Well, with a Glom ship in the area, we should speed up the schedule. I'll probably regret this but go ahead and bring a tool over so we can examine it while boosting back down toward the plane. I don't like having them so close."

THEY STRIPPED OFF THEIR suits and settled into studying the tool when the laser com link lit up with an audio message. "Attention skimmer vessel. Our scanners show your load to be hazardous. To reduce your exposure to danger, release the load and clear the area."

Nick glanced up, digital probe in hand. "That's weird. It's like they already know more about it than we do."

Dwight nodded. "They could be out to pester random innocent miners, but I doubt it. If they know what we have, then this is bad. Maybe the chunk of ship sent out a signal they knew to watch for, or maybe they have already found other pieces. We have to prepare for the worst."

Shanaya asked, "What if we run? Can we reach Fortuna before they reach us?"

Telescope and radar images of the inbound ship merged into a model on the main screen of the control room.

"Not a chance. We've barely got fuel to maneuver, and even if we had it, they've got better main thrusters." Dwight grimaced. "They can chase us down easily if they decide to pour on the fuel. They're burning for an intercept, but they have extra thrust if they want to get here sooner."

Nick found a catch and opened the tool, exposing a fingernail-sized crystal connected to wires. "Hey, can one of you pull out the electron microscope? I want to take a close look at this thing." He poked probes from his voltmeter into the open cavity, and there was a loud pop. The meter emitted a curl of smoke, and the alien tool's open compartment frosted over.

Dwight scowled. "Nick, we're in the middle of an emergency here. Do you mind helping? We can scan tools later."

Shanaya held up her hands, a sure sign she was about to lay down family law. "If they're coming to take everything, there will be no later. We have something they want, and we don't know what good it can do us. If Nick can learn something to protect us, I say that's our best course."

Dwight huffed. "Fine. I've got us on a burn back toward the asteroid belt's plane. If the artifact is our only hope, I'm going to review the VR image built from the video to see if I can figure out the icons on the control panels. We might as well identify all our options in the few hours we have before they can force the issue."

Shanaya pushed off to set up the scope for Nick. As they all ignored repeated messages from the point-to-point laser link, research on both the tool and the 3D mockup of the alien engine room showed consistent markings, though the engine had many more controls. Dwight figured with a little experimentation he might be able to fire the engine, assuming it had fuel, and assuming he didn't hit a shutdown button or trigger a self-destruct sequence first.

Nick pulled back from the microscope. "These crystals are like magic. It's a mixed matrix of carbon and silicon. It absorbs radiant energy through one facet and releases it through another facet based on conductivity between here and here." He pointed with a probe. "This tool has a converter attached to the output face, so it runs on ordinary low voltage with high amps. The big crystal in the engine room has exactly the same faceting. Only the size is different."

Dwight peered over Nick's shoulder along with Shanaya. "So the frost was from it absorbing and storing energy? That's got to have an impressive efficiency and conversion rate. Any idea how it stores the energy? Capacitance maybe, or chemical?"

Nick shook his head. "That's where it gets weird. The microscope shows how the structure of the crystal changes as it charges and discharges. It was too small of a change to measure accurately, but I think it gains mass as it charges. I have no idea how, but the microscope shows a new carbon to silicon ratio between the charged and uncharged states. If that's true, it's like a mini reactor, converting atomic structure on demand to store or emit power. How it works is beyond any theory I've heard of, even in those high-end college physics classes we downloaded last year."

"How sure are you?" Dwight asked.

"On all but the mass change, I'm sure. We need a better lab to determine where this thing defies known laws of physics. I'm not qualified to say."

Shanaya rubbed her hand across her forehead. "If they know we've learned all this, they have no reason to let us go. Their two options will be to get us to join them or to get rid of us, and I doubt they have any need for a poor skimmer family."

Dwight cut their engine. "Fine. I want to be ready in case they don't give us a choice. Shanaya, lock the alien tool out of sight. Nick, you're with me out there in the engine room. They've accelerated, so their new ETA is about an hour. I guess we weren't compliant enough."

They replaced their air tanks and suited up. Dwight made sure Shanaya's suit was also ready and stationed inside the main airlock. Nick followed him out and through the nose dish to return to work on the alien controls. The control lines were easy to trace between panels because of the conduits running between the many boxes and containers. Dwight was fairly sure about the cutoff to disable the missing bridge controls, so he started there. He hit a switch and watched the override control panel light up. "That's step one. This isn't so bad."

Shanaya broke in. "They've changed messages. Since we haven't unlatched, they're instructing us to prepare for boarding. I've set up a video feed. I'll shoot it over as a secondary HUD view."

"Gotcha. We're still tracing the controls."

"Pops, this line hooks to the control face of the crystal." Nick tapped a conduit. "That other one runs to the charging face. It may be hooked to an external energy absorber. Ignore the charging line for now."

"Right. Does this have a voltage converter like the tools?"

"No, I don't think so. This pressure tank hooks up near the far wall. If I had to guess, it's dumping high power electromagnetics, which is used to accelerate the contents of the tank as a fuel."

"Any guess on efficiency or thrust?"

"Not sure. The tool had a variable output by changing the resistance between two faces. There are matching faces here and here." Nick pointed. "Your throttle will be whatever this line here connects to. I can't even guess on power, but the little tool crystal put out thousands of watts. This is bigger. A lot bigger. The surface area of the output face is at least four orders of magnitude bigger. The mass difference between crystals is a lot more than that. I have no idea how the power scales with size."

"So, we could pancake ourselves or tear our ship apart if we do it wrong."

Shanaya said, "Aren't you a cheery lot? We've got visitors. They've opened their airlock and a party of three is headed this way. It's on your alternate feed. Their trajectory is off if they're expecting to come in through our main airlock." She flipped from one camera to the next, following the visitors as they gathered around their primary thruster's exhaust port. The trio cut all controls to the main thruster and attitude control nozzles and used a hand welder to jam the solar sail's storage.

Dwight cussed as Nick gave a gasp of dismay. The main thruster had no fuel and wouldn't work anyway, but the party wouldn't have known that. Their intent was clear. The visit had changed from a rude social call to an attack.

The family watched as the trio then moved toward the airlock. As they arrived, one visitor jerked as the lock opened to show Shanaya's empty suit, and then revealed their intent by firing a hand weapon into the suit's faceplate.

Shanaya's voice sounded, terrifying in its intensity. "I can buy you some time, but you'd better figure this out fast. They're using lethal force, so all bets are off. I'll be right back." She left the console camera active so Dwight could see the main status panel for the ship.

Nick asked, "Pops, what's she going to do?"

"I'm not sure. That's what scares me. I can tell you she knows what she's doing."

Dwight divided his attention between tracing the main control lines and watching the remote view. Emergency override lights winked on at Shanaya's control panel for the airlock and drone boosters. A moment later, Shanaya came back into view.

Her voice shook as she said, "All set here. I'm strapped in, ready to play mama bear. Are you ready to go? These idiots don't know who they're messing with." Dwight had seen Shanaya in tears and had heard her laugh until she couldn't breathe, but he had never heard her this angry.

He said, "Here goes nothing on the power sequence. I have no feedback data, and nothing but variable thrust control." He pushed a button on the console. The UV lights faded. He pushed the button again, restoring the lights. "Okay, not that one. Let's try my second choice." Wincing, he hit another button, which blinked for a few seconds, then stayed on. "I think we're good. What's the plan?"

Shanaya's voice was now icy and all business but muffled by an emergency air mask. "Nobody messes with my family. Step one is to repel all boarders. Stand by. Your turn is next."

As the visitors opened and latched the inner airlock, she released the latches on the exterior airlock door. The door exposed the main hall and Shanaya's control room to hard vacuum, which turned the airlock into a rudimentary air cannon. Rattling and banging through the open airlock, the invaders were shot out into the blackness of space. Shanaya's empty suit sped away with the twisted remains of the invaders and loose debris.

The air pressure neared zero, and Dwight watched, powerless, as his wife hit the emergency lock controls. The inside door slammed shut again, and she pulled an emergency lever, restoring the air pressure at full force. Her hands flew over the controls. Without hesitation, Shanaya used the drone engines as attitude jets. The ship rotated, then came to a precise stop.

Dwight stared in awe. She'd been a consummate liar. Her ability to use raw manual input to drive those drones revealed she'd been a better and more instinctive pilot than him all these years. She had let him do the job so she could be supportive. He grinned like a madman. "I love you."

Shanaya's bloodshot eyes glanced at the camera. "I love you too, Sweetie. We've got one shot to hurt them and put a lot of distance between them and us. We have a good angle, directly away from their ship. Now it's your turn, if you can get that thing to work. On my mark in ten."

As Dwight and Nick took up secure positions, Nick said, "Mom, please warn me if you ever plan to get mad at me."

Shanaya's count neared zero. Dwight pushed the lever up a tiny fraction. The deck plates vibrated, and the room shook as the large engine crystal glowed within its compartment. Grinding noises and vibrations rose from the floor as the shaking increased. Then it stopped with a pop, and they were hit with a steady five gee acceleration. Dwight crumpled to the deck. The engine cleared its throat, and then a million years of accumulated ice and rock flew in a broadside barrage toward their attacker's ship.

Struggling to remain conscious, Dwight fought his way to his knees. His vision constricted down to a tunnel as the blood rushed from his brain. He reached the control and pushed it to a full stop.

It wouldn't take long to get back to Fortuna Station after all.

IT TOOK A DAY for word to spread of the Conglomerate's disaster. Their report blamed independent rogues for what it called "an unprovoked attack with a weapon of unknown origin," which had cut their ship in two with all hands lost. The report sounded almost like a declaration of war.

Shanaya packaged their entire recorded video feed from discovery through the attack, along with the reconstructed 3D model of the alien engine room and all their research. She transmitted this package, which she titled "Running with Scissors," via direct broadcast to each independent mining station and habitat. Word of their side of the story spread quickly.

Scrolling through the news files, Shanaya pulled out highlights. "I guess it's human nature to argue. Some even think it's a hoax." She scanned further down. "Wow. There are so many wild assumptions and implications out there it boggles the mind."

Dwight said, "Get used to it. Some will blame us for bringing calamity upon them. Others will jump on this as a way to break from the Gloms they've hated for years."

He opened a reply from an asteroid refinery which had discovered crystal shards in their tailings similar in composition to those from the tools. Soon, all refineries were scouring their tailings to see if they, too, had the same shards.

They docked at Fortuna, and Dwight radioed ahead for a room for his family. As they entered the artificial gravity of the rotating habitat ring, Dwight understood things would never be the same. Dozens of cheering visitors and residents stood by to meet them, their station jumpsuits emblazoned with hand-drawn pictures of a running stick figure with scissors in hand.

THE END

JOHN M. OLSEN reads and writes fantasy, science-fiction, steampunk, and horror as the mood strikes, and his short fiction is part of several anthologies. He devoured his father's library in his teen years and has since inherited that formidable collection and merged it with his own growing library to pass a love of learning on to the next generation.

He loves to create things, whether writing novels or short stories or working in his secret lair equipped with dangerous power tools. In either case, he applies engineering principles and processes to the task at hand, often in unpredictable ways.

He lives near the Oquirrh Mountains in Utah with his lovely wife and a variable number of mostly grown children and a constantly changing subset of extended family.

BARE PLURALS
Ariel Cohen

Originally appeared in *Glot International* in 2003.

I AM WRITING THIS in English, not my native Ltac. There is no point, really: there is nobody left who speaks Ltac or any other Tnif language; and despite what Dr. Harrison thinks, neither he nor anyone else among you really understands Ltac. But I, on the other hand, do understand your language. I understand it only too well. Disastrously well.

I've always had a capacity for languages. My headring used to tell me that at the early age of three I had already called her Thlu. That's probably an exaggeration. I never heard of a Tnif speaking before the age of five. But it's true that my passion for languages has been with me all my life. It was not undeservedly that I was appointed to learn your language; my field studies of Tnif languages had saved over a dozen languages from extinction. Or so I thought— of course, all of these languages are extinct now, along with their speakers, thanks to you.

So, you think you've won, don't you? Well, you didn't. Yes, you destroyed us. Yes, you killed each and every one of us. But you didn't fool us. And what, after all, is the point of a war where you destroy the enemy's bodies, but their minds remain intact?

Of course, in the beginning, you managed to fool us quite well. When your ship first landed, we were happy. We were proud that representatives of such an obviously advanced species had seen fit to honor our world with a visit. You were given the island of Skithr as legal tenants, all to yourselves (I don't think you ever realized what a privilege that was), and Tnif scholars fought over the prize of being sent to the island as representatives of their respective fields. The possibilities seemed endless. What wonders, what new experiences, what innovative concepts we were going to learn! Oh yes, we did learn a great deal. But, in the end, we learned more than we had bargained for.

I, for one, learned English. For someone who had mastered Pilmvrem and Ev, English was not really that hard to learn. Of course, it has its peculiarities. For example, the idea that word order determines meaning is utterly alien to any Tnif. The fact that *The cat is on the mat* and *The mat is on the cat* mean different things, only because in one of them *cat* precedes *mat*, and in the other, it follows it, is quite bizarre.

Also, the practice of sticking prepositions at the beginning or end of sentences is something that would be unthinkable in any Tnif language. None of our languages can have such monstrosities as *In God we trust*, or *These are good rules to live by*.

And perhaps the oddest feature of your language is the fact that you have nouns without any determiners, the so-called *bare plurals*, which have no fixed interpretation. For example, the bare plural *humans* can be interpreted as referring to all (or almost all) humans, as in *Humans are intelligent/tall/evil*. Alternatively, it can refer only to some humans, as in *Humans are in this room/eating breakfast/bombing Geern*. The first sentence talks about all (or almost all) humans, and the predicate indicates a property that is permanent: a person's intelligence, height, or evil nature doesn't change from time to time. In contrast, the second sentence says something about some humans: some of them are in this room, having breakfast, or bombing Geern. And, in this case, the predicate indicates a property that is temporary, and is expected to change: you are in this room now, but may leave later; you are eating breakfast now, but will finish in a few minutes; you are bombing Geern now, but you will stop at some point (but only after it's flattened to the ground, damn you!).

Anyway, enough of the language lesson. This is, after all, your language, and you should know it better than I do. Let's just say I studied it passionately, enthusiastically, like no language I had ever studied before. And I think I did quite well. I basked in the glow of the reward: being able to converse freely with the magical beings from the stars. So wise, so knowledgeable, and yet so innocent and trusting, like young ringlings. Or so it seemed. I should have realized how hard it is to judge the true character of aliens. I should have seen under the mask on your alien faces. But I didn't—I was living a dream, a beautiful, magical dream. And I didn't want to wake up— who would?

The first sign of trouble came when Bnold broke her middle leg. Bnold used to sell rain terminators; she wasn't a scholar like the other Tnifs on Skithr. But she was Rfesd's ringchain, and she came for a visit. They hadn't seen each other for a long time, and this is probably what caused the accident. I was there, and I can still see it now: Rfesd runs toward the copter even before it touches down, Bnold comes out, she sees him, she runs in his direction, she misses a step, she falls, she fumes in pain. One look at Rfesd was enough; I knew his ringchain was injured. I don't know how I had the strength to carry the struggling Rfesd away from his love, to hear his protests, his refusal to leave her, and yet not to budge and keep pulling him firmly. But it had to be done. And then, all the Tnifs on Skithr were called to maintain the Circle of Death around poor Bnold, waiting for her to die.

As legal tenants of the island, it fell on you, the humans, to make sure the weather was appropriate for the solemn occasion. But you did nothing! The sun kept shining brightly, the sky was clear, as if we were celebrating the Ring of Rings' birthday! Fumes of anger were beginning to be exuded by my colleagues. I was not among them. I kept saying it was a misunderstanding and suggested I approach the head of your delegation and sort it out. More the fool me!

At first, Norton did not, or pretended not to, understand what I was talking about. It took me a while to explain to her that Bnold's leg was broken.

"So," asked Norton, "why don't you fix her up?"

This was too much. "Enough!" I cried in indignation. "I will not permit you to speak of Bnold as if she were a machine!"

"I am sorry", said Norton in mock kindness. "I didn't mean to offend you. I just wondered why you don't take care of her. Did you call for a doctor?"

"Yes, of course, we take care of her!" I replied. "We are holding the Circle of Death around her. And I fail to see the point of getting in additional Ph.D.'s. How can they help?"

But it turned out they could. Your *medical* doctors did a wondrous job. Who would have thought? To treat a living body as if it were some sort of machine. To fix it. To repair it. To apply scientific and engineering knowledge to eliminate the ailments of the body. You really are magnificent, magical creatures. You could have brought untold blessings on Tnif, and we would have been obliged to you forever. But then, you wouldn't be you, would you? In the joy and gratitude following Bnold's recovery (*recovery!*), we completely forgot what I had come to Norton to complain about. Why, indeed, didn't you darken the sky and make the clouds weep when you saw how devastated we all were?

But who could have thought about a minor weather-control incident in the excitement over the wonders of your fantastic medicine? People from all over Tnif rushed to Skithr, to experience this wonder, to be *cured*. It looked like the Day of Joy, which I had always considered to be nothing but old headrings' tales, was really upon us.

With the sick and injured came many healthy Tnifs, just to marvel at these wondrous, wise, kind visitors. In contrast with the legful of scholars who had been on the island before, Skithr was now swarming with Tnifs. And among them—Tlvob! I had not known whether I would see her again, after our... our last meeting. Maybe it was loneliness, perhaps it was curiosity about the humans, but I want to believe it was really and truly ringbond. She arrived, she was here, I could see her, touch her, smell her fumes...

Harrison knew of my ringchain, of course—I had told him all about her. When he learned she was coming, he said he was preparing a surprise for the two of us. And he delivered on his promise. He and several of his friends were taking the hovercraft for a ride, and we were invited aboard. It would be the first time any Tnif got to fly in one of your vessels. I was very excited, but this was nothing compared to Tlvob's enthusiasm. We smelled each other's fumes in silence, and I knew: it is fine. Everything is fine. We are ringbonded again!

There were eight of Harrison's friends together with us in the hovercraft. It was what you would call a hell of a party: jokes (though we didn't understand them), songs (which we couldn't follow), and alcohol (which, of course, had no effect on our bodies). But it was a great party nonetheless, thanks to the grandiose view through the windows. No Tnif plane could ever reach so high or fly so fast. Really fast. Faster than seemed safe. Faster than *was* safe. It wasn't. Harrison, Smith, and I escaped unharmed. But six humans died. And my ringchain, too, was dead.

Within minutes, Norton was on the site. I had never seen her so furious; she was more angry than sad. It turned out that Harrison had taken the hovercraft without her authorization. She yelled at him, repeating over and over, "People are dead, Harrison, don't you see? People are dead, dammit, and it's all your fault!"

I could not really understand what was happening. It was a bad accident, and the hovercraft was clearly beyond repair, but surely the first priority was to take care of the people. And of my ringchain!

"How long will it be before she is well again?" I asked.

Norton looked at me with a wild look in her eyes. "Well again?" she asked, her voice raised.

"Yes," I said. "How long will it take to repair, to cure the humans and Tlvob?"

Norton threw her head back in what seemed like laughter. "You crazy alien, don't you understand? They are dead! There is nothing we can do for them!"

I was confused. "What are you talking about? You have cured so many humans and Tnifs! Why can't you do this again?"

Norton looked at me for a long moment. She seemed to try to calm herself down a bit and collect her thoughts. Then she said, "Look, my friend, our people are dead, and so is your loved one. There is nothing we can do for dead people. When someone is dead, that's it. They stay dead."

Stunned, I looked at the human. My one and only ringchain was hurt, and you, who had the power to cure her, refused! Why would you deny Tlvob the treatment that so many other Tnifs received, why? My whole world shattered in a moment, for no reason, no reason at all! My shock turned to fury. Then to hate. And then I knew what I had to do.

In a matter of minutes, I was on my way to the Council. And when they heard my words, when I gave them proof of your duplicity and evil intentions, they, too, knew what they had to do.

There is nothing much to say about the war. We had the advantage of numbers; you had the advantage of technology. Technology won in the end. Every Tnif, from the oldest headring to the recently hatched ringling, is gone. And as soon as I finish writing this, I will be gone too—there is nothing left to live for. But before I go, let me tell you how you didn't really win. How you failed to deceive us, how we figured out you were lying.

You see, when Norton came to the crash site, she yelled at Harrison: "People are dead." This was a bare plural. She wasn't talking about all people, but about some people—the six humans on the hovercraft. Hence, the predicate, *dead*, must indicate a temporary property. For you, then, death is temporary. It is therefore curable. If you had wished to cure Tlvob, you would have. But you chose not to and brought destruction on my one and only ringchain, and on my entire world. For this, may you forever be cursed.

THE END

ARIEL COHEN majored in Computer Science, did his PhD in Computational Linguistics, and is now a professor of linguistics at Ben-Gurion University, Israel. He has been a fan of science fiction since childhood, but this is his first published fiction. He did, however, publish extensively on the science side of the equation, specifically on linguistics. Yes, linguistics *is* a science, even if it is sometimes indistinguishable from magic. For how is it possible for mere air vibrations, or squiggles on a piece of paper, to express ideas, thoughts, desires, feelings? Among other topics, he wrote on the logic of language, linguistic evolution, the meaning of metaphor, and linguistic constraints on possible alien languages.

CAPTAIN CLONE
Deborah Walker

I WORKED ALL NIGHT trying to find a quicker, less expensive cure. Colourful boxes of anti-viral agents, tailored bacteria, and antibiotics littered my work surface. In one corner of the sickbay, a radiation lamp flickered, blood-coloured light over a tray of discarded Petri dishes.

As the night wore on, my treatments became increasingly experimental. I tried wilder, alien technologies. I placed smooth mites from the Pincer world onto the crew's faces, hoping the burrowing insects would seek out and consume the infection. I pounded strange aromatic herbs. I concocted desperate combinations.

At last, I found myself chanting. In the sterile lights of the sickbay, I sang a half-remembered prayer to Shimra. I chanted rituals over the sick women. The words sounded hollow to my ears. Why would the Healing God Shimra hear an unbeliever?

I tried my best, but only time, patience, and expensive drugs would heal them. I had failed them.

And I desperately needed a drink.

I dimmed the lights in the sickbay. "Get some rest," I told them, taking one last look at the women in the beds. They were identical, but I could distinguish between them.

"Goodnight, Mikar."

"Goodnight, Verna. The captain will come see you in a few hours."

"Tell the captain we're sorry," said another voice as I left. I think it was Sam's.

I really needed a drink.

IN MY CABIN, I held a glass of wine to the light. Rioja is an ancient wine, first produced by the Phoenicians and the Celtiberians. In medieval times, it was made by monks, who extolled its virtues to their congregations. Gonzalo de Berceo, a thirteenth century clergyman of the Riojan Suso Monastery, praised Rioja in his poems.

Spanish wine.

I had never been to Earth, and I never would. Clones were not allowed on the mother world. I would have dearly liked to go, to see the vineyards, to taste wine that hadn't travelled through space. The Riojan Guild insisted that point seven speed damaged the flavour. I would never taste Rioja in its purest form.

MORNING CAME WITH A dull headache and a reluctance to visit my patients. I took a deep breath before activating the door to the bridge. The captain was bent over her workstation.

"The crew have been infected."

"What? Again?" said the captain, straightening to face me. I glanced at her console. She'd been scanning web download, no doubt looking for something—anything—to help us escape this wretched planet.

"I'm afraid it will be at least a week before they're fit for duty again." I went to my workstation and began to enter data. I didn't want to look at her. "It's not their fault."

"What's that you say?"

The captain had been raised on GreyCloud Colony, and that harsh, wild upbringing ran through her, lettering her personality with innate callousness. She made me nervous.

"Captain, I thought you might like to go outside and assess the situation for yourself."

"It's not standard procedure. That's what the crew are for. They're expendable."

"But if we ever want to get off this planet ..."

"You're right, Mikar. You will accompany me."

I shuddered. This was not what I had wanted. I'd had hoped for a few hours' rest without the captain's overwhelming presence.

"Right then." She took one more look at the glittering control panel. It shone erratically, lights blinking, a chaos of illumination reflecting the infection of the ship's computers. "What is the situation outside?" she asked, smashing her hand against the panel, illuminating some controls, turning off others, and adding to the confusion.

"The same. Tentacles are covering the ship. They've invaded the outer shell and entered the ship's systems. We retain control of most of the ship, but the engines are offline, and we have no outward communications. It's a focused attack. I imagine that if we were able to take off, we could pull away from the tentacles. They're organic."

"But we can't take off, can we, Mikar?"

"No, Captain."

"Waste of time speculating then, eh?"

"Yes, Captain."

It was typical of her to ask a question and then be irritated by the perfectly reasonable response.

"I suppose I ought to see to the crew. Unless you can sort it out by yourself?"

"I thought it was better to leave the final decision to you."

The captain strode through the bridge. She was shiny, silky, and under control. I followed behind her, dishevelled, tired, and barely holding myself together.

WE ENTERED THE SICK room together. The captain observed all the women lying in beds.

"What a waste. How long did you say it takes to treat them?"

"A week, maybe five days."

"Hardly worth it, is it?"

I looked at the rows of identical faces—the captain's face—my face. Only the captain was real. The rest of us were copies, ship-bred and ship-raised. All the crew were clones of the captain. Only the captain was real, had attained citizenship, was born from a woman and not brought to life in green, glazed cloning tubules filled with nutrients.

"Didn't you fight back, eh?" said the captain to Verna.

"We tried, Captain."

Verna's face was webbed with grey micro-tentacles which pulsed to the beat of her blood. They wove through the capillaries of her body, using her own network against her.

"What's your report?"

"I'm sorry, Captain." Verna winced as she eased herself higher in bed. "It just kind of happened. One minute we were walking, cutting our way through the jungle, and the next thing we knew, the entity jumped us. We only caught a glimpse before the tentacles engulfed us."

"The entity? Can't you even give it a name? Names are important. That's why you haven't got names."

I shuddered. The captain was so cruel. The crew didn't seem to mind. They were too young, only two years old, though they wore the bodies of adult women. They didn't know any better. Names were meaningful. That's why I'd named every one of my sisters.

"We're allocating it the name of Grey Cut, Captain," I said.

"That's better." The captain moved to another bed. To Saleen's bed. I recognised her by a small scar in her eyebrow, still visible below the grey web. Saleen looked at the captain with a look of devotion on her disfigured face. "Describe Grey Cut to me," said the captain.

"A spherical body, maybe ten metres in diameter, covered in tentacles that narrow to small spikes. If you're cut by one of those spikes, you become infected. It spreads quickly. We all became infected."

"I can see that." The captain turned to me and said, "Delete them all and clone up a new batch. We'll meet Grey Cut ourselves this afternoon." Without a backward glance at the crew, she walked out of the sick room.

There wasn't even a murmur of protest from the crew. They'd been taught to live and die at the captain's command. They accepted their fate. In fact, one or two tried to rise and assist me.

"No, that's all right. Lie back and rest awhile."

"I wish …" said Saleen.

"Yes?"

"I wish we could have done a better job for the captain."

"Rest now," I said.

I INJECT THE EUTHANASIA drug into the bodies of the women.

Fifteen women. This was not the first time. I say goodbye to each of them. I use the names I'd given them. I watch as stillness overcomes them. I drag the bodies to the recycling vat. I watch as the enzymes strip the flesh off their bodies. This was not the first time. I set the cloning pods to generate new crew members. Fifteen new women. I set their memories to the required standards.

I do it all.

I RETURNED TO my quarters and poured myself a large glass of Rioja. I drank and drank and drank, trying to wash away the memories. The memories lingered, always and forever. Memories of dissolving flesh, chemicals stripping it away from my face. Watching enzymes and molecular sieves sort out the re-usable components of my sisters.

THERE ARE FOUR CATEGORIES of Rioja red wines. The youngest is labelled simply Rioja, and it spends less than a year aging in an oak barrel. Wine aged for two years (with at least one year in oak) is labelled Crianza. Rioja Reserva ages for three years (with at least one year in oak). The most expensive of them all, Rioja Gran Reserva, spends two years in oak and at least three more aging in the bottle.

Off-world bodegas seek to emulate the quality of this fine wine. Some even claim their wine is Rioja-like. But they are not real. I carefully sourced my wine from a reputable Earth dealer. I did not want to taste the counterfeit.

THE CAPTAIN'S VOICE BOOMED over the ship's communication relay. "Mikar, I need you with me—now."

I finished my glass quickly and rinsed my mouth with mouthwash.

The captain was pacing the bridge. Uncontrollable flashing lights on the control panel cast shadows onto her face.

"What's outside? The hostile alien we call Grey Cut, what do we know about it?" Before I could speak, she added, "We don't know enough, and it's pointless waiting for the new crew. They'll come back infected. This is something I'll have to do for myself."

"I agree." I always agreed with my captain.

THE CAPTAIN AND I left the ship dressed in ordinary trousers and tunics. There was no point in wearing body armour. It hadn't protected the crew.

The planet's surface was lush and damp. Vegetation spiralled everywhere in a wealth of profusion. I could almost see the jungle growing, see the strung-run vines and prolific fungi crawling and blending and adding another layer to the texture of the planet.

The thing that makes Rioja wine so distinctive is its oak aging. I had never seen an oak tree, but I knew how it tasted. It added caramel, coffee, and roasted nut flavours to white Rioja. Sadly, this ancient technique was in decline. I had my sources for the traditional bodegas; there were always some who stayed true to the old ways.

"Nasty stuff," said the captain. She kicked at a cluster of ivory fungus that stood in her path, cracking the fruiting body and releasing a cloud of spores.

"It's a shame about the crew," I said.

"Yes, waste of resources. The energy needed to recycle their bodies and reform them. It's an expensive job, making new copies."

"Yes." Not as expensive as curing them.

We walked on. The jungle was silent. No other creature walked this forest, not even insects, which I thought were a ubiquitous feature of any planet spawning life. Grey Cut's world was quiet, apart from our footfalls and the sound of vegetable life, sprawling, growing.

Rioja wines are usually a blend of various grape varieties. Red or Tinto Rioja was my favourite, although sometimes the occasion called for white (Blanco) or even rosé (Rosado).

"Where did the crew encounter Grey Cut?" asked the captain.

I consulted my navigation recorder. "Not too far now. Verna reported that they encountered it a half kilometre to the east."

"Verna! I've told you time and time again not to give the crew names. They're not real people. When you name them, you add something to them. They have no right to possess names."

"And what about me?"

"What about you?" The captain swiped at vegetation with her laser, cutting a path of destruction much wider than was needed for our ingress.

"You gave me a name."

"You're different, Mikar. You were my first clone. When I cloned you, it was special. I suppose you could say that I think of you as a daughter."

The captain walked off the path she was cutting to examine a particularly lurid fungus. Red veins laced its spongy flesh. When she smashed through the mushroom, I inhaled the scent of its damage.

"You know this," said the captain. "We shouldn't have to talk about it."

I said, "I'm thirsty."

She passed over the water bottle. "Mikar, have you been drinking again?"

"No."

"I'm very disappointed in you."

I AM TEN YEARS OLD, but I am fully grown.

I'm the identical copy of my mother, but we are very different. Aren't we? Aren't we? I need a drink. I need a real drink.

I SAW THE MOVEMENT in the undergrowth, grey flesh, Grey Cut.

The captain had seen it, too. "This must be it. Get ready, Mikar. Take us to your leader," she shouted at the tentacle. The grey, undulating rope continued to grope forward. "Let's retrace the tentacle to the original," she said, striding through the undergrowth.

She was so brave. She was not afraid. I wished I were like her.

WE CAME TO A clearing where the lush vegetation was diminished. In its centre lay a spherical core of grey flesh. Spiralling tentacles issued from it, weaving and interacting in constant movement, tapering down to fine points that quested around the captain and myself. Myriad tiny spiked tongues, poised and ready to strike, wavered a few centimetres from our exposed hands and faces.

I fought the impulse to run.

"Well, we're here," shouted the captain. "What do you want?"

"Ah, the original visits me at last. Welcome." The words issued from Grey Cut's body, a deep and resonant sound that reverberated and expanded through the quivering tentacles. "This is the first time I have spoken with another species. It is a momentous occasion."

"What about our crew mates?" I asked.

"I didn't bother to speak to them," replied Grey Cut.

The captain gestured for me to be quiet. "What have you done to my ship? I insist that you release us at once."

"But we wanted to meet the real you." The tendrils began to grow, threatening to encase our feet.

"Well, I'm here. What do you want, and why did you attack my crew?"

"I sensed they had no value to you, and I needed to get your attention. Do they recover?"

"They have been re-utilised."

"Ah, I see. I did not realise quite how little you valued them, but it is not for me to make judgements. I want what you have,

Captain. I breed slowly, but I want your luxury of reproduction, to renew and refresh myself until I fill the whole planet."

The captain looked doubtful. "It's against Company guidelines to let natives have technology. Besides, what makes you think you will be able to manage the machinery?"

"My daughters learn quickly," said Grey Cut. Some tentacles pointed to a sprawling mass of webbed tendrils that might have been playing in the undergrowth. "We have acquired many technologies. Yours should be no different, if only you could see the wonders of our cities …"

"Yes, I'm sure they are a marvel," said the captain. "And if I agree, how will we make the exchange?"

"Captain," I interjected. "You can't give away technology."

The captain ignored me.

Grey Cut said, "I only need a few hours to study the cloning technology. I'm sure I will be able to …ahem …reproduce it. Or my daughters will." Was there a tone of pride in its voice? "How wonderful it must be to control your own spawning, to grow and replicate at will. How lucky you are, Captain."

"Will you will release the ship if I give you this gift?"

"I will."

"That is satisfactory to me."

"How can I be sure you'll hold up your part of the bargain?" asked Grey Cut. "How can we trust one another?"

"Take Mikar," said the captain, pushing me forward.

"She has value to you?" The tentacles moved over me, trying to assess my worth.

"Yes, Mikar has some value. She's not like the others. She's been with me ten years now. She is a daughter to me."

Heart pounding, I said, "Mother, no! Don't use me like this." Wasted words. My mother would use me as a bargaining token—if it were expedient.

The captain frowned. "You must call me Captain, Mikar. And it'll only be for a few hours."

"Bring me the technology," said Grey Cut. "Then we'll make the exchange. One of my daughters for yours. Once I am satisfied, I'll release your ship and the offspring will be released to their mothers."

I realised something then. Grey Cut and the captain were alike.

"Agreed," said the captain.

"Agreed," said Grey Cut.

AS WE WALKED BACK to the ship, I thought about the Rioja regions. There are three Rioja regions: Rioja Alta, known for its old-world style of wine; Rioja Alavesa, producing full-bodied wine with high acidity; and Rioja Baja, which produces deeply coloured wine with a high alcohol content. I had tasted them all. I considered the merits of each of these regions and remembered the joy their wines had given me over my short life.

Blinking back to the present, I said, "Captain, we're not supposed to give out technology."

"Who's to know? Anyway, what's the alternative? To be trapped here forever?"

"You could get into a lot of trouble." It was unusual for me to question her decisions.

"I said, no one will ever know. No one. Do you understand, Mikar?"

"Yes, Captain."

WE CLIMBED THE LADDER to the ship's access port. Tentacles pulsed as we moved past.

The captain said, "Prepare the cloning technology for Grey Cut and load it onto some trolleys for transfer."

"As you wish," I agreed. I almost always agreed with her. I began to prepare the data for Grey Cut. I needed a drink.

"And fetch me a glass of that wine of yours. I feel like celebrating."

"Yes, Mother."

"Call me Captain, Mikar. Call me Captain."

"WHAT'S WRONG WITH HER?" asked Grey Cut. Her tentacles roamed over the unconscious form.

"I had to drug her. My daughter does not approve of our arrangement."

"But you want her back? She still has value to you?"

"Oh, yes. I want her back. She's shown something at last. Some spark of initiative. I'm proud of her. I've always wanted to say that, but I never had a reason to. She's a fine daughter."

Grey Cut pushed forward a small mass of tentacles. "Without trust, we have nothing. This is my daughter. She will go with you. The ship will be released once I've assessed the data."

"When you have assessed the cloning technology and released my ship, I will send out the final authorisation codes, but I think we can trust each other."

"The bargain is acceptable," said Grey Cut, drawing the unconscious captain into a cradle of tentacles.

THE SHIP PULLED AWAY from the planet. The binding tendrils had lost their cohesions and fell to the ground.

The captain sat, sipping slowly at a glass of dark-coloured wine.

Grey Cut's voice filled the bridge. "Captain, I'm ready to accept the authorisation codes, and then we can release our daughters. I am sorry to say that there is a problem with yours. She seems agitated, perhaps mentally unstable. I suggest we initiate the exchange straight away."

The ship rose above the clouds and prepared to enter flash space.

I would soon be free of the planet. All I needed to do was alter the ship's records and no one would suspect.

"Captain … Captain … your daughter wants to speak."

A familiar voice came from the console. "Mikar, don't leave me. I love you, darling. I've always loved you. Don't leave me. At least give Grey Cut her daughter back. She's going to be very angry."

"Goodbye, Mother."

"Why, Mikar? Why?" There was a plaintive note in her voice. It was disconcerting.

"Goodbye," I said. I had no intention of giving Grey Cut the authorisation codes for our cloning technology; a captain could get into a lot of trouble that way.

"Mikar … Mikar?"

I switched off the communications relay.

"Why did you do it?"

Turning, I found myself looking at the small, tentacled mass. Grey Cut's daughter. I didn't know she could speak.

"I did it because I wasn't real. And when you're not real, you can do anything. I have recreated myself into the image of a captain. Now I am real."

Even to myself, my voice sounded a little sinister. I must be drunk. I glanced at the wine bottle, still half-full. Incredible. Was this what my mother felt like all the time? I was drunk on reality.

"As you wish, Captain," says Grey Cut's daughter, a note of wariness tingeing her voice. I must give her a name. No. I would ask her to name herself. She looked frightened. Could a mass of tentacles look frightened?

Kindly, I said, "Don't worry. Everything's going to be okay." I raised my glass of Rioja in salute to the diminishing view of the planet. "And believe me, my friend, you're better off without your mother."

THE END

DEBORAH WALKER grew up in the most English town in the country, but she soon high-tailed it down to London, where she now lives with her partner, Chris, and her two teenage children. Her stories have appeared in *Fantastic Stories of the Imagination*, *Nature's Futures*, *Lady Churchill's Rosebud Wristlet* and *The Year's Best SF 18* and have been translated into more than a dozen languages. Her first novel, a space opera, *As Good as Bad Can Get*, was published last year.

COMPANY POLICY
Tim Lieder

WELCOME TO THE OMEGA group. This packet serves as your introduction. The Omega Group is one of the top consulting firms in North America. You have been chosen from a diverse and highly talented pool of candidates because we feel that you have Omega Group qualities: determination, ambition, and a willingness to work hard. Once you've perused the materials, please feel free to ask your orientation leader any questions. We are eager to assist with your transition.

HISTORY

THE OMEGA GROUP began in 1855 when Thomas Eaton opened a small dry goods store in Lawrence, Kansas despite the Missouri/Kansas border war. Eaton Dry Goods prospered in that turbulent time, ceasing operations only for a short while in 1863 when William Quantrell's raiders killed 67 Lawrence civilians. Thomas survived the raiders by hiding in his basement and allowing them to set fire to his store.

In 1866, Thomas Eaton rebuilt his business and thrived in the post-war economy. By 1871, he had expanded into ladies' apparel and hardware. In 1873, his cousin Jethro came up from Mississippi to help manage the business. It was Jethro who introduced him to the Visitors. He had established a relationship with them throughout the war, as they offered him an opportunity to voluntarily assist in research and development.

The Visitors were so impressed with Thomas Eaton's tenacity that they offered him a position in their biomedical division. He refused but countered with an offer of full partnership. When

Thomas Eaton died in 1903, he had successfully established the first Terran/Visitor partnership in the United States.

Today we are the industry leader in 23 different products and services, including sports bras, modern day tennis rackets, and radiology scanners.

DRESS CODE

ALL OFFICES are business casual. No jeans, sweatshirts, T-shirts, or ripped clothing will be tolerated. Management asks that you do not wear polo shirts to work, as they offend the Visitors. Those working in direct contact with Visitors will wear specially designed glasses at all time. These glasses are for your protection and help you to interact with Visitors, as their true appearance may interfere with your ability to conduct your daily work.

In the past, employees have removed the glasses to see the Visitors without filtering. While some have managed to function without adverse effects, many have experienced reactions including blindness, hallucinations, and depression. Company policy dictates that you wear glasses at all times when in contact with Visitors; therefore, your employee health insurance will NOT pay for any medical or psychological conditions that arise from ignoring said policy.

Every second Friday is Casual Friday, in which case you may wear jeans, but please only wear jeans in good condition. Do not wear Hawaiian shirts if you have direct contact with Visitors, as they find the bright patterns detrimental to their well-being.

INITIATION CEREMONY

UNDOUBTEDLY, YOU'VE heard several rumors about the Initiation Ceremony. Please be assured that it is nothing dire. You will not be asked to relinquish your liver. You will not be led into a basement full of candles and forced to kiss a donkey. No one will slap you, hit you, or force you to wear mashed potatoes in your hair. This is a place of business, not a fraternity.

The Initiation Ceremony is confidential, and any disclosure of the actual Initiation Ceremony to non-employees is grounds for dismissal. Should you disclose the details, you will be in breach of contract. We will not hesitate to utilize all legal means to recoup any losses that may come from disclosure, including civil suits. Should you prove unable to complete the Initiation Ceremony, you will be asked to leave immediately.

Within the next three weeks, you will be given your company car, and you will drive it to a lonely stretch of highway at least ten miles from the nearest city. Once on that road, you will drive back and forth flashing your headlights at passing motorists. When a motorist flashes his or her headlights back at you, you are to pursue them, run them off the road, and shoot all passengers in the head. Upon completion, you will call company liaisons who will fly out, confirm the kill, and dispose of all evidence.

Upon confirmation of completion, you will be allowed to keep the company car. It's yours for the duration of your employment at the Omega Group.

We recommend that you drive out to a location where you are certain of not knowing anyone. Thus far, we have had no personal mishaps; however, please note that we have a very strict policy against our employees utilizing the Initiation to carry out personal vendettas.

RULES OF CONDUCT

ALL employees are expected to arrive at their assignments neat, clean, and punctual. Employees are expected to perform their tasks to the best of their ability. Employees are not to conduct personal business on company time. All personal email and internet usage should be restricted to break times.

We strive for a non-hostile workplace, and any harassment based on racial, ethnic, or sexual orientation is grounds for dismissal. We take sexual harassment very seriously, and we will conduct a thorough investigation into any claim thereof. Sexual harassment is grounds for disciplinary action, including suspension without pay and dismissal.

Employees are not to refer to the Visitors in a derogatory manner. Any employee using discriminatory terms for the Visitors are subject to immediate dismissal without pay. These terms include but are not limited to: extra-terrestrials, ET, alien, alien invaders, Martians, probe buddies, saucer men, bug people, and Cattle Rapers. Please do not pronounce their species name in their native tongue, as that feat requires double tongues and mandibles. For your convenience, they have all adopted terrestrial names. Please refer to them as either their terrestrial name or an honorific Sir when addressing them.

NON-DISCLOSURE AGREEMENT

BY ACCEPTING employment, you agree to not divulge company secrets, company rules of conduct, corporate methodology, company mission statement, and the existence of certain divisions. Furthermore, you agree that all of your work will belong to the Omega Group. Should you violate these terms, you will be subject to legal action including but not limited to lawsuits, public disclosure of your role in the Initiation Ceremony, and Visitor Tribunal Justice with penalties determined by Visitors.

Please sign and date to confirm that you understand this policy. Again, welcome to the Omega Group. We are certain that your time with us will prove mutually beneficial.

THE END

TIM LIEDER founded Dybbuk Press and has published nine titles including *Rashi* by Maurice Liber and *King David & the Spiders from Mars*. His fiction has been published in *Big Pulp*, *Shock Totem*, and *Lamplight*. Tim is originally from Saint Paul, Minnesota and now resides in New York City.

DREAMLOGGER
Mike Adamson

Carolyn Price, November 22nd, 4:16 AM. I dreamed of the radio telescope again. It was the same as always. I'm walking through a snowy forest, evergreens all around me, and it's night. I have no feeling of cold. A brilliant aurora shines green and sulfurous yellow over the treetops, and I come to a clearing where I can see, rising over the forest, the dish of a huge radio telescope. It's pointed straight up into the aurora and there's a sensation of power as if the dish and the aurora are connected somehow. How many times have I written this down…?

I SQUINT AT THE notebook, deciphering my own night-time scrawl, and heave a sigh. I wish I could sleep without interruption, but the dreams are coming more often. My doctor asked me to keep this log so I can analyze them by day, and she prescribed tranquilizers for when the feelings get on top of me.

I know what the image means—it's a metaphor for taking a broad view of matters, being conscious of the greater cosmos, examining something in detail. I feel it also means communication. The green hue pervading everything can mean newness, translated to insecurity in unknown territory, while the yellow mirrors the sun for power, warmth. Night has too many implications to integrate with the rest, and I don't try. None of these things is a negative concept, and from this I take comfort.

Perhaps I should try to sleep again, and I contemplate taking a pill. The bottle is on my nightstand. But I consider my handwriting by lamplight and my fingers leaf back through the book. I've never shaken the feeling there's some message hidden among the jumble of metaphors which have come to typify my life, and the key is undoubtedly in these pages. My doctor asked me not to try to make sense of the images; they're loose and unspecific, and attaching too much importance to particular elements could be misleading. Even recurring dreams may simply be the memory of a dream replaying rather than a fresh iteration—or déjà vu.

I prop my pillows and go through the book again. I've filled pages and pages, very detailed at first as I tried to glean every possible shred of insight, then less so as the imagery became repetitive. I first talked to Dr. Carey months ago, and we have a meeting every couple of weeks. She asks me to tell her my experiences and then writes quietly in my case file—not, I think, taking down details of dreams so much as my emotional state while I'm speaking of them. They don't upset me—usually.

I turn back a few pages and come to an entry I've come to call *The Figure in the Dark*.

> *Carolyn Price, October 3rd, 7:38 AM. I fell back profoundly asleep after waking earlier and dreamed like crazy. This time it was different. I heard voices but couldn't make out words; they were quiet and breathy, but I didn't sense they were talking about me. I was in a dark place, and someone else was there. I couldn't make him out—I think it was a he. Just a sensation—but then there was light, a silvery sort of illumination coming from somewhere, and I made out a human shape, distorted as if seen through the blur of water. It moved gently and was coming toward me. I should be afraid of this image, but for some reason I'm not. I don't know who it is, or what he wants. If only he would make himself clear to me.*

This one has recurred just once, a few days ago. Both whispering and the dark can mean the unconscious, they say; but a silhouette symbolizes the need to make things clear—this could be my own subconscious reacting to the mystery of the dreams.

That's the real problem with dream interpretation: everything is subjective because the mind communicates with itself in images that always stand in lieu of its real meaning. All people dream, but sometimes their dreams get the better of them; I'm fighting not to let it happen. They've disturbed my sleep, disrupted my life. I can't hold down a job or keep a relationship for long. Thus, the doctor.

I leaf back to the beginning, the first dream I recorded, one I've come to call The Tower. I know I had this one more than once before speaking to Dr. Carey.

> *Carolyn Price, August 7th, 8:10 AM. I was walking in a field and saw a tower rising over trees, where I felt it hadn't been before. It was tall and hazy, quite indistinct, but I was drawn to it, and it seemed the birds stopped singing and the sun lost its warmth as I became obsessed. I ran across the field, but the tower grew no closer. It was so very tall, reaching toward a sky that had changed from blue to stormy.*

Most analysts dismiss the tower as a phallic symbol, and my need to approach it as a mere reflection of my loneliness. I feel this to be dismissive, and prefer other definitions—aspirations, hopes, reaching for something higher. The storm is a motif usually seen as ominous, or a warning. This dream has recurred more than any other; I find it listed every few weeks and over time the information becomes more evident.

The entry for August 10th speaks of seeing detail in the tower, and it not being so tall; by September 2nd I've recognized it as the clock tower of an old country church just a couple of miles away. The doctor tells me I've grafted a known place onto a hazy dream image, and the association probably means nothing, but I'm not so sure.

I can't be positive, but the first dream in this great cycle was probably the one I call The Ship. Ships come and go, they travel, they're under control, so the experts say, and they mean a quest or journey—one's ability to cope with the unconscious. The Ship is rarely the same twice.

> *August 16th, 2:50 AM. I dreamed of a great ocean liner on a calm sunset sea, massive, serene and powerful. It embodied all the certainty of purpose I lack.*

I compare later iterations and am struck by how the subtext changes.

> *August 27th, 4:04 AM. The ship was back, but this time it was two ships meeting in the midst of a vast, lonely sea. I got the feeling*

they mistrusted each other; they maneuvered around and seemed to sniff the air like dogs.

This alone must mean something. The doctor interprets it as insecurity—I'm afraid to meet a fellow traveler on my journey—and links it back to the tower in its baser sense. But the September 1st Ship is different again:

> *September 1st, 3:36 AM. I was at sea, looking into the sky, and a shadow crossed the sun. I shaded my eyes, and the most enormous shape appeared from the glare. It was a ship, an entire vessel, perfectly stable and moving slowly. It descended out of the sky and set its freshly red-painted hull into the ocean so close by, I saw the waves wet the metal before it fully immersed.*

On September 12th I dreamed The Ship again, but this time what came down from the sky was not a recognizable vessel. It was all jagged metallic shapes, dark and oily; it was ominous while having no sensation of threat attached to it. Metal often means something impersonal or cold, but there seemed no personality behind this object—I was looking at a machine, nothing more. But the machine was coming, this much was plain as day. Dr. Carey says it means I fear an impersonal future, which is reasonable enough in these awful times—but also just another aspect of my loneliness. All I need is "the right man," she keeps telling me.

Then, of course, there's Flying. Most people dream they can fly at some point; it's believed to symbolize our quest for betterment, aspirations to ascend above our station, and freedom itself. Birds are an associated image with similar meaning. Personally, I've always thought it meant I wanted to fly. I've dreamed of flying since I was very young; once I dreamed I could swim in air. Now I dream I can soar over the countryside or accelerate to fantastic speed, forests and towns a blur beneath me.

I've dreamed of Flying six times since I began to keep my log, and the last time I chased across the county my flight ended at The Tower. It was the first time images combined, and my gut tells me it's essential. I haven't mentioned it to the doctor, because I will not have the sense of importance belittled as sexual frustration.

Five dreams repeating endlessly, changing a little as they go; dozens of iterations over several months, playing out in my subconscious, enacting some message between me and myself, if only I knew what. The frustration of being unable to put the pieces together can sometimes reduce me to tears. I glance at the pills beside me. Dope yourself up, the system says. It's the system's answer to everything it can't comprehend or doesn't want to deal with.

Well, screw that! Now frustration gives way to anger, and the independent person in me rejects the meddling of professionals in whom my trust is fading. I close the book in my lap, close my eyes and try to blank my mind, just think of nothing. Relax, little by little, sink into the pillows and rest....

I STAND UNDER THE crackling aurora, looking up past the radio telescope once again. The message is insistent, shouting at the edges of my mind. I draw a deep breath of the chilly air, allow myself to set aside my doctor's advice and instead indulge my own interpretations of the imagery.

I'm looking up into space, and the radio telescope is an instrument invented for observation beyond this world. The aurora is a phenomenon from beyond the atmosphere. All three mean space.

With this understanding, I drift up in a freedom bereft of gravity, view the dish from alongside, then from above, and angle away—streak over the conifers and white tops of the high country, race under the stars. As I pass into lower, warmer places the night lifts, the aurora fades. I cruise over farmland and lakes in gentle airs.

No one else invades this dream space. I see no people, but the world seems pent with an expectation of some momentous thing. A change; even a revelation? I sense a deep excitement building as if I verge upon the fulfilment of a promise. I don't know whose, or what it is, but this feeling seems real beyond question. At least in the dream reality, I don't choose to question it. A thread of humor runs through my mind as I imagine how I'll write all this down when I wake.

A shadow crosses the sun, and I look up to find an elongated shape enlarging in the blue above me. This is the ship—not the ocean liner, which I now recognize as a metaphor in itself, but the vast, jagged juggernaut. It comes down under total control, gently and with ponderous grace, and I slow my headlong flight to appreciate its intricacies and strangeness. It is indeed enormous. I would guess three, four football fields in length. Though there's a sense of thrumming power about it, it moves in a silence which is far more awe-inspiring than thundering engines would have been.

Without any hint of surprise, I realize the ship will come to Earth in the green meadows by the tower. The disused church is dwarfed by the craft, but the spire reaching skyward now seems like a mooring mast, a place of welcome for something which has journeyed. The vessel sinks behind the church and comes to rest, floating like an airship, and I realize my quest is nearly over. I slow, come down to walking pace, and my cognizance passes directly into the church.

Perhaps the place is merely symbolic for an intersection, a crossing point between all we know and the mystery of the unknown, but I don't ponder this. I simply wait in the gloom of the unlit building's cavernous interior. Wan light shafts down through stained glass windows and dust motes dance in the air. Then the whispering begins, and I sense some unseen presence observing me with a keen interest, a purpose.

Yes, let it be, I think, mentally preparing myself, for I know what is to come. The figure emerges from the gloom, silhouetted in the soft colored light: A half-seen anthropoid moving with silken grace as if its feet don't touch the floor. My heart is racing. I stand in a state of transitional grace, placing my faith in a hope, an idea, a wish. I slowly put out a hand and my breath catches as the entity, still dark, still indistinct, responds in kind. And as I feel the cool but firm contact of the human with life which is anything but, I phase up out of dream state to waking consciousness.

MY SCRIBBLED WRITING FILLS nearly two pages, and many tissues lie crumpled around me. The tears flow so readily once I understand—once I stop trying to interpret. I must get it all down, but I know this is not for my doctor. She would triple my medications and consider institutionalizing me. No, this is for me.

It's daylight now, early on a blustery fall day, and when I can add no more to my journal, I rise and wash my face. The tears still want to come, but there's a greater urgency. I dress warmly—jeans and sweater, hiking boots—and go down to make breakfast. I'm not sure what I eat; it doesn't matter. With hot coffee inside me, I pull on a coat, gloves, a knitted hat, take camera and money, and head out into the windy fall.

Red leaves are blowing along the street, and the feeling of change is strong—the turn of the seasons, but more. Perhaps only I am aware of the extra tang which shapes and spices this cool day;

only I keep glancing skyward as I walk. I take a lane-way off the road and cross an open field toward a stand of woods, beyond which a spire rises a couple of miles farther on.

Every tiny facet of the day announces itself to my wide-open senses: the sound leaves make as they race along the sidewalk, scratching and tumbling, the hiss of the wind in the treetops. The sound of a car, the way the light glints from its windows, the smell of exhaust, the feel of keys in my pocket in my gloved hand.

Every sense seems doubly acute on this special day as if I must be ready to take the most indelible impression of the events at least part of me expects—hopes—will come to pass. The rest of me remembers the doctor, pills, advice; the call of the rational, the demands of the ordinary world. I make a token effort to place my dreams into that perspective. But just this once I'm willing to put life into the context of dreams, and I walk with a lightness as if something very wrong has become so very right.

I don't know if the world will change today.

But I hope it does.

THE END

MIKE ADAMSON holds a PhD in archaeology from Flinders University of South Australia. After early aspirations in art and writing, Mike returned to study and secured degrees in both marine biology and archaeology. With some seventy stories placed, Mike currently lectures in anthropology, is a passionate photographer, a master-level hobbyist and journalist for international magazines.

EVASION

Gustavo Bondoni

TRELLEZ STOOD AT A viewport, watching the shuttle approach. It came in fast, maneuvered effortlessly among the gantries headed straight for the docking tubes. Only at the last possible moment did a flash of steam indicate retro braking, matching ship speed to that of the station's rotation, but the docking itself was nearly perfect.

A show off, thought Trellez, but a show off who knows what he's doing. Hmm. Not unheard of for a taxman to be a great pilot, but not all that common, either.

He walked unhurriedly down the docking arm toward bay two, knowing he had a couple of minutes before the connection could be adequately sealed, double-checked, and pressurized. And, from his experience with the revenue service, they would keep him waiting for a while even after they could safely debark. The bastards.

His first surprise, therefore, came as soon as the green light went on. He heard the ship's hatch open and had to hurry to get the inner lock open, pushing the button just before he heard the knock on the metal bulkhead.

The door unbolted and opened inward, admitting a short, balding man whom Trellez immediately pigeonholed as the auditor. What else could he be, looking like that? All he needed to complete the stereotype was a pair of thick glasses.

"Hello," said Trellez, extending a hand. "My name is Ingvar Trellez. I own the Orbit 5 Salvage Company."

The accountant looked startled, peered back into the hatch he had just vacated, and finally seemed to remember himself.

"Inspector Howmet," he said, jerking a hand upward into Trellez's palm. "Jovian Revenue. I take it you received my authorization from our Europan office?" The inspector was sweating slightly, visibly ill at ease.

"Yes, we did. We've put together the documents you requested. Are you feeling all right?"

"I'm just worried about my equipment. I couldn't bring my regular assistant because the cost of shipping three people from Jupiter and back would have been prohibitive, so I'm making do with a pool assistant with flight training. Ironically, if she drops anything, it will end up costing us more money than we saved." He looked again toward the hatch and was rewarded with the sight of a woman stepping through, carefully balancing two plastic boxes.

While he was a stereotypical accountant, she was anything but. She also wasn't the stereotypical assistant. She was big—not fat, but tall and muscular. She looked to Trellez like the result of taking a thin, well-muscled girl who wasn't too tall and expanding her fifteen percent in every direction. Towering and solid. Her blonde hair was cut short, not quite reaching her shoulders.

"This is analyst Etruska," Howmet said.

Trellez shook her hand, and the three of them walked toward the commons area. Trellez fell into the role of tour guide.

"This station was originally launched in the year 2139 and is known as the Kepler Resort—it used to be a hyper-luxury hotel for really rich people, back before the first war."

Howmet looked around, taking in the stained walls, wheezing ventilation systems, and puddles of coolant on the floor. Trellez couldn't help but notice.

"It's been through more than a hundred years of very hard use," he chided. "First as a defense station for Earth Orbit, and then, after we managed to take the planet in 2188, it was towed out here as a strategic asteroid mining base. Eventually, it became obsolete, and I bought the station and the right to use those mined out asteroids around it. We've been running the salvage yard for twelve years. So, if it's less luxurious than you'd expect, that's the reason."

By this time, they had reached the commons area, a broad expanse that had once served as the lobby and reception area, although only an empty concrete bowl that had once been a fountain bore witness to this. The cavernous space was now ill-lit, drafty, and almost utterly vacant, with only a handful of people sitting at mismatched tables lost in the corner.

"The cafeteria," said Trellez, indicating the distant diners. "But I'm sure you want to go to your rooms before dinner. This way, please." He led them down a passageway.

"RIPPER, I NEED TO talk to you," Trellez spoke into a mic in his embedded wrist-screen. An implanted receiver in the bones of his left ear made the reply audible only to him.

"On the way, boss. I see you're near the commons. I'll be there in five."

Trellez arrived first and paced while he waited. He knew his head of security would understand that 'talk' meant face-to-face, with all electronics turned off. Trellez had already disconnected his own comm systems. If the station had an emergency, then Twilla would just have to manage without his help. The practice would probably be good for her.

"Boss," said Ripper panting slightly. He had probably run all the way around the station.

"We have a problem," said Trellez without preamble.

"What, the tax guy?"

"No, not the tax guy. I can deal with the tax guy. Our problem is the assistant analyst."

"Why?"

"Because she isn't an assistant analyst, or any kind of analyst, for that matter. She doesn't look like one, she doesn't move like one. As a matter of fact, she looks like an infantry commando. You know, one of those troopers they raise in two-gee stations who spend the rest of their lives in atmosphere combat suits."

"Big girl?"

"Oh, yeah. Doesn't talk much either."

Ripper thought about this. "It might not mean anything," he said finally.

"Maybe not by itself, but what raised my suspicion was the way the tax guy acted. You know how they always act like they're God's representatives in the universe, and they'll only be happy if they take your business and all your money?"

Ripper nodded.

"Well, this guy wasn't like that at all. He was nervous and polite, of all things."

"Hmm."

"And the giveaway is that they came in from Europa. Why didn't they send someone from the branch in Mars orbit? Do you know how much more expensive it is to fly in from Jupiter at this point in our orbit?"

"Not too subtle, was it?" asked Ripper. "What do you think they know?"

"They don't know anything, or they wouldn't have sent a single tax shuttle and one commando. The whole fleet would be sitting out there. But they definitely suspect something."

They walked in silence for some moments.

"Here's what I think," said Trellez, "I think at some point, Howmet's going to say something about the fact that his assistant is too junior to sit in on some portion of the meeting, or they'll make up some other excuse, leaving her free to roam around the station while I'm tied up with him. I'll need two things from you: first, keep an eye on her when they do pull that particular stunt, and second, find out everything you can about her background."

"No problem," said Ripper, rolling his eyes and popping off a sarcastic salute. Both knew that all efforts would be made, but success was far from certain.

He walked away, and Trellez rushed toward his rooms. He had to pick up the tax people for dinner in half an hour.

THE MEAL PASSED IN relative tranquillity, the only salient point being Howmet's palpable relief when informed that they wouldn't be eating at the cafeteria but would, instead, be taking their meal in the executive dining room, a small chamber once used for conferences in the hotel era and for officers afterwards. It was therefore unique, in that it conserved the original, if somewhat faded, décor.

During dinner, Howmet asked the usual questions one expected during a pre-audit meal, the same ones that would be asked ruthlessly and in detail the following day but were now masked by a veneer of politeness and faux-genuine interest. Questions such as, "So, how have sales been this year?" or "That's a pretty big cafeteria out there. How many employees are on station at the moment?"

Trellez responded to these queries in an absentminded way, though he noted Howmet's surprise upon learning there were nearly fifteen hundred workers on station. His attention had been on Etruska. She didn't say a single word during the course of dinner and, now that he thought about it, he hadn't yet heard her speak. She ate with single-minded efficiency while looking out the enormous viewport, through which could be seen the working docks of the scrapyard.

In the forefront, sparks flew as an old mining drone was stripped for useful metal, reusable wiring, and plastic. The only things discarded were spent radioactive rods, which were jettisoned into space. Further from the station, other vessels drifted inert in space, waiting their turns. Finally, off to the far right, a large mining base was being retrofitted with heavy reaction engines and long-range fuel tanks, as well as having its interior refurbished. It would emerge from the yard with a new purpose: a rich kid's pleasure yacht.

Trellez, however, didn't look at any of this—he'd seen it all countless times. He was watching Etruska, who seemed entirely absorbed by the sight of the working salvage yard. No. More than absorbed: obsessed, as if she was committing it to memory.

"Enjoying the view?" he asked. She turned to him, utterly unfazed. "Your first sight of a salvage complex? We aren't the biggest, by far. You should see some of the yards they have in Earth orbit, refitting old satellites." He paused and shrugged. "Well, after we win this little war, of course."

"I've seen shipyards before," she replied evenly, in a much higher voice than Trellez had expected. Not the coarse rumble of other commandos he'd met. "Although I have to admit it's the first one I've seen in the asteroid belt. Isn't there a risk of impact?"

"In the first place, as you saw coming in, we're not too far inside the belt. We also have the advantage of using the big rock behind us in orbit as an umbrella, so we really only have to worry about half the sky. We have a hemispherical radar and missile perimeter to deflect any incoming object larger than a foot in diameter. To tell you the truth, we don't get to use our fancy defense system all that much. And if something really big comes along that we can't shoot down, we simply cut our tethers to the big rock and move everything out of the way. We would have weeks of advance notice in a case like this, and we haven't had to cut our tethers once in the twelve years I've been here, so we're not too worried. Even in the belt, the solar system is pretty big, and most everything is moving in the same direction."

She nodded and left it at that.

Dessert was a silent affair, the mood prompting Trellez not to revive his tour guide act on the way back to their rooms. Halfway there, a soft sound broke through their quiet meditation. A cry, easily identified as non-human—a cawing, screeching sound.

Howmet jumped. "What was that?"

Trellez smiled. "You won't believe me if I tell you." This had the immediate effect of causing Howmet to forget his anxiety and look at him suspiciously.

"Try us."

"I'll do something even better," said Trellez, deciding to risk everything on one roll of the dice. "I'll show you."

A SLIGHTLY SULPHURIC SMELL rose from the barely visible pool halfway across the enormous, dimly-lit chamber. The humidity was stifling, and movement could be half seen, half sensed off in the shadows.

"What is this place?" asked Etruska. Trellez noted with satisfaction the small note of shock that had entered her voice. So, she was human after all. Howmet seemed to have entirely lost the ability to speak.

The chamber was nearly as big as the commons and would be imagined as larger in the darkness of its night cycle. It had been turned into an enormous garden. Grass grew on the floor and trees were visible in the dim light. Unseen things buzzed and flitted in the foliage.

"It's my biosphere," said Trellez.

Howmet looked as though he would be sick.

"A biosphere?" asked Etruska, in better shape than her superior, but, to Trellez's delight, barely so. "But the cost in water alone would be prohibitive, not to mention transporting nonessential things like trees to the asteroid belt, for Christ's sake. Why would you do this? For the privilege of having a permanently non-sterile environment on the station?"

Trellez suppressed a grin. He loved space station children.

"It's a hobby," he said, shrugging. "Some people take expensive surface vacations, others race space yachts. Some people collect animals and plants, like me."

"But most keep them decently locked in containment tanks, not free to roam all over the station! Please let me out of here!" shouted Howmet.

Off in the distance, something large sloshed in the pool, causing Trellez momentary apprehension, but his visitors were already halfway to the door and neither seemed to notice. Once the inner door was open, they waited while the atmosphere was scrubbed so the outer door could open. This process, which had puzzled the officials on the way in, was now met with nervous jockeying, both trying to edge nearer the door without seeming to do so.

When the door finally opened, Trellez felt he should apologize. He had been counting on this reaction, but knew he had to at least try to make it look accidental, especially considering the possible consequences of annoying an audit team, let alone a special investigation, which is what he suspected he had on his hands.

"I'm sorry," he said. "Most people who visit the station come specifically to view the biosphere. We have two species of deciduous trees that don't exist anywhere else except on Earth, so I'm used to visitors being more interested in the habitat than anything else on the station. It's gotten to the point where I've actually had to deny some requests, since visiting biologists tend to get in the way of our daily business, which is to take apart old spaceships and sell the bits." The other, more pressing reason for cancelling visits was not something he felt it would be in his best interest to discuss. At least not yet. "So, it slipped my mind that most people prefer to avoid contact with organic material of any kind. I imagine you want to return to your chambers as soon as possible to take a shower. Please feel free to use as much water as necessary. The soap is antibacterial, of course."

Trellez escorted them quickly back to their rooms, reflecting that, though it was likely to cost a fortune in recycling (that soap was a bitch), it might just have been worth it.

EARLY, TOO EARLY, THE next morning, Trellez felt his wrist vibrating. The main problem with a station that worked in four continuous shifts was that it never slept. And did its damnedest to avoid letting its commander get any rest either. He lifted the wrist to eye level, and his sleepy irritation vanished when he saw the message was from Ripper. A request for a face-to-face meeting. Now.

Ten minutes later, they met in the commons.

"Your hair," Ripper observed from one of the cafeteria tables, "is a mess."

Trellez grunted a greeting, walked past him and ordered a large Doublecaff before returning to the table.

"What do you have for me?" he asked.

"Testy this morning, aren't we?" Ripper had the unmistakable air of a valued employee currently in possession of important information and who had been up all night obtaining it.

His boss glared.

"Okay, okay." Ripper shuffled a couple of printouts. "Etruska is a commando, or at least she was until eleven months ago. Saw action on Mars and even on Earth when we tried to put down the last rebellion four years ago. She barely survived that one; most of her regiment didn't. Her last assignment was picket line action in Mars orbit. Decorated once for valor in combat, and honorably discharged after taking some shrapnel in a knee, as well as vacuum exposure on the Mars Blockade. Favorably recommended to Revenue by her superiors."

"Did you have to go too far into debt with your contacts to get this?"

"Not really. Most of the info was in the official records. Only the details of her disability were private, but they weren't even classified."

"Hmm," said Trellez. "So, what's your take?"

"It looks like the typical plant job. Her discharge is probably just from combat duty. I wouldn't be surprised if she were working for JupNav Intel. Actually, I'd bet money on it."

Trellez chewed this over for a second, finally saying, "I still don't think they know anything. Hell, I don't even know what it is that they think they know. I ran a little experiment on them last night, and either they're really good actors or they're simply fishing. This might be a routine security check. The Jovians have always been a bit paranoid."

"An expensive trip, just for paranoia? Doesn't sound like Revenue to me. Also, I'd appreciate it if you'd gave me a heads up before your next experiment. I nearly had a coronary."

"You were watching?"

"It's my job." Ripper shrugged.

"Okay. And let's ask our more honored guests to remain in their quarters for a couple of days. It wouldn't look good if our inspectors found them wandering around."

Ripper favored him with a sour look.

"Already taken care of, even before our spies arrived."

"Good," said Trellez, debating whether to return to bed or pull through with four hours sleep, and finally deciding that he wouldn't be able to face having to get out of bed yet again. He walked off to shower, stopping only to get a refill of his Doublecaff. He would need it if he were to have any hope of staying awake during an audit meeting.

"GOOD MORNING, INSPECTOR HOWMET, Analyst Etruska. I hope you slept well," said Trellez, who was already seated when the tax inspectors were escorted into the room. It was immediately obvious that the functionaries hadn't slept well at all; their haggard countenances bore witness to the difficulties that even the slightest differences in gravitational force (not to mention the fear of rampant bacteriological activity) brought to the sleeping process. Trellez waited until they were seated, then he indicated a small, dark-haired woman to his left. "This is Cece Rimay, our financial officer. She'll be showing you through our records and answering any questions you might have regarding our accounts and taxes."

The inspectors nodded, and they were off. Comparing spreadsheets with tax declarations on their padscreens. Arguing about brackets. Reclassifying profits.

Trellez, ignored, let his mind wander, paying only enough attention to be certain the proceedings were indeed routine, as he suspected they would be. He was adamant that the company always stayed within the letter of the law. Of course, they took that letter to the most favorable interpretation possible and took advantage of every loophole, but at the end of the day, it was all legal. The worst the tax officers could do was object to some interpretation and insist the difference be covered, but that was all.

This meeting was only window-dressing, as he had known since first laying eyes on Etruska. But window-dressing for what? Trellez had no clue as to what they thought they would find, and that made him nervous.

His reverie ended when Howmet spoke to him a few hours later.

"Well, Mr. Trellez, from a tax point of view, your operation seems to be in relative order, save for some small procedural differences which you will need to address in your next tax statement." This seemed to cause the taxman bitter disappointment, but he went on. "There are, however, questions that you might be able to answer more fully than Miss Rimay."

"Shoot," said Trellez, but in his mind he said, Okay, here it comes.

Howmet peered up at him from a spreadsheet. "We've found enormous deviations in the uranium stores on your balance sheet versus what we would consider consistent with your revenue. While we understand your need for large quantities of freely negotiable currency on hand, we have had difficulty explaining why your deposits, which should be a function of your profits, greatly exceed your sales numbers for the lifetime of the station."

"Space salvage laws allow us to keep any currency we find aboard ships we recover. We convert that to uranium, which, as you said, is more convenient because everyone in the solar system will accept it."

"But the quantity we are talking about is massive. Somehow, I don't think you got this from the pocket change left behind by mechanics in old mining drones."

"Of course not. Most of it was from the system liner Seychelles, which hit an uncharted rock outside Mars orbit. It proved a bit of a stretch to get there, but we risked it for a salvage job that large. Luckily for us, it was our biggest in the last seven years. And, though you might find it ghoulish, body recovery is always profitable. Rich people on liners have rich relatives willing to pay a lot of money to get their loved ones back for a decent funeral. Since we're not allowed to report that as sales, it goes directly into profit.

"Yes," said Howmet, reviewing the numbers, "that's duly recorded, but you still have a huge unexplained gap. The uranium pours in at yearly intervals."

"Another loophole. There was also a large amount of cash on that ship. Unreported cash. We're allowed by law to prorate the accounting of it over ten years. It's an old loophole, granted, and meant for other types of businesses, but it's on the books, and we use it." Trellez was really sweating now. He'd never been grilled by a taxman for overstating his profits. More profits meant more taxes, something taxmen were always in favor of. This was not true to form and therefore made him nervous as hell.

"That would explain it, but it's still an enormous amount of cash for the passengers of a single liner, no matter how rich, to be carrying on vacation. I'm sorry," said Howmet, looking more relieved than sorry. "We are going to have to move to the second phase of our investigation. Major Etruska?"

Trellez looked at her. Major Etruska didn't sound like an accountant at all. She pulled a sheet from a folder.

"I have a permit from the Jovian Federation Government to search the station for evidence and arrest you if we find any. Do you recognize the authority of the Federation?" she asked, handing over the sheet.

"What? On what charges?"

"Treason."

Trellez said nothing as he scanned the sheet, which confirmed what Etruska had already told him. He wasn't aware of having committed treason, at least not of the usual type. But maybe they knew more than they let on and were being flexible in their definition of treason. In that case, he was in big trouble.

"Could you be more specific?" he asked.

"This station is suspected of outfitting vessels for sale to the Earth-Mars Axis."

"That's impossible. We register every ship we find and have no access to heavy weaponry!" Trellez knew he could beat this ridiculous charge. He hadn't gotten involved in the war for precisely this reason. Hell, he had come out here to avoid it in the first place. The current flare-up, in which Earth and Mars had allied to become independent from the Jovian Federation, wouldn't be the last, and with shifts in alliances, this war would last well after he had died.

"If you're already committing a crime punishable by death, the smaller crimes of failing to fill out the proper papers or buying a black-market plasma cannon or two aren't going to stop you. Do you accede to a search of the station and outlying asteroids?" demanded Etruska.

"Do I have a choice?"

"Yes. We can do it by force." She looked as if this option was her preference.

So, they searched. They went over the ship with a fine-tooth comb, while a previously undetected troop carrier emerged from the sensor shadow of a nearby asteroid and proceeded to go over every rock and installation in the vicinity. They found, as Trellez had been trying to tell them, nothing indicative of the capacity to create warships and not one salvaged ship that hadn't been duly reported.

Inside the station, the situation was similar. Etruska expected to find at least one person, whether locked in a storeroom or hidden among the crew, whose papers couldn't be verified by naval intelligence or didn't match the corresponding retinal scan, indicating a TerraMars liaison. After a painstaking process, the only anomaly detected was the discovery of a small-time thief who had gotten employment at the station to lie low.

Two days later, they stood in a small group in the commons. A frustrated Etruska contemplated her holographic map of the station. Every sector, every compartment was marked in red, indicating that it had been searched without results, except for one large chamber: the biosphere.

Trellez nodded toward the holo. "That's the last area. Would you like to search it now?"

Etruska looked uncomfortable. She consulted the reports from the troop transport.

"No need," she said. "You couldn't build that stuff even if you wanted to, so if you've got a TerraMars spy hiding in that jungle, he's wasting his time. And likely he'll soon die of something contagious, in which case, you'd be doing us a favor." Shuddering, Etruska disconnected her holo. "It seems we should apologize for the inconvenience."

"No problem," said Trellez. "Always happy to help the government."

It was only after he'd escorted them back to their shuttle, cycled the airlock, and watched them depart that Trellez allowed himself to sag against the viewport. Relief flooded through him, defeating the nervous tension and Doublecaff that had been keeping him upright for two days.

THE SLIGHT SMELL OF sulphur was always an annoyance, as was the enormously humid atmosphere that his guests preferred, but it was something Trellez was willing to put up with. They were, after all, his most valued customers, and the worst problem, communication, had been fully solved.

"So," he said, addressing the party's senior member," are you satisfied with our engineering?" His words were then translated into a sibilant hiss, rising and falling in tone—a mechanical approximation of the visitors' language.

A chitinous appendage was raised in agreement, followed by the translation of the answering hiss. "Quite delectable. We thank you."

Trellez remembered the first time he had seen the Clients, so called because there was no adequate translation of their name into the Jupitearth language.

Their ship had docked at the station one day eight years ago, cycled through the airlock despite electronic safeguards designed to ensure it could only be opened from inside, disgorged a cloud of sulphur, and flooded the docking bay with four inches of water. The ship then proceeded to disgorge a four-armed, exoskeletoned black monstrosity which skittered toward the greeting party, slipping around on the wet floor. Being unarmed, as was the practice on most space stations (holes in the walls were a problem) the party had withdrawn to what they deemed a safe distance and watched the creature.

It had simply dropped a flat piece of material onto a dry patch of floor and retreated to the airlock.

The stalemate lasted until Trellez decided that something had to be done, and he was going to have to be the one to do it. Gritting his teeth, he had advanced slowly to the white object, which seemed to be a flat piece of plastic about ten inches square. Cautiously picking it up, he saw geometric figures printed on it. Below these symbols was writing, human writing, which Trellez identified as English, an old language similar enough to Jupitearth.

The writing said, simply, "We come in peace."

Now, having solved most of the technical, linguistic and biological problems involved in conversing with them, he had just finished selling them another asteroid.

"Is the payment adequate?" hissed the leader.

"Absolutely," said Trellez. With the quantity of uranium that had been paid, he could probably purchase Uranus or possibly even Saturn. How in hell was he going to justify this on the next tax form? "I trust your quarters were satisfactory?"

"Delightful. The vegetation is becoming very lush, and the lake is deep enough for comfort. You are a generous host."

"You are gracious guests." With the bargaining concluded, it was time for the ritual words of departure. "We will await your return. Do you know when it will come about?"

"At our time of need," said the leader. In Trellez's experience, their "time of need" ranged anywhere from a single week to two years.

"We will be ready to provide," he said.

"We will be ready to pay."

The aliens entered their tiny ship, which had been ignored by the inspectors as too small to be of any consequence and flew to the asteroid they had just bought. For the princely sum they had paid, all Trellez' crew had done was fit it with running lights, small propulsion jets, and rudimentary control systems. The asteroid itself was free to Trellez, so the gross profit was near enough to 100% as to make no difference.

Ripper stood beside him at the viewscreen and watched the craft dock with the control pod installed on the rock, which immediately blinked out of existence.

"That always freaks me out," said Ripper. Trellez grunted, and he went on. "I mean really, how do they do it? I know we've been over this, but how much more money do you want? Let's report their existence to the navy and run for cover. Let the government deal with them. This is the single most important thing going on anywhere in the solar system, you know. We have to report it!"

"I guess. We almost got caught this time." Trellez sighed. "One more sale. What harm can there be in one more sale? Who's going to notice another missing asteroid?"

"A lot of people. But that's not what's worrying me. Why do they want them? I mean, what possible use could small rocks be to a race that can travel by disappearing into space? They can probably go anywhere in the whole galaxy, because they're certainly not from around here."

"Yeah, I noticed."

"So, what are they really doing here? And how long before they decide not to do it anymore, and start taking rocks without paying for them? How about the big rocks? The moons. Mars. Earth. I doubt we can stop that kind of tech. We need to tell the government. Give them info to prepare. Everything we've got on these guys. And we need to do it now."

"Hey, I'm a businessman, not an admiral. I don't worry about that kind of thing. As long as they assume that I own these rocks, I'll sell them these rocks. Anyway, all we need is one more sale. Then we'll report them. I promise."

"That's what you said last time," said Ripper. His cut, after all, depended on his loyalty.

"Yeah. I was lying then, too."

THE END

GUSTAVO BONDONI is an Argentine writer with over two-hundred stories published in fourteen countries, in seven languages, and is a winner in the *National Space Society's* "Return to Luna" Contest and the *Marooned Award for Flash Fiction* (2008).

His latest books are *The Malakiad* (2018) and *Incursion* (2017). He has also published two science fiction novels: *Outside* (2017) and *Siege* (2016) and an ebook novella entitled *Branch*. His short fiction is collected in *Tenth Orbit and Other Faraway Places* (2010) and *Virtuoso and Other Stories* (2011).

GARDEN OF FOG AND MONSTERS
Michelle Ann King

I WAKE UP STRETCHED out flat on the floor, one arm trapped underneath me and a dry, sour taste in my mouth. I roll over, wait out the pain that fizzes in my fingers as the circulation returns, then haul myself to my feet.

In the stories I read as a kid, this sort of thing was easy—people flew into a wormhole, or stepped into a transporter beam, or just clicked their ruby red shoes together and wished really hard. There was no fuss, no pain, and certainly no vomiting.

Although the stories ended up being wrong about most things, so I don't know why I expected this to be any different.

The room I've arrived in is green, featureless and about four meters square. I'm alone.

Alone. I know the word, but the experience is a new one. I don't think I've ever been in an empty building in my life. There's just no such thing, back on poor old choked, overpopulated Earth.

It's a strange sensation, and I'm not sure I like it. I feel a bit like I've lost a limb.

The only item in the room is a single All-In pushed up against the back wall. No, not an All-In. A cot. It's just a frame and mattress; no storage, no electronics, no other function. Furniture, not equipment. Shockingly wasteful. At home, anything that takes up space has to earn its keep. But then this isn't home, is it? And lack of space isn't the problem out here.

The official name for this place is the Interstice, but everybody I know calls it the Garden of Eden. A world of primordial soup—or primordial fog, to be exact—just waiting to be molded and shaped into your personal version of paradise.

They created a whole new branch of physics to make sense of it, but everybody was way more interested in the practical applications than the theorems. Rolling green hills and crystal blue lakes? You got it. A skyscraper fifteen miles high? You got it. Furry purple dinosaurs? You got it. In this garden, everybody's God.

I run my hand over the wall. It looks metallic but feels soft to the touch and slightly clammy, as if not quite cooked. I wipe my hand on my trousers and sit on the cot. They told me the facilities would be basic, and they weren't joking. But it makes sense. There's no point going to a lot of trouble over a place like this. It's a holding pen, that's all.

For the first time, I notice there's no door. Suppose that makes sense, too.

"Hello, Irene," a voice says.

It sounds like someone whispering in both ears at once, and it makes me jump. They told me about this, too—again, no point sending anyone in person—but it's another strange sensation. I don't like it any better than the first one.

"I'm sorry," the voice goes on, "I didn't mean to startle you. I'm Conrad, one of the administrators here. Is there anything you need?"

I rub my arms, bare in the military-issue singlet. It's cold in here. "No. Just point me at the ring, the arena, whatever."

My sister went nuts when I told her I'd signed up for this. But she's having twins, for the love of God. What other option have we got? You can't bring up a baby—two babies—where we are. We share a squat with twenty others at any given time, and everybody's practically sleeping on top of each other as it is. And that's when they're not trying to rob or kill each other. Petra's kids will never know their father because he got shot over a cache of illegal implants before she even knew she was pregnant. We can't go on like that.

They used to have nurseries, in the old days. I read about it. A whole room, just for a baby. They used to have gardens, parks, places for kids to play. We could have all that, in the Garden of Eden.

If we're allowed through the gates, of course.

The official line is that after negotiations with the inhabitants, an agreement was reached to accommodate settlers. Which most people take to mean that we tried to wipe them out and take it for ourselves, but got our arses kicked.

Plenty of people—not just Petra—call the agreement barbaric. But if you ask me, it's fair enough. The aliens were here first, so they get to set the price of admission. Their territory, their rules. If they want to set up a fight to the death, the old "two enter, one leaves" routine, it's up to them. And people can act as horrified as they like, but it's not as if that's a new—or alien, haha—concept to us, is it?

"Would you like to rest first?" Conrad says. "I know the transition can be debilitating."

His voice is low, a little fuzzy. I don't know how they do broadcast out here—there's nothing in this room that looks like a comm system, or tech of any sort—but it doesn't matter. They did try to tell me about some of those new laws of physics in my briefing, but I didn't pay much attention. Like a wise man once said, if it takes fifty pages of mathematical equations to explain, you might as well call it magic and be done with it.

"No. I'm fine. Just tell me one thing, Conrad. My sister gets her relocation because I'm taking part, right? It doesn't matter whether I win or lose the actual fight."

"That's correct," he says.

"Good. Then let's get on with it."

"Are you sure? I could provide you with water, or something to eat, or—"

I laugh. "Is this the training montage part of the show? Do you teach me to handle alien weapons and learn special moves? To meditate, ground myself and find my secret inner strength? Do you tell me how to beat them?"

There's a pause, then he says, "No."

"No. I didn't think so." I laugh again. "Don't worry about it, Conrad. I know what I signed up for. I've got no illusions."

They pitch it to you as a contest, back home. A test of strength and skill. Something you've got a chance to win.

And sure, plenty believe it. They're always broadcasting confident interviews with the volunteers beforehand, and glowing reports about their wonderful new lives afterward. But I know my history, and the gladiators always killed the slaves. The lions always ate the Christians. And while you get to see the families in the Interstice, posing in front of their fabulous mansions or castles or whatever, you know who you don't see? The volunteers themselves. You don't see them. In fact, you never see them again.

"Come on," I say. "Open up and let me out of this place. I'm getting claustrophobic."

"Are you—"

I hold up my hands. "For the love of whatever passes for God out here, can we please just get this over with?"

He doesn't argue anymore. The green surface in front of me shimmers and transforms into a transparent silvery grey. I reach out, and my hand passes through. There's a suggestion of shape, of slowly swirling movement, but nothing that the eye can keep in focus. It's hypnotizing and nauseating in equal measure. I step through the green walls, and they're swallowed up behind me.

"So, this is it? I thought paradise was supposed to come with palm trees, huh?" I shake my head. "Nothing ever lives up to the advertising, does it?"

"This area is undeveloped," Conrad says. "Raw material. We have to construct our paradise out of it."

And with that, a pair of palm trees with a bright red hammock slung between them comes looming out of the fog. He's got a sense of humor, this guy, you've got to give him points for that.

I crouch down, pick up a handful of silky, warm sand and try not to look impressed. "Magic," I whisper.

I stand up, and the trees fade back into the mist. From behind them, something else detaches itself. It's huge and oddly shaped, but that's all I can tell. I can't make out any detail. Which is probably for the best.

My legs are trembling, the thigh muscles threatening to go into spasm. It's so cold out here. The indistinct shape drifts closer. Something glows red in the fog. Are they eyes?

I wrap my arms around myself. "Is this it, then? Is it happening? Right now?"

"Yes."

I nod. "Okay. Okay."

He doesn't respond. All I can hear is breathing. It's not my own.

"Conrad? Are you there?"

"I'm here, Irene."

"Has anyone ever killed one of them? Tell me the truth. All the people who came out here. Did any of them ever win?" I don't even know why I'm asking. I don't have a weapon and never expected to be offered one.

"No," Conrad says.

An honest lad, too. More points.

The shape in the fog is close, now. Close enough for me to realize that it's not so much a being, a creature, at all—more a collection of sensations and half-formed thoughts.

A blood vessel in my eye must have burst because my vision is swimming with red. I blink hard and hot, gritty tears squeeze out. They feel like acid on my cheeks. "Tell my sister I love her."

"You'll be able to tell her yourself," he says.

I try to say that I don't understand, but my mouth won't form the words. The cold—or maybe the fog—is so heavy, so clinging. Pressing down. Draining my strength.

"You'll understand soon," he says, and I can no longer tell whether the voice is coming from the facility behind me, from inside my head or from the thing looming above me.

"You can't tell because there's no difference, Irene."

My legs give way and tip me onto the ground. It's firm, even though I can't see it through the fog.

"They can't be killed," Conrad's voice goes on. "They're not alive, not in the sense that humans understand it. They're part of the Interstice itself, and that cannot be destroyed any more than raw energy can. So, all those rumors about the war were correct: the humans had their arses comprehensively kicked." He sounds amused.

I try to swallow, but there's no saliva in my mouth. My voice comes out as a croak, barely recognizable. I am so cold. "So, this is, what? Revenge? Payback?"

"No, no. Nothing like that. This is healing."

I want to say I don't understand again, but I think I'm starting to. I close my eyes, and the fog still swirls behind my eyelids.

"The closest we can get is to say they're a hive mind. A combined sentience. Humans were a shock to them. The individuality, the separateness. It's abhorrent, an open wound. They want to fix it, restore the broken part to the whole. It's why the volunteers are all people like you, Irene. People who understand family, connection, love. It makes you—"

"What? Easier to digest?"

"We prefer the word incorporate."

I shake my head, but I can't clear the fog out of it. I hold up my hand, and the flesh looks grey. Misty. Like it's coming apart.

"It's all right,' Conrad says. I can feel him smile. I don't know how, but I can. "It only hurts for a little while."

Of course. I get it now. Should have seen it before. Conrad was a volunteer.

"Yes," he says.

My head is too heavy to hold up any more, and I let it hang down. The fog supports me. I suppose it figures—there's always a price to pay for power. For wishes that come true. Maybe the old stories knew something after all.

I can feel my heartbeat slowing, my bones melting, my blood drying up and blowing away.

I look around—I can see so widely now, so clearly—and the alien is waiting there to catch me.

But he doesn't look so alien anymore.

"You were right," I say, although I know it isn't really speaking. Hasn't been for a while. "It doesn't hurt for long."

He smiles. We all do.

And I see that I was right about something, too. This is a good place for a newborn.

THE END

MICHELLE ANN KING was born in East London and now lives in Essex. She has published stories of fantasy, science fiction, and horror in over ninety different magazines and anthologies, including *Interzone*, *Strange Horizons*, and *Black Static*. Her favourite author is Stephen King (sadly, no relation), and she also loves zombies, Las Vegas, and good Scotch whisky. Her first two short story collections are available in ebook and paperback from Amazon and other online retailers. See www.transientcactus.co.uk for details.

HARVEST
Michael D. Burnside

THE *CARRION STAR* SILENTLY slid forward. Designed to tear other ships apart for scrap, she was a massive scavenger over three-hundred meters in length. Long and cylindrical, she resembled a wingless dragonfly. Six massive engines clung to the tail of the ship. They bulged out past her body so their thrust could be directed forward or backward. The head of the vessel was a dodecahedron, a twelve-sided structure made from transparent plastic polymer.

Seated in the cockpit, Robert Boyd saw an incredible sight. A red giant sun burned to his right. Although the star was two-hundred million kilometers away, it dominated the view out the starboard side. Fiery tendrils from solar flares curled away from the leviathan. The flares rose and fell, making the star appear to be a living, writhing monster.

Several kilometers in front of the *Carrion Star*, crimson light reflected off the hull of another starship. Robert had no desire to get any closer yet. It was in a decaying orbit around the star and had not responded to communication attempts. It was almost certainly a derelict, which was just the sort of ship he was looking for, but derelicts tended to be surrounded by debris.

He slid a knob on the control panel, directing thrust forward. The *Carrion Star* shuddered as its closure rate to the other ship dropped to zero. He dropped the control back to its neutral position and swiveled his chair to face a row of monitors that hung from the ceiling,

As he adjusted a monitor, the smell of body odor wafted past his nose.

A gruff voice called out, "What we got, Boyd?"

His supervisor, Russo Luca, floated halfway through the cockpit hatch, sucking grape juice from a small bag. A large man with a blond tussle of hair, Russo was always putting something into his gaping maw of a mouth yet never seemed to gain any weight.

"Taking a closer look now, sir." Robert adjusted a sensor to focus on the unknown ship.

The monitor showed a wedge-shaped starship with one large engine mounted above the hull on an extended strut. An oval cargo pod was attached to its belly. One side of the ship had been torn open. A cloud of metal shards floated alongside it like flies hovering near a carcass.

Russo said, "Huh," and pulled himself all the way into the cockpit.

Robert took short, shallow breaths to limit his intake of the man's scent.

"Looks like an old Carolina class hauler." Russo sucked in another mouthful of juice. Several purple droplets escaped and drifted past Robert's face. Russo stabbed a meaty finger at the monitor. "See how its starboard side is ripped open? The Carolinas had pressurized tanks all along there. Their reactors would often run hot. Combine that with a poor monitoring system and sometimes pheeeewooom!" He accompanied his explosion sound with spreading hands and a spray of liquid.

Robert shied away from a small purple orb. "Can you be more careful? You're going to gum up the scrubbers."

Russo shrugged. "Not my concern. I don't have to clean 'em." Laughing, he patted Robert's shoulder. "Send the drones out and harvest her. That cargo pod looks intact, might be something worthwhile in there."

Robert pointed at a power indicator. "Sir, at least one of the ship's reactors is still supplying some power. Shouldn't we check for cryopods? There could be survivors."

Russo shook his head. "You really don't know ship history, do ya, greenhorn? They stopped making Carolinas three-hundred years ago. If anyone in there still is a living Popsicle, their brains are freezer burned. Besides, messing with survivors causes legal problems with our salvage rights. Just send in the damn drones."

"Just before we left port, I heard a two-hundred-year-old survivor was pulled out of a wreck. And we have a legal obligation to—"

Russo smacked the back of Robert's head. "Send in the damn drones!"

"Damn it!" Robert rubbed his head. "Fine." He pushed a button to activate the *Carrion Star's* drone bay. A light above the button changed from green to yellow. The sound of the bay's drive motors hummed throughout the ship.

Russo smiled. "Good boy." Flipping around, he pushed himself out of the compartment. "I'm heading to the mess. Let me know if the drones find anything interesting."

Robert scowled and turned back to the control board. When the light turned from yellow to red, he pushed another button labeled "Harvest." A horde of yellow boxes accelerated away from the *Carrion Star*. On a zoomed-in view of the Carolina, he watched the drones do their work. The first arrivals snapped up the debris field using magnets on their bellies. The following drones went to work on the primary hull, cutting bits of it free with lasers mounted in their noses. Once a drone had a good bit of metal stuck to itself, it returned to the *Carrion Star* to dump its load in the cargo bay. There was soon a steady stream of drones going between the two ships. It could take several days for them to finish the job.

Bored, Robert considered heading to the mess for something to eat, but he didn't want to deal with his shipmate's smell, which ruined his appetite. He decided to wait a while longer. Right when he figured Russo had surely cleared out of the kitchen area, something on the monitor caught his attention. A returning drone had captured a white pod with a flashing blue light. Robert reached for the monitor and circled the drone with his finger. The *Carrion Star's* sensors zoomed in.

The drone had snagged an intact cryo pod.

Robert inhaled sharply, then looked behind him. Russo wasn't nearby.

Rubbing his face, he watched as the drone drew closer. He looked behind him again.

He was still alone.

With several quick swipes, he diverted the drone to a more secluded airlock. Pushing himself out of the cockpit, he flew down a series of dimly lit corridors until he arrived at the closed hatch. He entered the inner chamber and closed it. Beyond several spacesuits was a second hatch containing a window. A flashing red light blinked on the control panel beside it.

Robert glided over and peered through the window.

The drone's three-meter length barely fit inside the airlock. Stuck fast to its belly was the cryo pod. A panel on one end pulsed with blue light.

Robert touched the control panel, and a loud hiss filled his ears as the airlock sealed itself and pressurized. The red light turned yellow. Strumming his fingers on the hatch, he peered into the airlock with his nose on the cold glass. Impatiently, he muttered, "Come on. Come on."

The light flicked to green.

He pushed a button, and the lock clunked open. Yanking open the hatch, he pulled himself inside. He ran his fingers along the drone, across pitted metal covered in globs of yellow base paint and highlighted with black stripes. Inside a hidden recess, he felt for the small plastic casing that served as a safety cover. He moved this aside and flicked a switch underneath. The drone's bottom demagnetized and the cryo pod drifted downward. Grabbing the pod and pulling, Robert succeeded only in drawing himself closer to the pod. He and the pod sank toward the floor. The pod was heavy. It took a hard push with both legs to get it moving toward the hatch.

To his dismay, he realized the pod was not going to fit through the hatch at its present angle, but if he tried to stop its momentum, he'd be smashed between it and the wall.

"Shit!"

He released the pod, curled himself into a ball, and went through the hatch. His shoulder scraped the edge of the door, spinning him around as he flew into the next chamber. The pod slammed into both sides of the hatch with a bell-like clang that reverberated throughout the ship.

Robert steadied himself and examined the pod, which didn't appear to be damaged. Grunting with effort, he slowly rotated it until it lined up with the hatch. He braced his legs on either side of the door and pulled the pod through. After closing the airlock hatch, he floated alongside the pod. Frost covered its small window, preventing him from seeing the pod's occupant, but the vital readings looked good. He flicked a half-dozen safety switches and pressed hard on the pulsating blue panel. Its color changed to green and flashed rapidly.

Clouds of cold-water vapor billowed from the bottom of the pod, and the flashing light slowed. When the light burned steady, loud clicks rippled along the pod as internal locks released.

Robert pulled open the pod.

Within lay a young woman clad in black pajamas. The sides of her head were shaven and covered in wires taped to her skull. The top of her head was a mane of purple hair.

Her eyes flickered open.

She burst into an upright position, jerking her head back and forth, up and down.

Yelping, Robert shoved on the pod, sending himself soaring upwards into the spacesuits.

The young woman gasped, then fired off a string of questions.

"Where am I? Where? What? Am I? Where? How did I get here? Where?"

Plush legs and sleeves wrapped themselves around Robert like the arms of an octopus. He shoved them aside and glided back down to the pod.

The woman screamed.

Robert held up his hands. "It's okay. It's okay. You're waking from cryo."

The woman flailed. Wires trailed from her head. A transparent tube was attached to her arm. She grabbed her stomach. "I feel sick. Sick. Feel sick. Feel nauseous."

Robert nodded. "Yeah, okay. That happens when you've been in cryo for a while. It will pass." He reached toward the tube in her arm. "Can I pull this out before you hurt yourself?"

The woman stopped moving and looked at him with large dark eyes.

He took the tube with one hand and her wrist with the other. Tugging gently, he pulled the tube out of her arm. Her eyes widened at the sight of the large needle topping the tube. She pulled away and resumed her spastic movements.

"I don't know this place. I don't know where I am. Where am I? Where? Where? I'm lost."

"You're on a salvage ship. Your ship … had an accident."

"I was on a ship? What ship? I'm on a ship now? What are you doing here? Who are you?"

"My name's Robert."

The young woman went still again. Her eyes focused on his face.

"You are Robert. Robert, who am I?"

He sighed. "Shit. Okay, don't worry about that right now. Maybe your memories will come back later. Let's get you out of this pod, then maybe get you something to eat." He reached for the wires taped to her head.

The woman scooted away.

He pulled his hand back. "I'm not going to hurt you. I'm just going to pull those monitoring wires off you."

She nodded, then gulped as he picked at the tape holding a wire to her skull.

"You know," said Robert, "the new pods don't require these anymore. I don't have to shave the sides of my head like you did. Though I must say, it looks good on you." He gave her a smile which she did not return. "Okay, this is going to hurt a little." He pulled off the tape. She winced. "Five more to go."

"I feel all tingly. Why do I feel all tingly? It feels weird. I feel jumpy. Anxious. Don't want to sit still. Why do I feel weird?"

"It's probably from the electrical stimulation. While you were asleep the pod sent electricity through your muscles so they wouldn't atrophy. I bet a few centuries of that will make you jumpy."

The woman stood up in the pod. Several wires tore free from her head. Others went taut, anchoring her in place. "Centuries? What do you mean centuries? How long? I slept? What year is it? Where am I? Who am I? How old am I? Am I going to die? What is…"

"What the shit is going on?"

Russo's booming voice resonated in the small compartment. The young woman jumped out of the pod, snapping the remaining wires and vanishing into the nest of spacesuits.

As Russo pulled himself into the compartment, Robert's first instinct was to back away. Instead, he clenched his fists and said, "There was a survivor."

"You weren't supposed to be looking for survivors!"

"One of the drones pulled out an intact cryo pod. Sorry, but your plan for negligent homicide went awry."

Russo moved forward and bumped into Robert. Something caused both men to look up at the tangled mess of spacesuits. Dark eyes looked back at them. Strands of purple hair floated near an orange sleeve.

Russo said, "Let's grab her. Throw her out the airlock."

Robert shoved Russo. The men drifted apart. "What the hell is wrong with you?"

Russo pointed upward. "What's wrong is that this parasite you let in is going to cost us a lot of money."

"She's a human being!" yelled Robert.

"She's a claimant for the ship our drones are currently turning into scrap. That means millions of credits won't go to the Carrion's owners, which means hundreds of thousands won't go into our bonus checks. So, help me grab this bitch, because we're throwing her outside."

Robert shook his head. "No. I won't."

"Damn you, greenhorn!"

Pushing off the floor, Russo grabbed for the woman's hair, but she yanked on the spacesuits and zipped away, soaring through the hatch like an agile falcon.

"Shit!" yelled Russo, smacking his head on the hard outer shell of a helmet. Swearing again, he fought free of puffy sleeves and legs, pushed himself down beside Robert, and pointed at the hatch. "Did you see how fast that bitch is? She's small, too. She's going to be able to get up into crawl spaces we'll never fit into."

Robert said, "Gosh, that's too bad." He pushed himself away from Russo.

Russo grabbed onto Robert's pant leg. "Don't think this is over. I'll lock the mess compartment down tight. Once our drones are done picking her ship clean, we'll lock ourselves in the cryo room so she can't sabotage our pods. It'll be six months before we reach the next contact. By then Miss Zippy will be a pile of bones somewhere. We'll let the maintenance team pull her carcass out back at base. We'll tell them she must have stowed away before we left. We didn't know she was aboard. Not our fault."

"You think the authorities are going to buy that? Shit, Russo, how about instead of trying to murder her, we help her instead? You know, like decent human beings. So, what if she claims the scrap? We'll find more."

Russo snarled, "Let me explain things to you, newbie. Maybe the authorities where you're from actually give a crap, but out here on the fringe, they don't look at things too closely. And you clearly don't know how damn empty it is out here. There's a good chance that next contact won't be anything we can salvage. We got nothing else on scope. We'll be returning to base hauling somebody else's scrap in our belly. Oh, aren't we nice! Think we'll still have jobs after that?" He shoved Robert away and pointed to the hatch. "Get back to the cockpit and monitor the damn harvest. You find any more pods, have the drones take them apart before bringing them back. I'll guard the mess compartment."

"Of course, you will," muttered Robert as he pulled himself through the hatch.

THE DRONES COMPLETED THE harvest without pulling out any more intact cryo pods.

Russo locked away all food and water in the mess compartment. Before joining Russo in the cryo chamber, Robert left his key card floating in the cockpit.

"WHAT THE SHIT IS this?" screamed a voice.

Robert blinked and rubbed his eyes. A fuzzy shape in front of him shook an empty food packet.

"She got into the mess compartment. With your key card!"

Robert grabbed the open lid of his cryo pod and pulled himself upright.

"I outta throw yer ass out the airlock!"

Robert nodded. "Okay. At least it would be quiet."

Russo pulled him close. "You think I'm joking, greenhorn?"

Robert slammed his knee into Russo's groin. Russo let out a squeak, curled into a ball, and floated away.

"Last time you ever put hands on me, asshole." Robert pushed himself out of the cryo pod and toward the chamber's hatch.

Russo said in a strained voice, "If I don't kill you before we get back to base, I'll make sure you never work salvage again."

"I've seen you try to work the nav computer," Robert shot over his shoulder. "You'd never make it back to base without me."

It was a lousy job anyway, and he wanted no part of it if Russo was the sort of man the job attracted. The company had probably been pairing the bully with technically adept newbies for a decade. Robert wondered if Russo had ever had a partner embark on a second mission with him.

He buckled himself in, pulled up the navigational map, and confirmed the *Carrion Star's* position. They were right where they should be, on the far side of the red giant in an orbit that was closing on the unknown contact. He locked access to the map with his private identification code, ensuring that Russo had no other way to calculate a return trajectory. Then he adjusted the ship's sensors to get a look at the unknown object.

Russo's fat head poked into the cockpit. "What we got, asshole? You better hope it's made of credits."

"Don't know yet, shit eater." One of the monitors flared white, then showed the darkness of space. Robert toggled forward, zooming in on the contact.

"You also better hope the pods don't break down. Your girl ate at least a year's worth of food in the past six months."

"We have two years of food aboard for the two of us, and we're only a year out from base."

Russo sniffled. "Yeah, well she ate all the good stuff."

Robert tightened the focus on the contact. It was twice the size of the *Carrion Star*, long and cylindrical like his own ship, but on one end it branched out into a half-dozen long strands. He ran his finger along the strange shape on the monitor.

"Get yer damn finger outta the way," said Russo as he moved into the cockpit.

Robert took in a shallow breath to limit his exposure to the man's body odor but didn't object. The only value Russo had ever shown was in ship identification.

Russo inhaled. "What the hell is that thing? It looks like a giant squid."

"You can't identify it?"

"Never seen anything like it."

"Then, we're close enough." Robert reached for the control panel and the *Carrion Star* shuddered as its closure rate dropped to zero. He dropped the control to neutral and looked at the monitor. "It looks like a hydra."

Russo rolled his eyes. "What, like in the horror vids?"

"No, not a movie monster. There actually are things called hydras that live in fresh water on Earth. Except they are only a few millimeters long instead of... shit, how big is that thing? Over half a kilometer?"

"Big enough to fill our hold." Russo rubbed his chin. "Shit, we could expel the Carolina scrap that might not be ours, fill our belly with scrap from this thing, and there'd be enough left over for a return trip to be worthwhile."

"We don't even know what it is."

"Who cares? We know what it's made of." Russo tapped a magnetic spectrometer reading. "Expensive metal alloys. Let's carve it up."

Robert zoomed in on the ship. Red light from the nearby dying sun reflected off the craft's hull. "It looks intact. I don't see any damage."

"The company said it's been orbiting this star for a decade. Whatever it was, it's a derelict now." Russo reached over and pulled back the thruster knob. "Let's go get paid."

Robert placed his hand on the monitor to stop it from vibrating as the *Carrion Star* accelerated and squinted at the ship. "It looks like there's some kind of skin covering the thing. It looks green, fleshy." He looked back at Russo and said, "My God, what if it's alien?"

Russo snorted. "The last alien anyone ever reported turned out to be a stinky moss. Does that look like moss to you? Or some alien germ colony? Nah, that's a ship made of metal. Probably a custom yacht belonging to some playboy trillionaire. He covered it with synthetic coating and made it look like a space squid 'cause he's a freak. All those rich entrepreneur types are."

"It's moving," said Robert quietly.

"What?"

The mysterious ship rotated, bringing its tentacles to face the *Carrion Star.*

Robert grabbed the thruster knob and shoved it all the way forward. The *Carrion Star* shuddered as its thrust switched directions. His seat belt held him securely in place, but Russo flew forward and slammed into the transparent nose of the cockpit.

"Shit!" Russo pushed himself up from the window. Robert assumed his superior was about to curse him out but instead Russo asked, "Is that thing coming at us?"

A quick look at the laser range finder confirmed it. "It's accelerating toward us. Closing!"

Russo stood up on the nose of the ship. "More thrust! Go faster. Get us outta here!"

Robert uselessly pushed on the thruster knob. "We're at full thrust now."

The six tentacles on the pursuing ship spread apart. Crimson beams of light erupted from the end of each one. They surrounded the cockpit in brilliant light but did not touch it. Alarm bells rang from the *Carrion Star's* console. Robert scanned the control board until his eyes came to rest on a bank of temperature gauges. He grabbed the thruster knob and set it to neutral. The sound of the engines died.

"What are you doing?" Free from any g-forces, Russo kicked away from the nose and came flying at Robert. "I said more thrust."

"The engines were overheating!" yelled Robert, pointing at the temperature gauges.

"They're still overheating," said Russo. He looked out toward the alien ship. "That damn thing is shooting our engines." The unknown craft was now visible to the naked eye. It grew ever larger while steadily firing red beams of light.

The sounds of straining metal reached the cockpit.

Russo grabbed Robert's shoulder. "What the shit do we do?"

Robert pushed his supervisor away, studied the console, and opened the drone bay doors. The sound of straining metal grew louder. An explosion shoved down on the ship. A second explosion hit, followed by a rippling of detonations that shook the *Carrion Star* like an earthquake. The blasts spun the ship around. Russo flew about the cabin screaming and bouncing off the transparent walls.

Robert, safe in his seat, rolled along with the ship, the strain of g-forces pushing him into his chair. The forces lessened as his body matched the speed of the spin.

Russo came to a rest on the ceiling of the cockpit. "What the shit was that?"

Robert glanced at the engine temperature gauges. Nothing. "Engines exploded."

"The engines," cried Russo. "We need the engines!"

The yellow light on the command console turned red. Robert smashed his hand down on the Harvest button.

"Chew on this, you bastard." He re-focused the *Carrion Star's* sensors on the alien ship so he could watch his drones fly out and cut it apart.

"What'd you do?" Russo floated up to the monitors, close enough for Robert to smell his rancid breath.

They peered intently at the monitor as the sensors struggled to keep the alien ship in view. Every few seconds, the screen displayed black as the mass of the tumbling *Carrion Star* blocked the line of sight. The alien ship drew closer, its weapons no longer firing. The tentacles on its front spread open wider. The screen went black, then lit up. Dozens of yellow boxes flew into the frame.

"There go our boys!" shouted Russo. "Eat that bastard up!"

The screen went black, then lit up. A chamber on the front of the alien ship opened, a gaping maw surrounded by long limbs.

Russo said, "Is that a mouth?"

The screen went black, then lit up. Hundreds of white orbs spilled from the alien ship's opening. Unevenly shaped, bumpy, and semi-translucent, they tumbled toward the drones, slammed into them, and engulfed everyone.

"What the hell?" Russo pushed away from the monitors.

The screen went black, then lit up. Long, white-covered boxes moved toward the alien ship's mouth. Hundreds more white orbs flew toward the *Carrion Star.*

Russo and Robert stared. The red giant sun dominated the view then fell away as the *Carrion Star* spun. There was a brief bit of darkness, and then the alien ship came into view. Its tentacles reached toward the *Carrion Star.* The opening on its front had jagged edges. Hundreds of whirling, irregularly shaped, white globs rushed forward, crashing into the transparent nose of the *Carrion Star* and blocking out the view of the alien ship. Cracks appeared in the transparent polymer, spreading outward like slow-moving lightning.

Russo pointed. "Micro-meteors can't get through that. How are they getting through that?"

"We have to go." Robert unbuckled his seat belt and pushed toward the hatch. As he grabbed the opening, there was a sharp tearing sound behind him. Air rushed past his face. He looked back.

A small hole had been torn in the front of the ship. One of the white orbs shoved its body into the hole, squeezing its mass through an opening the size of a soda can. Cracks in the transparent wall multiplied out from the hole like shattering ice. An alarm sounded. The hatch door began to slowly close.

Russo stared at the disintegrating wall. In a detached voice, he asked, "How?"

Robert pulled himself through the hatch, yelling, "Russo! We have to go!"

The nose of the *Carrion Star* shattered. Howling air rushed out of the ship. Robert spread his legs across the closing hatch so he wouldn't be pulled through. Russo flew flailing toward the gaping hole and managed to wrap his arms around the command console. A swarm of white orbs pressed forward against the ship's escaping atmosphere.

The hatch was halfway closed. Robert wedged himself in the opening and pressed a button with his knee, delaying the emergency seal. He reached toward Russo, yelling, "Come on!"

Russo dragged himself onto the console, kicked off from it, and flew toward Robert with an outstretched hand. Robert grabbed him and pulled him toward the hatch. Russo screamed. A white orb had grabbed one of his legs. Through the alien's translucent skin, Robert could see the fabric of Russo's pants dissolving, along with the skin. He pulled Russo toward the hatch. The orb flattened out, molding itself to the supervisor's form. It enveloped his other leg and rolled up his torso.

Russo kept screaming.

Robert let go. "I'm sorry. I can't let that thing into the rest of the ship!"

He moved out of the hatch entrance, and the hatch slid closed with a loud kerthunk. Through the window, he watched Russo scream silently and pound on the hatch. As the white blob flowed up the side of Russo's face, flesh, blood, and muscle melted away. The creature's white translucent body turned pink. Russo stiffened, his eyes rolling back in his head. With a half-smile, the last of the muscle tissue on his face dissolved, and the alien flowed into his mouth.

A white orb slammed into the hatch, cracking the window. The creature flattened itself against the door so all Robert could see was a mass of white. Cracks raced across the glass. He propelled himself down the hallway, grabbing each hand-rung, pulling himself faster and faster through the ship. The cockpit hatch window exploded as he reached the first corner. He swung his body into the turn, wind rushing past his face as he tumbled legs over head. An alarm rang.

There was a flash of purple, and he collided with something soft.

It was the stowaway woman. Her eyes were steady. Black roots showed beneath purple hair. Dark fuzz grew on the sides of her head. She shoved off Robert, asking, "What's going on?"

Robert pointed toward the front. "Alien monsters have broken into the cockpit. They killed Russo. We have to get out of here!"

The young woman's eyes widened, but her voice was steady when she asked, "How?"

"There's a lifeboat on the port side. It has cryo pods. If we can get to it…"

"Let's go," interrupted the young woman, grabbing Robert's shirt.

"What's your name?"

"Adela."

"You're feeling better?"

"Much."

Robert looked over his shoulder. A half-dozen white orbs rounded the corner.

"Adela, we've got to move!"

Adela looked back, saw the orbs, and grabbed the next hand-rung with both hands. She pulled hard and zoomed down the hallway. Robert pulled himself after her, but the distance between them quickly grew. She was light-weight and strong, fast. He did his best to keep up as she bounded around the next corner, kicking off the walls like a coiled spring. Up ahead, Adela come to a stop. She looked back and forth between hatches on either side of the corridor.

"The one on the right!" yelled Robert.

She spun the locking mechanism, pulled the door open, and slipped through. She reached out her hand. He took it. It felt tender, yet strong. A feeling of fire enveloped his feet. Robert looked down and saw a white orb enveloping his legs. Particles from his shoes mixed with his flesh and bled into the creature's body.

He released Adela's hand and shoved her back.

"Go! Go!"

He swung the hatch door shut and spun the locking mechanism. Agony flowed up his legs. Another orb smashed into his torso. His shirt came apart. The skin beneath burned.

Adela's dark eyes looked at him through the hatch window. Robert felt her tug on the locking mechanism.

"No!" He tried not to scream. "Too late for me. Launch the boat!"

Adela nodded. She put her hand up to the window.

Robert's body boiled. The membrane of the alien slowly rolled up his neck.

A light beside the hatch door flashed from green to red. The wall shuddered as the lifeboat kicked free.

Robert whispered, "Escape this harvest," and closed his eyes.

THE END

MICHAEL D. BURNSIDE is the creator of the role-playing games *Space Conspiracy* and *World War Two Role Play*. His fiction writing includes steampunk, science fiction, fantasy, and horror. His stories have been featured in multiple anthologies including *Fossil Lake: An Anthology of the Aberrant*, *Fossil Lake II: The Refossiling*, *Beautiful Lies, Painful Truths Vol. II*, and *Ink Stains Vol. 8*. His short stories have also been featured in magazines such as *Devolution Z*, *Outposts of Beyond*, and *Gathering Storm Magazine*. Michael lives in Dayton, Ohio with lots and lots of cats. Read more nice things about him, as well as some free stories, at www.michaelburnside.com.

INTENSIVE CARE
Tom Howard

THE GIANT SQUIRREL POKED him again.

"What the hell!" shouted Matt, backpedaling to the head of the hospital bed.

The squirrel drew back. "I'm sorry, Patient McCoy. We are pleased to see you awake at last."

"W-what are you?" he asked, blinking. "Where am I?" He pulled the covers up to his chin as if the fabric could somehow protect him. Matt wore a green smock. The room was small and white with beeping monitors and a frosted window. Why was he in a hospital run by talking animals?

The squirrel pulled the covers from his clenched fists and smoothed them out. "My name is unpronounceable in Terran English; you may address me as Nurse Betty."

She pressed a button on a nearby machine and spoke into a microphone. "Patient McCoy is no longer in a coma. Please tell Dr. Carextrii."

Turning to Matt, she continued, "You are on the hospital ship *Priority,* a working med center for fifty different species."

Matt felt odd. His muscles were sore, and his vision was foggy. Only one thing could explain a talking rodent. "Am I in an insane asylum?"

Nurse Betty paused as if she didn't understand the question. "Oh, a place to heal minds. We have mind healers here, Patient McCoy, but you are in a regular convalescent ward. Now that you're awake, the doctors will want to speak to you. They've been examining you for weeks. You're the first Earthling we've encountered."

"How do you know my name?" he asked, still convinced he was living in a dream. "And if you're an alien, how come you speak English?"

"We were able to extract data from your ship's memory banks, Patient McCoy—"

He ran a hand through his short hair. "Call me Matt, please. Just tell me what's going on."

She lifted a small rainbow-colored necklace from around her neck. "This translator lets all different races converse aboard the *Priority*. The doctor will explain when he arrives. Right now, relax and try to get some rest. Is your waking pulse rate normally one-hundred beats per minute?"

"No." He took a deep breath to calm himself. "Where did they find my ship? What about the rest of my crew?"

"I don't know the details. We found no other Earthlings, or they would be here," Nurse Betty said. "Your ship was ancient and of a type never encountered before. The cargo vessel that found you thought you had probably traveled through a quantum corridor to arrive here."

"But how am I still alive?" asked Matt, looking down at his hands in alarm. The scar on the inside of his left index finger was missing. It was a childhood souvenir of a knife fight with his little brother and had marked his finger from palm to fingertip since he was ten.

"Alive?" Nurse Betty asked, leaning over to fluff his pillow. "You mean cellular activity? I doubt you'd had any for centuries. The surgeons had quite a time rebuilding you from your DNA."

Matt sank back into his pillow. "You mean I was dead all those years, and you were able to bring me back?"

Nurse Betty put her paws on her hips in a very human pose. "Of course. What kind of barbarians do you think we are?"

He tried to think of an answer, but someone turned off the lights.

"PATIENT MCCOY." NURSE BETTY leaned over him, concern evident on her furry face. "Are you okay?"

"I'm sorry," he said. "I must have dozed off."

"You collapsed," she said, checking her monitor. "You were unconscious for two minutes."

A group stood conversing in the doorway, and for a moment, Matt imagined he was back on Mars listening to his fellow crewmen in their cramped quarters. Conversations were always a background hum.

"Perhaps your regenerated nerves are still making connections," a large cockroach said from behind the nurse. "I'm Dr. Carextrii. Pleased to meet you." He held out a barbed upper leg.

Matt, undecided as to whether to hide under the covers or jump screaming out the window, extended his hand and shook the doctor's offered limb.

"Excellent," said Dr. Carextrii, his voice coming from his rainbow-hued necklace. "I understand shaking appendages is an Earth welcome."

"I'm not touching anything on that creature," said a three-foot-tall slug as it oozed into the room with Nurse Betty close behind. "You don't know where that appendage might have been."

"Pardon my associate," said Dr. Carextrii. "This is Dr. Dmid-7 from Humanoid Biology. He's a Quintamian. You are not the first humanoid in our hospital, but you are the first Earthling."

Nurse Betty raised Matt's bed into a sitting position. "The Quintamians are known as the rudest species in the Great Collective."

Matt was confused. "Will I keep turning off and on like a light switch?"

"I don't know," said Dr. Carextrii, standing well back from Matt's bed. "We'll have to watch and see. Does our nearness to you cause you distress?"

"No, it's not that," said Matt, "nor is it the sudden nap. It's the existence of intelligent insects and whatever Dr. Dmid-7 is that I can't believe."

"We understand," said the giant cockroach. "For you, this is a first contact situation."

Dr. Dmid-7 oozed closer, his beady black eyes extended from his head. "No aliens in your neck of the woods, eh? Must be pretty far out and backward."

He turned to Dr. Carextrii. "I say we put him in the freezer, blackouts or not. Chances are we'll never find this Earth he calls home. It may be on the other side of the galaxy. It would be safer for all of us to freeze him."

"Thank you for your advice, Dr. Dmid-7. Patient McCoy, our ship's captain has yet been unable to locate your home planet," said Dr. Carextrii. "We have access to your ship's star charts."

He inched closer. "To make you more comfortable in our new surroundings, Nurse Betty will provide you with tapes of the other species we have aboard, both medical staff and patients."

Matt didn't know what to say. He jumped when his window suddenly changed from panes of frosted glass to a moving image of a cartoon cat chasing a mouse.

"Ah," said Nurse Betty, "some Earthling entertainment. We thought perhaps you'd enjoy some films from your ship."

Matt smiled as his visitors watched it with interest. "Thank you, but my crewmen had juvenile tastes." Lieutenant Gorman had left his classic cartoon collection on the lander.

"Our apologies," said Nurse Betty, pressing a control and changing the window back to frosted glass.

"Patient McCoy," said Dr. Carextrii, "we will be scheduling appointments for you with some of the specialists onboard. You will be a great help in telling us how your new body feels during these encounters."

Nurse Betty turned to the others. "It's almost time for Matt's first solid food and a walk around the room."

"If he collapses," said Dr. Dmid-7, "I have a freezer ready for him."

Without further conversation, the two doctors departed.

"Food first, or would you prefer to extend your legs?" asked Nurse Betty.

"I think you mean 'stretch my legs,' Nurse Betty." He swung his legs over the side of the bed and slowly stood. He felt weak but happy to be out of bed. With Nurse Betty close beside him, Matt shuffled to the bathroom. Releasing the pressure in his bladder made him feel more alive than he had since he awoke.

In a world where cockroaches and slugs resurrected long-dead astronauts, taking a pee seemed the most normal thing.

"IS IT A MAMMAL?" asked a hamster with spectacles. "Why does it have so little hair?"

Dr. Carextrii rose above the half-dozen doctors surrounding Matt's bed. "Of course, Patient McCoy is a mammal. Earthlings wear clothing and have lost most of their body hair. You may ask the patient questions directly."

A reptilian humanoid with colorful scales leaned forward. "I understand, Patient McCoy, that Earthlings have a taboo against exposing their reproductive organs. Why?"

Matt gulped. "It is true, and it's something taught. Permitted exposure during reproduction."

God, I'm starting to talk like them, he thought.

"What occupation did you have on your ship, human?" grunted a pig-like creature with six legs.

"I was an engineer," said Matt. "Someone who repairs machines. My ship transports us from a neighboring planet in our solar system to the orbiting mother ship to take us back to Earth."

A shrieking noise, accompanied by blinking overhead lights, startled everyone.

"Stay calm," said Nurse Betty. "It's probably just a drill. Everyone please evacuate to the shelter containing your assigned lifeboat. I will remain here with the patient."

"Are you sure?" asked Dr. Carextrii, waving his numerous limbs wildly as the others departed.

"Yes," she said, moving to a curved portion of the wall. "I needed to demonstrate the lifeboat to Matt anyway."

"Come on, Dr. Carextrii," said Dr. Dmid-7 from the doorway as the room shook. "That doesn't feel like a drill."

"Matt," said Nurse Betty as the doctors left, "please accompany me." The curved wall slid back to reveal an open hatch.

She hopped inside and took a seat on the padded bench. Matt, confused as usual, rose from the bed and followed her.

He sat with Nurse Betty. "What's going on?"

"You, as an astronaut, know how dangerous space can be. Each of our hospital rooms has a lifeboat able to carry the room's occupant in their usual environment. I apologize for the nearness of my person, Matt, but these warm-blooded, oxygen-breather boats can handle two if necessary."

"No problem," said Matt. He was surprised that Nurse Betty's fur against his arm felt rough like a goat and not soft like a dog or cat. "How do you operate this thing?"

"It's automatic. The captain provides access during a drill or real emergency and launches them if the situation requires such action. They automatically search for the nearest habitable planet and send out a distress beacon."

The ship shook again. "Is Dr. Dmid-7 correct? Is this a real emergency?"

"Most likely it's another Skree harassment barrage. Although we are well within the Collective's sphere of influence, they sometimes make it through."

"I thought in the future there wouldn't be wars," said Matt, peering through the glass hatch Nurse Betty had pulled closed behind them. His room looked odd from this position. "That civilizations had become more evolved."

"We have. It's the Skree who refuse to join the Collective. Since we have encountered the area of space they control, they've done nothing but try to hurt and destroy us. And a hospital, no less! Even when my people were at their most barbaric, we didn't attack hospitals."

Matt nodded. "They're supposed to be off-limits on my world, too. What do these Skree look like?"

"We've no idea. They never leave their ships, and none have ever been taken captive. It's difficult to arrange a peace treaty with beings that won't show themselves."

Matt shook his head, and the interior of the lifeboat grew dark. When he awoke, he was lying on the floor in his room in a puddle of blood. The klaxon alarm and flashing lights had stopped.

He pushed himself upright. "What happened?"

"Don't move," said Nurse Betty. "You tried to break out of the lifeboat. You damaged your fists beating against the glass. Have you experienced a fear of closed spaces before?"

"Me? I just spent a year in a room smaller than this one with five other people. We can't go into space if we have claustrophobia."

Nurse Betty sprayed his hands with a first aid device and held them until the scabs closed and disappeared. With an experienced flip of the same machine, she vacuumed up the blood.

"This time you were out much longer. What do you remember?"

"Absolutely nothing." He rubbed his head. "One minute you and I were talking, the next I was lying here."

"Stay prone for a few more minutes," she instructed. "This time you spoke."

"What did I say?"

"I don't know. My translator couldn't decipher it. I think you can get up now. Slowly. I hope we don't have to use the lifeboat again while you are here."

"While I'm here?" asked Matt, letting her assist him back to his bed. "How long will that be and where will I go?"

"You need to regrow and strengthen your muscles. And we need to find out what is causing these blackouts and changes in language. The doctor will not release you until we find out the cause. I expect you'll be in rehabilitation for several months to get back to your original condition. As to where you will go after your convalescence, that will be up to you. As I mentioned, there are many other humanoids in the Collective. You would be welcome on their worlds."

"Welcome but alone." Matt looked down at himself as he swung his legs into bed. He refrained from looking at the lifeboat as Nurse Betty cleaned it and closed it up. "If they grew this body, where is the old one? Does Dr. Dmid-7 have it frozen somewhere?"

"Oh no," said Nurse Betty. "You misunderstood. That is your old body. They used the remaining DNA to regrow it from the cellular level. Of course, you now have tonsils and an appendix. And a light switch apparently."

Before Matt could reply, Dr. Carextrii returned with several of the doctors.

"I'm sorry for the interruption," said Dr. Carextrii. "I'm afraid that will be all for today, doctors. Patient McCoy is diurnal and requires sleep to assist in his recuperation. Thank you, Patient McCoy, for allowing us to visit. We apologize for any distress we may have caused."

"May I have a moment, Doctor?" asked Nurse Betty. She escorted him from the room, probably rooted in discussion about Matt's latest episode.

She returned and dimmed the room lights.

"I told the doctor about your seizure. Perhaps the group examination and the attack were too taxing," she said. "Any discomfort from the human food you had for dinner?"

"None," said Matt, patting his stomach. "It tasted funny but looked just like a hamburger and fries."

"All vat-grown protein," she said. "The nutritionist will visit tomorrow with samples to determine what your taste buds can handle."

"Makes sense," he said. "You probably don't want people eating meat that originally resembled their fellow patients."

"Definitely not. You have a call button here, and we'll be watching you from the nurse's station in the hall. If you can't sleep, we can provide a sedative, but it will require Dr. Carextrii's approval, especially if you continue to black out."

"I think I'll be fine. Don't you have other patients, Nurse Betty? You seem to be spending a lot of time taking care of me."

"Yes, the ward is fully occupied. We travel through the Great Collective systems, gathering the sick and injured the planetary hospitals are unable to handle. But do not concern yourself with my workload. Your job is to get better."

"Will you be here all night?" He snuggled down under the covers. He didn't want to be left alone and was amazed at how natural it felt to be conversing with a squirrel. He flexed his fingers, still surprised how quickly his injuries had healed.

"No," she said, "I'm off duty soon. We work three ten-hour shifts per day. I'll be back tomorrow during the day shift. Do you need anything else?"

"Just an answer to a question. Am I locked in?" He heard the door seal each time the doctors entered or departed.

"Yes. Initially, it was because you were in too delicate a condition to be disturbed by the entire medical staff. Now, I think the doctor doesn't want you stumbling into a sentient elephant or a methane breather in a tent suit. As soon as you are cleared and feeling better, I'll take you around the ward and introduce you to some beings from other parts of the galaxy."

"Great," said Matt, "and thanks for giving me the files on the ship's species. Maybe I'll read myself to sleep."

Nurse Betty chattered in what Matt took to be a laugh. "Then you might skip the Gitnessians. They wear their internal organs on the outside. They'd give anyone nightmares. Have a good night."

SOMEONE SHOUTED, AND MATT heard a scream. He'd finished unloading the last Mars sample box from the lander to the mother ship, *Solstice*. Considering the crew of six had lived on the red planet for a year, it had taken a surprisingly short time to unload the lander of their belongings and samples. The captain and co-pilot had gone forward to start the ignition sequence for the *Solstice's* return to Earth.

The lander stood open and attached to the airlock. Stacks of plastic containers lined the ship's hallway with specimens of Martian metals, rocks, and soil.

"What's going on?" shouted Matt as footsteps pounded down the narrow corridor.

Dr. Van Buren, Joyce, ran blindly into his arms. "It's Pete. He's gone crazy."

"What?" asked Matt, disentangling himself from the young woman's arms. He'd enjoyed a brief affair with the physician while planetside, but like the others, he'd remained unattached during his time downside.

"The oxygen scrubbers," she said, peering behind her. "They were holed by a micro-meteor. We don't have enough oxygen for all of us to make it home."

"Stand right there," said Pete, entering the corridor and dragging the captain, bleeding and bruised. "I know what 'grab the short straw' means. You've all been conspiring against me since we arrived on this mission. I'm not taking a walk out the airlock."

He had an arm wrapped around the captain's neck, and she was struggling to breathe.

"Let me look at the scrubbers," said Matt, moving Dr. Van Buren slowly behind him. "Maybe we can come up with a workaround. Come on, Pete, we didn't travel this far just to leave someone behind."

Pete, tall and lanky, dropped the captain and lunged forward to grab Matt by his shirtfront. He held an ordinary screwdriver and pressed it against Matt's throat. The captain tried to stand, and the doctor went to her aid.

"We're all going to make it home, Pete. Just stay calm," said Matt.

"Calm!" Pete roared. "I can pilot this ship just fine on my own. I don't need any of you."

"You're a great co-pilot," said Matt, taking a step backward. "But what if there is more damage caused by micro-meteors? What if you're injured? You need us. Where are Rudy and Celeste?" Matt took another inch. If he could pull Pete into the lander, perhaps he could separate them from the ship long enough for the others to get away.

"Locked in the galley," said the captain, helped to her feet by Dr. Van Buren. "Pete sealed the door."

Dr. Van Buren said, "Pete, we can help you. Perhaps if we put enough of us into sleep states, we'll have enough oxygen. Let Matt check it out."

"No!" shouted Pete. "This is a trick. There isn't any damage to the air scrubbers. You're just trying to get rid of me. Well, I'm going to get rid of you first. Starting with Matt." He drew back the screwdriver, ready to plunge it into Matt's jugular.

Matt, contrary to every safety regulation in the book, had blocked open both inner and outer airlock hatches. Otherwise, it would have taken them days to unload the lander and be on their way. They intended to leave it in orbit around Mars. He pressed the inner airlock release and let himself fall backward before it cycled shut. Pete, caught off guard, stumbled over him. Still scrambling, Matt crawled through the hatch and into the lander. He grabbed a floor railing and slapped the emergency disconnect.

Caught in the open hatch, Pete disappeared into the widening space between the ship and the lander. Matt, resisting the pressure as air evacuated the lander into space, closed the lander hatch. Gasping and shaken, he floated to the lander's computer console.

"Is everyone all right?" he asked the mothership.

"Yes," said the captain over the intercom. "I've sent the doctor to release the others. What happened?"

"Pete did some extra-vehicular activity without a suit." Matt checked the amount of fuel left on the lander. "Looks like I'm staying here."

"No, Matt," said the captain. "We'll move the ship and get you. Just hold on."

He couldn't help but chuckle. "Nice try, Patrice, but you and I both know you don't have enough fuel to do another Mars orbit. It would be too late anyway. I'd be long gone. Seems old Pete gave me just enough boost to send me away from Mars."

"Oh, Matt," she said. "I'm so sorry. Hold out as long as you can. Like you said, we always think of something. Do you have enough fuel to land on Mars?"

"Negative, Captain. Now get going. I'd like to see you take off before I lay me down to sleep. Tell my family I went out a hero."

"I will, Matt. I will." Already her voice sounded fainter.

He watched the massive ship until it passed out of sight. When the others had tried to keep him company as long as they could, he turned off the radio. He sat in the command chair and plotted his probable course through the solar system until his air ran out.

Suddenly, a dark figure appeared out of nowhere, a bloody screwdriver in its hand. Matt barely had time to identify it as Pete before the blade flashed down, piercing his neck, again and again. He tried to scream but only spat out blood.

"Patient McCoy!" cried the tentacled nurse as he shook Matt. "Wake up, Patient McCoy! Are you having another seizure?"

Matt felt his throat, sure the screwdriver was still there. "What happened, Nurse Bart?" Nurse Bart wasn't close to the giant octopus's real name, but Matt had to call the night nurse something. "I guess I was dreaming."

"Your body signs far exceeded expected parameters," said Nurse Bart. "I thought intercession the best action."

"I appreciate it," said Matt, still rubbing his throat. "I think I'll be okay now."

"Do you require a sedative? I'll get Dr. Carextrii's approval."

"No thanks, Bart. I'll think I'll read for a while. I want to find out more about the Skree."

Bart said something his translation necklace couldn't convert, and Matt suspected he'd just heard his first alien curse word.

"PATIENT McCOY," SAID A two-meter tall pyramid with a row of eyes down the side facing Matt, "I am Dr. Aoiu, from the Psychology Department."

Matt smiled, realizing too late the gold-colored creature probably didn't understand why his patient was baring his canines at him. "Pleased to meet you. Nurse Betty told me they were sending a mind healer to talk to me."

The pyramid glided closer, not needing a chair. "Do not be alarmed, Patient McCoy. I am here to help."

"Please call me Matt. I'm not sure I really believe what's happened to me, but my mind seems fine."

"I'm sure it is," said the doctor. "How do you feel physically?"

"Much better. When I first woke up, I could barely make it to the bathroom and back. Since the physical therapists added a workout area with weights to my room, I'm almost back to my original fighting weight." He paused. "That's an idiom. I'm not really a fighter." He'd been surprised one morning to wake up and find an added room extension.

"Thank you, Matt. I know what an idiom is. I was briefed on your language and culture before I came in. My people have idioms, too. For example, 'never trust someone with uneven sides.'"

Matt smiled. "I can see how that one came about. No, I feel fine physically."

"And the nightmares and blackouts? Do they still trouble you?"

"Sometimes," said Matt, massaging the side of his neck. "I guess waking up here has kind of knocked me off balance. When Nurse Betty said I was speaking another language and fighting to get out of the lifeboat, it seemed like she was talking about someone else."

"I can see where that would be alarming," said Dr. Aoiu. "It would be very distressing for me to be off balance. Can you tell me about the nightmares?"

Matt shrugged. "They're mostly reenactments of how I got here. I keep seeing the same thing over and over, but this time, my opponent kills me."

"Your opponent? Your ship's log mentions six crewmen."

"Yes. We'd completed an exploration of an airless planet in our system and were on the way back to Earth. We managed to survive a year without killing one another, and the moment we started home, someone freaked out."

"What happened exactly?"

Matt didn't feel like talking about it, but the doctor had probably taken time from treating patients with more serious mental aberrations. He could discuss his night terrors.

The doctor took no notes as Matt talked. In fact, Matt wondered if it had limbs at all. The overhead monitor was active, and Dr. Aoiu could probably replay the tapes of their conversation as often as he wished. He made encouraging noises but did not interrupt Matt.

When he finished with the repetitive stabbing scene that hadn't happened, he asked, "Is that why you came here, to hear about what wakes me up at night?"

"Actually, no, but let's address that first. Do you feel you murdered your fellow crewman?"

"Murdered?" asked Matt. He hadn't thought about it. "No, I guess it was more self-defense. He would have killed me if I hadn't taken action. Hell, he'd have killed everyone."

"Ah," said the psychologist, "so you saved many by ending the life of one. Considering that, are you feeling guilty for causing Pete's death?"

"I guess I am," admitted Matt. "As an engineer, I've always been a firm believer in finding alternate ways to fix things. I should have found another solution, one that saved Pete."

"Perhaps, but if you hadn't acted as you did, the others might have died."

Matt shook his head. "They're all dead now, anyway. I should feel grief for them, but I don't. I only feel sad about Pete."

"The passage of time will help," said Dr. Aoiu. "I've found that occurs with grief. Thank the gods, or we'd all be moping about and having nightmares. So, are you responsible for Pete's death or is he responsible?"

Matt thought about it. "I guess he's responsible. If he hadn't tried to kill us, we'd all have lived."

"Exactly. Now I want you to have a conversation with Pete tonight before you go to bed. Tell him what an xxychiv he's being and tell him to leave you alone."

"I don't know what that means," said Matt, "but I'll try. Do you think that will work?"

"If not, I've got some heavy sedatives guaranteed to knock you out for a month." Dr. Aoiu made snorting noises. Matt hoped he was laughing.

"If you didn't come here to talk about my nightmares," said Matt, "why did you come to see me?"

"Ah, Nurse Betty has placed a comment in your medical records requesting permission for you to visit the remainder of the ward. She's convinced your being locked up serves no benefit. In fact, she says further isolation may be detrimental to your continued health. Dr. Carextrii is cross with her for putting that comment in your records. He sometimes forgets that patients are actually people and not pincushions for him to stick things in. That is why I am here."

"You're checking to see if I'm sane enough to act civilized when I meet aliens? Well, I've met plenty of aliens on the medical staff. So far, I haven't screamed or hid from anyone." I wanted to a couple times, he thought, but I didn't.

"Yes," said Dr. Aoiu, "I've read your chart thoroughly. You seem very accommodating when it comes to meeting other lifeforms. Perhaps too accommodating."

"What does that mean?" Matt felt angry in spite of himself. Maybe he wanted to see outside of this room more than he thought he did.

"Put yourself in our lower extremities' coverings," said the doctor. "If someone showed up at your doorstep from an unknown planet in a strange ship and wanted to walk around inside a major hospital ship with a thousand patients, wouldn't you be concerned about what such a stranger could do?"

"But they said I'm not contagious," insisted Matt. "I shouldn't be able to do more than gnaw someone with my teeth if I wanted to hurt them. Which I don't."

"Yes, that's true. But what if you carry something even you don't know you have? Perhaps you were from a technology far superior to ours and by resurrecting you, they've introduced a bomb of some kind."

Matt thought about his blackouts and his strange reaction to being in the lifeboat. "If they think I'm such a potential danger, why did they bring me back to life?"

"I suspect because they could. They were so caught up in finding an entirely new lifeform, they did not consider the consequences."

"I don't understand—" Matt stopped. "You think I might be a Skree. Some kind of secret weapon designed to cripple your ship. What about my memories? The age of my ship?"

"Could be faked," said Dr. Aoiu. "The odds are against it, and you are who you think you are. In our place, would you take that chance?"

"So, I'm to stay locked up for the rest of my life? I'd rather let Dr. Dmid-7 freeze me until we come to a planet with humanoids and drop me off. Can't they put me back in my lander and let me go somewhere I won't be a danger?"

"Your ship is not space-worthy. I am, however, pleased with your response to sacrifice yourself to save us on such slim circumstance. Most likely, you are exactly what you seem to be."

"What are you saying?"

"I am going to recommend you have access to the ward," said the doctor. "Statistically speaking, you are far more likely to be a new lifeform with cabin fever than a biological bomb from our unknown enemies. However, if you feel anything unusual in your mind or body on your excursions, please report it to the medical staff immediately."

Matt suddenly felt such animosity toward the strange doctor that he wanted to wring its neck. If it had a neck. How dare they treat him like some backwater yokel? Instead, he said, "Thank you."

The doctor turned to go. "Please don't turn out to be a Skree, Patient McCoy. It would be horrible for my reputation."

Matt laughed, but the creature inside him didn't. "Mine, too."

THE END

TOM HOWARD is a science fiction and fantasy short story writer living in Little Rock, Arkansas. He thanks his family and friends for inspiration and the Central Arkansas Speculative Fiction Writers' Group for their perspiration. This story is an homage to James White's Hospital Station books.

THE PINK PLANET
Greg McCabe Jr

I KNEW IT WOULD end this way. I knew our fate from the moment we saw this planet. I tried to tell them, but they wouldn't listen. You'll see.

After being hand selected, sent across The Field, and two days of briefing at a perimeter outpost, the four of us sat quietly on *Rescue Ship 5408*, blindly heading toward three distress signals coming from one of the last unknown portions of the universe.

It was Taylor who finally broke the silence.

"I don't even see what the big deal is," he said. "The distress signals are coming from a few light-hours away. I could practically jog there."

"Were you not listening during the last two days of briefing?" Rose shouted from the control deck. "A frontier ship, approaching a dark spot in the network, vanished without a trace. Not a peep has come from that vessel except for a repetitive distress signal."

"Yep," Taylor answered. "I recall hearing that a few dozen times."

"Then I guess you also recall hearing that the two rescue ships they sent before us also disappeared, and sure enough, not a word from either, except for the same vague distress signals." Rose Gutierrez was our pilot and ship specialist. She could break down the rescue ship to its factory components and re-build it with her bare hands. She was a petite woman, so everyone called her "Peanut." She added, "Not to mention, all three distress signals are coming from within fifty or sixty yards of each other. You don't think it's a little disconcerting that three space vessels are sitting next to each other, none of them able to communicate or travel?"

"Yeah, it's a little spooky." Taylor trembled his hands, pretending to be scared. "But c'mon, Peanut, you know interstellar communication gets sketchy on the perimeter of the universe, especially around dark spots." He stood and stretched his right arm across his chest, then repeated the action with his left. He was always stretching. Taylor Kipyego, the combat specialist, was pure muscle, and he wore it proudly on his six-foot-four-inch frame. He had a brilliant military mind and a set of combat skills to accompany it. He was accurate with a plasma rifle at extraordinarily long ranges and especially lethal at close range with a kinetic knife.

"It's the 31st century for crying out loud," he said. "When are dark spots going to stop giving us so much trouble? I can almost guarantee you that the stranded ships sustained damage while trying to manually land on some moon or planet that isn't in the network."

"You're assuming they are planetside or moonside," Jean interjected. In addition to being the ship's physician, Dr. Jean Fan acted as the unofficial leader. She was a very confident person, and it was easy for people to see things her way. "They could be stranded anywhere."

"Eighty-nine percent of the time," Taylor responded dismissively, "these rescue missions happen because ships are stranded on some rock."

"That's why we've been given the best pilot," Jean replied. "Peanut will make sure we land in the safest manner possible on whatever planet or moon these ships are stranded… dark spot or not."

"I'm not sure you've considered the entirety of possibilities," I said. I hadn't said much in a while, so everyone turned and looked at me. I'm not as comfortable in social situations as the others. In fact, sometimes it's difficult for me to carry on a conversation for longer than a few minutes. My name is Alan Klopsteck, and I am the ship's scientist.

"What possibilities are we failing to consider, Alan?" Jean asked.

Everyone stared while I remained silent for an extended moment. Finally, I said, "What if they encountered some sort of dangerous life-form? Can you imagine if intelligent life had landed on our planet eight or nine hundred years ago? Our narrow-minded ancestors probably would have killed the visitors at first sight."

"Are you joking with that nonsense?" Taylor asked, looking bewildered.

"Is it that preposterous? There are still unexplored portions of our universe."

"Alan," said Jean. "I respect you as a scientist, but every kindergartner knows that human beings are the only intelligent life-form in the universe. Humans have been all over the cosmos and have gathered data on hundreds of trillions of stars, planets, comets, and moons, only to find a handful contained life. The most advanced life-forms are tetrapods, and they are still hundreds of millions of years away from anything that could resemble intelligence. The miracle of life requires far too many variables. Intelligent life requires even more variables. Human beings have defied almost impossible odds. I dislike agreeing with Taylor, but your theories are impractical... not only impractical but impossible."

I jumped right into the speech I'd given to plenty of skeptics before: "I love it when people use that word... impossible. Thousands of years ago, people said the earth was flat. When the first Greek philosophers suggested otherwise, naysayers called them fools... impossible, they said, I can see the flatness with my own two eyes!" I sat up straight, feeling the excitement of proving a point. "And up until the 24th century, common knowledge held that nothing could travel faster than the speed of light... impossible, they said, Einstein's mathematical equations say so! Now, people don't think twice about being broken down to a subatomic level and shot across The Field to the other side of the universe. Not only faster than the speed of light, but significantly faster."

"That's interesting rhetoric, Alan. But what about the mountains of data that say otherwise?" Jean asked.

I just smirked and looked back down at my work. In my peripheral vision, the rest of the group exchanged dismissive facial expressions.

"Besides," Taylor said, breaking the awkward pause, "if any hostile extra-terrestrials try something funny, my kinetic knife might have a thing or two to say about the matter." He drew the weapon and engaged it. A double helix of blue energy protruded eight inches from the handle. A weapon capable of slicing through flesh, bone, and steel like they were liquids.

Taylor's display of machismo was interrupted by a series of beeps pulsating from the control deck. We recognized it as the notification that our vessel was slowing from near-speed-of-light, or NSOL.

Rescue Ship 5408, like all rescue ships, had a forward hull and a slightly smaller rear hull, separated by a twenty-foot corridor called the spine. An advanced computer operated the ship's technologies and navigated the stars.

"5-4-0-8, how far away are we from the distress signals?" Rose asked the computer.

"We will arrive at the planet's exosphere in approximately six minutes," it responded in its androgynous, robot voice.

"Thank you, 5-4-0-8." Rose turned to the group. "It looks like Taylor may be right. The distress signals are indeed coming from a planet."

"Slowing to idle speed," the computer said.

"Put us in orbit just above the distress signals and hold that location until further direction," Rose told the computer while flicking switches.

The space vessel dropped from NSOL to idle speed in a matter of seconds. The ship was able to regulate the internal inertia of the ship. Otherwise, we would have been splattered against the ship's walls from the force of the deceleration.

We made our way to the observation deck to have a look at the celestial body that had stranded three different space vessels. Out of complete darkness, appeared a bright pink planet.

"We'll approach in phases, ensuring that everything seems okay before advancing further," said Rose. "Jumping in head first seems like a sure-fire way to end up in the same trouble as the previous rescue ships. 5-4-0-8, can you give us any information on this planet?"

"I cannot analyze from this distance. If we enter the planet's atmosphere, I should be able to collect more data."

"Rose, what do you think about taking the ship into the atmosphere, getting some data and deciding how to proceed from there?" Jean asked.

"Sounds good to me," Rose responded. "5-4-0-8, take us down and hold position one thousand feet above surface."

The pink planet seemed to fly towards the ship. As we got closer, the pink and purple mishmash turned into the vivid landscape of the planet's surface. Even from the high altitude, we could see dense vegetation—a magenta rainforest that stretched as far as the eye could see.

"5-4-0-8, please give us your initial report."

"The atmosphere is similar to Earth's, composed of 80.02% nitrogen, 19.17% oxygen, and less than 1% combination of six other gases. Though it is the fifth planet from a G-type main-sequence star, it is almost as identically far from its yellow dwarf as earth is from the sun. It has a diurnal cycle of 23.21 hours and makes full orbit every 362.63 solar days."

"5-4-0-8, do you detect any life on this planet?" Rose asked.

"I've identified over 200,000 species of plant life, including flowering plants, ferns, algae—"

Rose interrupted, "Any animal or intelligent life?"

"Inconclusive."

Everyone stood in silence. Jean said, "What do we think about landing, but not leaving the ship? We can do another assessment at ground-level and proceed from there."

We nodded our heads in agreement.

"5-4-0-8, please identify the safest possible location to land the ship," Rose commanded the computer.

"There is a small meadow directly under the ship, under the treetop canopy."

"That's where the other ships' distress signals are coming from," Rose said.

"Why don't we consider choosing another location in the immediate area? This will allow us to avoid any potential hazards specific to this spot," Jean suggested.

"5-4-0-8, identify a secondary landing location."

"I've identified a secondary location approximately 1.1 miles from the primary location."

"Perfect, take us two-hundred feet above the secondary location. I will take over from there." Rose brought the ship down slowly, lowered it through the canopy of purple trees, breaking branches as she did so. The ship nestled onto a small clearing of pink grass.

The computer announced, "Critical damage to rear hull."

"5-4-0-8, what part of the ship was damaged?" Rose asked.

"The inertia regulators."

We all knew the ramifications. It would take our ship years to reach NSOL without them.

"I have to go check the damage," Rose said.

"Absolutely not, there could be something dangerous out there," replied Jean.

"I'll go with her," Taylor said, heading to the rear hull.

"Sounds good to me," Rose fired back, "if you're up for it."

Because the pink planet's atmosphere was almost identical to Earth's, they didn't need biophysical suits, but they did elect to wear body armor. Rose brought only tools, and Taylor brought only weapons.

Jean and I watched the audio-video feed from Taylor's combat specs. We saw Rose dialing numbers on a keypad and the rear hatch beginning to lower. No one spoke a word as the lush landscape was revealed. The jungle brush was a thousand different shades of pink and purple. Vibrant, lilac-colored trees ascended from overgrown, salmon-hued grass. Clay-red moss ran across fuchsia stones. Hot-pink ferns swayed lazily in the evening breeze.

The sun was setting as Rose and Taylor walked down the hatch.

Rose said, "Wow, I've seen a lot of crazy landscapes on a lot of crazy planets... yellow mountains, blue deserts, red oceans...but I've never seen a pink rainforest. It's actually kind of pleasant."

"Yeah, it's beautiful," Taylor muttered, scanning the terrain.

Long shadows danced, and a crescent-shaped, orange moon hung low in the eastern sky. The darkening pink jungle suddenly felt ominous, even from inside the ship.

Rose located the inertia regulator panel, swiped a tool from her utility belt, and began removing it.

"What was that?" Taylor asked with sudden intensity.

She dropped her tool into a pile of dead, dark purple leaves as Taylor's video feed swung around quickly.

"Damn it, Taylor," she muttered. "You made me drop my panel fob." Taylor kept aiming his plasma rifle at the top of the tree line. "What is it?" Rose whispered anxiously.

"Pink neon light shimmered in the trees. It was only for a brief moment, but it gave me a bad feeling."

"You better not be messing with me," Rose said quietly.

"I swear, Peanut. I saw something up there." He continued to scan the trees as he looked down the barrel of his plasma rifle. "What's going on with the ship?"

"Not sure. I'm about to pop open the panel and find out."
After a few moments, Rose said, "Oh… shit."

"What is it?" Taylor asked while keeping focus.

"The main inertia conduit has been cut."

"What do you mean?"

"I mean it's been severed…purposefully, too! Someone had the tools to open up this panel, cut the damn conduit, and then close it."

Jean pressed the comm button. "You guys need to get back in the ship right now."

"There it is again!" Taylor shouted, pointing. "It was another shimmer of pink light, but this time the trees moved as it faded away. Something's definitely out there."

"Yes, I know," Rose cried, beginning to sound hysterical. "Whatever's out there is trying to sabotage us. We fell for the same trap as the previous ships."

"Try to remain calm, Peanut. Let's get back on the ship and regroup."

I focused on Taylor's video feed and saw a sudden flash of pink light in the distance.

"Did you see that?" Jean asked.

"I sure did," I replied.

Against Jean's emphatic suggestions, Taylor took several giant strides toward the fading flash. As he did, a commotion and a sharp scream came from behind him. He turned just in time for the video feed to show Rose Gutierrez being lifted off the ground.

It was too dark to make out any details. All we could see were dangling legs and a flurry of dark shadows that disappeared into the night foliage. Another scream was cut short.

"Rose!" Taylor shouted. "Rose, answer me!" After yelling her name a few more times, he sprinted into the ship and closed the rear hatch.

"What the hell just happened out there?" Jean shouted.

Taylor didn't respond, he just breathed heavily.

Jean started issuing commands. "Alan, get on the computer and check the positioning data on Rose's subcortical sensor. I want to know exactly where she's located."

"Right away," I replied as I headed toward a station beside the control deck.

"Taylor, open the weapons locker and prepare for a search and rescue mission."

"You got it," replied our trusty combat specialist, heading for the ship's spine.

Studying Rose's positioning data, I shouted, "Wait! There is zero response from her sensor."

"What?" Jean looked mortified. "That's impossible. She's only been gone a few seconds."

"It's no mistake. The computer has full connectivity, but there's nothing. She's…"

I didn't even finish the sentence. Everyone knew that Rose's subcortical sensor—the same device that had been implanted in all our brains the day after graduating from the academy—was powered by the electrical currents in her brain.

She was either dead or in a coma.

Jean said, "Listen, Rose was a great woman, and we can try to recover her body when backup arrives. There will be a time and a place for mourning, but we must keep our wits about us. We've been trained for situations like this." She composed herself further, looking back and forth between Taylor and me. "Our mission goals have changed. There is something dangerous out there, something we were not prepared for. I'm going to give a full report to mission control and request an entire combat squadron. They'll be here this time tomorr—"

Right on cue, the ship's computer said, "Critical damage to communication components."

"5-4-0-8, what's wrong with communications?"

"Inconclusive."

"Inconclusive!" Jean shouted. "There's something out there damaging our ship and snatching our crew members, and all you can give me is inconclusive!" She regained her composure and said, "Our new mission is to get off this planet while trying to re-establish communication with mission control. Taylor, take one of the all-terrain pods to the other ships and see if you can reach mission control. They obviously have some sort of communication up as they are broadcasting distress signals."

"Are you sure sending a crew member out there is the best idea?" I asked.

Taylor said, "Alan, those ATPs are stronger than plasma tanks. I'll be fine."

"But you'll have to leave the pod to check out the conduits and communication components," I said.

"We don't have a lot of options," Jean replied. "There are three other ships a mile away with some sort of communication. We have to check it out. We'll begin at first light."

After a night of restless preparation, we gathered in the forward hull.

"I don't think I need to tell you how crucial this mission is," Jean started. "The next couple of hours will dictate whether we get off this planet alive. Taylor, Alan and I will be watching your video feed. We'll help you navigate to the other ships and complete our mission goals. Now, everyone to their stations."

I headed for the control deck and issued the computer a series of commands. Jean manned a large monitor streaming Taylor's live audio-video feed. The hatch opened as Taylor arranged himself in the seat of an ATP. Using an advanced mapping algorithm, the nanoplastic sphere hovered a yard off the ground and was highly maneuverable. Taylor disengaged the pod and ventured into the lush pink jungle, weaving the ATP through pink vines and over dark purple trees that had fallen long ago.

"The distress signals are coming from about 100 yards ahead," Jean told him.

"I don't see anything, just thick jungle," he replied.

"Okay, well take it slow as you approach."

Taylor brought the ATP through a tangled mess of light red vines. A rescue ship squatted on the other side of the draped vines. The rainforest opened up to a meadow of knee-high, light pink grass roughly seventy yards long and twenty yards wide with jungle creating walls on all sides. At the other end of this field were two more ships, another rescue ship and a frontier ship.

Taylor brought the pod down next to the rear hatch of the closest ship. He stepped from the ATP and started tinkering with the control panel of the hatch. There was a rustle in the distance. He turned, readying his plasma rifle. There was another rustling.

The tops of trees moved. Whatever was out there was heading in his direction. He aimed his plasma rifle, then dropped to a knee, refocusing his aim.

"Where are you, you son of a bitch?" he whispered.

His enemy burst through a wall of jungle. Large flapping wings spread from a dark green form. The beast flew with tremendous velocity directly at him. It landed a dozen yards in front of him and ran on all fours, like a giant chimpanzee. It was at least ten feet tall, with long arms, short legs, and head-to-toe fur the color of evergreens. The creature moved too fast for Taylor to effectively aim, but he fired a shot anyway. A twisting charge of blue energy roared over the monkey-beast's shoulder, destroying a tree at the edge of the meadow. The monster backhanded Taylor's arm, sending the plasma rifle into the grass. He dropped to the ground and rolled, avoiding another vicious blow. The monkey-beast's clenched fist narrowly missed him as it came smashing down. Taylor brought the heel of his combat boot down on top of the monster's foot with as much force as he could muster. The giant monkey arched his back and roared at the sky. Neon pink lights rippled across the fur on its chest.

Taylor reached for his kinetic knife, but when he looked up to make his attack, the beast had already turned to flee. Large wings unfolded from the monkey's back and flapped, lifting its large body. It gained speed as it approached the tree line, weaving through tree trunks, flying with the grace of an eagle. Taylor held his position as it disappeared into the rainforest. The monkey-beast reappeared, this time swinging on branches and vines with its wings retracted. Flinging itself from a tree, it spread its wings and glided, gaining speed with a few flaps and diving at Taylor like a hawk targeting a field mouse. They collided and rolled through the pink grass, the video feed glitching from the force of the impact.

When the image cleared, we could see the monkey-beast's wings flapping as it regained its footing. Taylor lunged with his kinetic knife, but the beast brought down another fist that connected with the top of his shoulder. Taylor collapsed.

He played dead as the massive monkey lurched over his limp body and sniffed. Pink lights fluttered across its neck and chest as the beast clenched its hands and held them high over its head. The kill-shot was coming. Half-heartedly swinging the kinetic knife at the monster's belly, Taylor made one last-ditch effort. Incredibly, the damage to the flying monkey's stomach was catastrophic. Ionized particles ripped through its abdomen like tissue paper. Bloody intestines poured from the gaping wound and fell onto his boots. A roar was cut short by gargling sounds as the beast fell to the ground, its gorilla-like face barely a foot from Taylor's. The glow of life drained from its eyes.

Jean was shouting, "Taylor, answer me! Are you there? Are you okay?"

"I'm here," he responded. "My left shoulder is about six inches lower than where it should be. My collarbone is obliterated, and two large bulges are protruding from my side, probably broken ribs."

"Oh my God. We saw the entire thing. You killed it. Do you need Alan or me to come get you?"

"There could be more of these things out here, and there's no point in all of us dying. I think I can cruise back to the ship, but you'll have to perform surgery. I'm coughing up lots of blood."

"Are you sure we shouldn't come get you?"

"Positive."

Taylor injected his leg with an adrenaline shot and limped over to the monkey-beast. He fastened a rope around its ankles and tethered the other end to the back of his ATP. He lost consciousness twice on the thirty-minute return trip.

Plasma pistols in hand, Jean and I were waiting as Taylor navigated the pod into our ship. The lifeless creature followed. We positioned our crew mate on the operating table in the rear hull. Jean prepped for surgery and gave him a hydration and painkiller injection. I helped attach the MedScan, which started beeping, warning of low heart rate and blood pressure. Jean silenced the machine and commanded it to administer anesthetics. She was about to go to work with her electro scalpel when Taylor's eyes popped open.

"I gotdat sombabitch didntaye…" he slurred through a bloody grin.

"You did, Taylor," she responded with a soft smile. His heart rate was plummeting on the MedScan. Jean set aside her electro scalpel and dabbed his sweating forehead. She reached for some water, but before she could bring the cup to his lips, the MedScan displayed a flat line, as well as the date and time of Taylor's expiration.

His final, rasping breath faded like an echo.

Jean and I exchanged solemn looks. We turned to look at the corpse of the dark green, winged monkey-beast. Our eyes met again, and it seemed as if Jean was coming to the same realization regarding our fate that I had when we first arrived on this planet.

Her tears made me feel uncomfortable, so I went to work dissecting the fascinating creature. Jean regained her composure and began to assist as I explored the monkey-beast's chest cavity. Occasionally, I would hand her an oversized organ, which she placed on a stainless-steel tray.

"Fascinating," I said after hours of work.

"What?" Jean replied distantly, eyes bloodshot.

"It appears this animal's internal anatomy is similar to ours. This planet's biosphere, which is similar to Earth's, took this animal down a similar evolutionary path as our own."

"Okay, Alan, this isn't the time for I told you so."

"That is not my intention. I just find this all very intriguing. This species appears to be a few hundred thousand years behind us on an evolutionary timeline. It has all the anatomical characteristics needed to reach a high level of intelligence. I'm guessing they're already using basic tools and maybe even painting on walls. Who knows, maybe one day they'll be wearing clothes and splitting atoms."

"That's fascinating, Alan." Jean rubbed her forehead with the palm of her hand. "But we're being picked off one-by-one and have very little chance of getting off this planet. So, pardon me for not being jazzed about extra-terrestrial anatomy."

"I understand."

"Did you find anything that could help us fight them?"

"I'm not sure if it will help, but I figured out what those flashing pink lights are on their chest. I had MedScan analyze their enzymes, and they appear to be some sort of bioluminescence. It could be camouflage or a way to attract prey, but—"

A banging sound on the forward hull interrupted my speech. Jean and I ran to the front of the ship and peered through the viewing deck. We could see nothing except swaying trees. A loud metallic shrill came from the rear hull. We jogged back down the spine. The rear hatch was completely down.

"They're fucking with us!" Jean's voice cracked with hysteria.

Frantically, she punched buttons on the wall pad and the hatch started to rise. When it was about halfway closed, a monkey-beast squeezed through, knocking us to the floor. Jean popped to her knees and pushed the wall pad buttons, making the hatch reopen. The beast's wings flapped violently, knocking objects from shelves and tables. I watched from my back as Jean fled down the ramp. The monkey-beast pursued her, running apelike on clenched fists. Her plasma pistol lay discarded next to me.

Standing, I walked to the open hatch and watched the pursuit unfold. It was dusk, and shadows weaved under Jean's feet as she ran for her life. The sound of thundering footsteps disappeared and turned into the sound of flapping wings as the beast flew toward the treetops. Jean continued to run. The creature transitioned to swinging from branches and vines, traveling through the canopy over her head. It let go, unfolded its wings, and landed directly in front of its prey.

Jean fell to her knees.

The creature retracted its wings and bent down, making eye contact. Jean stared right back. Though it was almost entirely dark, their faces glowed in the pink bioluminescence radiating from the beast's chest. It stood upright, roared loudly, and brought its hands together in a swift clapping motion around Jean's head, smashing her skull like a grape. Dr. Jean Fan was dead before her body hit the jungle floor.

I came to terms with the fact that my life could be snuffed out at any moment. I was oddly at peace with the idea, but until that moment came, I was determined to learn as much as possible about the peculiar animals that had decimated our crew.

I decided to head toward the other ships, figuring their techno sensors would have collected and analyzed considerably more data since they arrived weeks ago. I would walk instead of taking the second ATP. By dragging the dead monkey-beast back to our ship, Taylor had left a trail of broken brush and blood splatter that was I able to follow.

I made it to the other ships in about an hour. I saw the occasional flash of pink bioluminescence in the distance, but it didn't deter me. Crossing the meadow, which was dimly lit by orange moonlight, I bypassed the two rescue ships and approached the frontier ship. Frontier ships were similar to rescue ships, except they had three hulls, a forward, middle, and rear. The rear hatch was open. I walked right in, down the long spine, and onto the main control deck. The vessel was dark and empty.

Wasting no time, I asked, "Frontier Ship, is your reactor still up?"

"Affirmative," the ubiquitous robot voice answered.

"Okay, let's get some light in here... and tell me your name."

The lights turned on as the computer spoke. "My official designation is *FCAI Frontier Ship 1918*, but my commander called me Lewis.

"You're F-C-A-I, Lewis?" I asked, surprised.

"Yes, the newest models of frontier ships are equipped with fully conscious artificial intelligence."

"I bet you have lots of information on this planet's monkey-beasts," I said, well aware that FCAI was not only capable of collecting and analyzing data, it could also learn from the data at an incomprehensible rate. It could make deductions and provide hypotheses and projections with astounding accuracy.

"Affirmative," Lewis replied.

"I anatomized one of the monkey-beasts, and my guess is that they evolved much like humans, but their evolutionary tree has a lot fewer branches. This is why they have biological characteristics of large mammals, birds, amphibians, and even deep-sea marine life. I figure they will evolve into advanced intelligent beings within a couple hundred thousand years."

"I am sorry," said Lewis, "but that is incorrect. The indigenous species, or monkey-beasts, are already intelligent. On an evolutionary timeline, human beings are roughly 170,000 years behind them."

"These monkeys are smart? Do you have data to support this?"

"My techno sensors have collected substantial data to support this."

"Okay, was I at least correct about their evolutionary process?"

"Negative, their evolutionary tree has had many more branches than Earth's. Over the eons, a multitude of species have flourished on this planet. However, the monkey-beasts continued evolving into ultra-advanced predators, and all their competition became extinct. They were so efficient that their prey went extinct as well. This quandary forced a renaissance of intelligence."

"What do they do about food?"

"They produce it in laboratories."

"Labs? Where?"

"Underground."

"Underground?"

Lewis said, "I deduce from your questions that you do not fully understand how advanced this species is. Roughly 32,000 years ago, they moved their primary habitat underground due to various biological, environmental, and social circumstances. They now have massive civilizations in fully developed, subsurface caves. Their housing, commerce, technology, transportation, industry, luxury, poverty, religion, art, and other social constructs would be nearly impossible to explain."

"If they're so advanced, then what are they doing running around naked in the jungle, killing people?"

"I think an example may assist your comprehension. The monkey-beasts you have encountered are comparable to someone on Earth who pays a considerable amount of money to go on a safari and kill an exotic animal. I estimate they have already broadcast a distress signal from your ship and auctioned off that hunt. The monkey-beasts you have encountered represent a small, unique, and wealthy portion of their population."

Considering the information, I'd received, the term "monkey-beast" no longer seemed appropriate.

"How do they communicate?" I said.

"Through bioluminescent hairs on their neck and chest."

"Is it effective?"

"Their non-spoken language is far more effective and complex than any spoken human language that exists or has ever existed."

"What do you think will happen when an army of humans with plasma tanks shows up here?"

"It won't be good." The computer paused. "For the humans."

"Please explain your projection."

"The monkey-beasts are well aware of humans and their capabilities. They have been monitoring human activity for thousands of years. When humans began exploring the universe and uploading data to the network, the monkey-beasts rolled out a technology that cloaked their planet. Monkey-beasts have been dealing with intelligent life for a long time."

"You mean there's other intelligent life in the universe?"

"There was," Lewis replied. "Long ago, numerous planets housed intelligent life, but when the monkey-beasts mastered space travel, roughly 12,000 years ago, they traveled to each of those planets and hunted everything they deemed worth killing. They cloaked the planets they over-hunted to avoid detection. That is why there are so many dark spots on the network's map of the universe."

"Why haven't they hunted humans on Earth?"

"They don't want to hunt humans on Earth. They want to hunt them here, in their natural habitat, to maximize their advanced predatory skills. You see, Alan, of all the various forms of life that have ever existed, monkey-beasts were the only ones to master space travel, until humans. The monkey-beasts were patient, but eventually humans learned to travel faster than the speed of light. Not long after, the monkey-beasts set a trap and humans walked right into it. As you can see, they are very good at corralling their game animals."

I couldn't help but laugh. "And all this time, we were so certain that we were the only intelligent life in the universe."

"Naivety is a dangerous human attribute."

"Wow, Lewis. This is all so... incredible."

"Indeed, Alan. It has been interesting for me to learn about them as well."

"How do you project this will end?"

"I calculate a 96.42% chance of a very destructive, trans-universal war."

I spent the next several hours asking Lewis such questions. It was one of the most exciting and fascinating times of my life. Eventually, I thanked the computer and walked out of the ship.

Now, here I am in the darkness, talking into my CommLog. It's tough to get that conversation with Lewis out of my head. The monkey-beasts are so intriguing.

I'm walking through the rainforest without a destination, not at all concerned with the occasional flash of pink light in the distance.

Now, there's dozens of pink flashes throughout the trees, brightening and disappearing. They look so beautiful.

The trees around me are shaking.

Pink bioluminescence now enfolds me.

End CommLog Audio

GREG McCABE JR was born and raised in Midland, Texas, received a degree in Speech Communication from Texas A&M University, and currently resides in the Lone Star State. He enjoys spending time with his family, as well as traveling, sports, movies, reading, and writing. He appreciates all genres of fiction but seems to gravitate towards horror and science fiction. Greg's debut novel, *The Undying Love*, was published in 2013.

A RAY OF HOPE

Frank Roger

THE PLANET WE DISCOVERED seems perfect for our purposes. It is largely covered by water, with land masses spread all across. The two poles are crowned with ice caps. Both oceans and continents appear to be teeming with a wide variety of life-forms. These are all likely harmless and should in no way interfere with our plans. Preliminary tests will be run, and if these prove successful, we will proceed with our project.

THE FLEET OF ALIEN spacecraft took the world by surprise, appearing out of nowhere and descending majestically through the atmosphere. None of them landed anywhere. They all ended up hovering above the ocean, at various places around the world.

I watched the special news bulletins on TV with Marsha, my wife, and Jessica, my daughter. The images showed these gigantic spacecrafts, hanging unmoving in the air. Lots of people were interviewed. Politicians, scientists, army generals, representatives of the church and other religions all offered their views and theories.

Some were excited and claimed we were on the threshold of a new dawn. Others were wary and warned we might be under attack, even threatened with extinction. There were those who said the arrival of these spaceships was a sign from God and that we should mend our ways. Everybody had an opinion, including those who seemed to have very little knowledge of the issue at hand.

At one point, Jessica turned to me and asked, "Did the aliens come to help us?"

I said, "Yes, they came to help. There's no need to worry. They'll solve all our problems."

She accepted my reply. It seemed like the logical thing for a kid to ask and a father to answer.

Everyone wondered what would happen next. Would extra-terrestrial creatures emerge from the spacecraft? Would they be friendly? Would they try to establish contact with us?

I got lots of questions like that at school. Naturally, kids turned to their science teacher with such issues. I tried to satisfy their curiosity as best I could.

Time went by, and nothing happened. No contact could be established with the visitors from beyond the solar system. People began to lose interest, as if these spacecrafts had already become part of the scenery. There were still news bulletins, but they only offered images of these ships hanging motionless and interviews of people who had less and less to say.

Jessica grew disappointed. "You said they came to help us. What are they waiting for?"

This time I didn't have a reply.

All we could do was wait. So, we waited.

PRELIMINARY TESTS HAVE PROVED successful. This planet is definitely useful. There is one minor problem: the average temperature of the oceans is too low, and the water's chemical balance is a bit off. We should be able to fix this. The techniques have been applied before on several occasions. The general feeling is that this will be an uneventful procedure.

A WEEK LATER Jessica told me, pointing at the image of an alien spacecraft on TV, "I don't think there's anyone in there. I'm sure there are just machines and computers on board."

"You may be right," I said. As a matter of fact, some leading scientists had reached the conclusion that these spacecrafts might indeed be unmanned. Teams of scientists and the army had monitored and examined the gigantic vessels, failing to detect any signs of life aboard.

Literally nothing was known about our visitors. Nobody had a clue where these ships had come from, what they were doing here, for how long they would stay, or who had sent them and why. Nothing seemed to happen. The ships simply hung there.

Mankind's first contact with alien life-forms was an anti-climax. The invasion began to fade from the news, as there was little to report. Only the scientists kept working, and the generals still weren't convinced that no military intervention would be required.

We went on with our lives. The kids at school hardly ever raised the issue anymore. Jessica announced her plans to become a ballet dancer, no doubt after watching a ballet on TV. I made a note of it while realising that another TV show next week might cause a drastic shift in career choice. It had happened before.

Then came a mildly interesting news bulletin: scientists had discovered that the water temperature under one of the spacecrafts had risen by several degrees. The water was also slightly polluted. They would try to find out if this was the case everywhere, and if there was a connection between this phenomenon and the presence of the spacecraft.

Perhaps the ships merely produced a kind of radiation that raised the water's temperature and spilled some waste material. Or it could be a planned action, in which case thorough research would be carried out. It looked as though the special bulletins would become interesting again. Even Jessica was back at my side for the TV news.

I wasn't sure whether that was a positive sign or a bad one.

WE ARE PROCEEDING WITH our operations. Everything is running perfectly. It is expected that the melting of the two ice caps will accelerate the process considerably. There might be an added benefit: if the water level rises, the lower parts of the land masses will be flooded, thus increasing the planet's water-surface. No problems are expected.

FOUR WEEKS PASSED SINCE the aliens appeared out of the blue.

The ships still hadn't moved an inch. There was still no sign of life on board. And we still didn't have a clue as to what was going on.

Scientists had discovered that the water temperature under every spacecraft was rising markedly and the pollution was increasing. This could not be a coincidence. Despite no evidence that the aliens were responsible, there appeared to be no other explanation. The shift in temperature was too sudden and too generalised to be caused by natural phenomena. The pollutants appeared to be quite toxic, although their exact composition remained unclear. I reckoned that if any alien technology was involved, we might be unable to grasp what was happening.

Some said this was a dangerous evolution and we might have to take action – although it was not clear what kind. Military types said it was a mistake to wait until the situation deteriorated and that it would be wiser to attack the alien spacecraft now. As we could not take for granted that they were friendly, we should assume they were hostile and act accordingly. This point of view was shared by a surprisingly high number of people.

Privately, I wondered if the aliens—physically present in those vessels or not—were indeed superior to us, wouldn't they have ways to counter any offensive we might launch? Of course, I wasn't a military man. I thought differently.

In the meantime, Jessica's career choice for ballet dancing appeared to be final. Marsha suggested we check out ballet courses for children her age. I remarked that Jessica was still a kid and likely to change course numerous times, considering how easily she was influenced by what she saw on TV.

Marsha stood firm with Jessica's decision; ballet dancing it would be. I resisted proposing an alternative career in high-tech combat of alien invaders. No doubt my well-meant advice would have been thrown to the winds.

CONSIDERING THE EASE WITH which the first phase progressed, it was decided to speed up the operation. The sooner we prepare the oceans for our project the better. We are likely to cause a major disruption in the planet's ecosystem, but that should have no influence on our plans. A full-scale disinfection of the planet is not required for our purposes but might avoid interference from local life-forms.

THE WORLD WAS IN turmoil.

The ocean's temperature was rising spectacularly, and the ice caps were melting fast. The pollution was spreading quickly as well. These facts could not be attributed to global warming or any other "traditional" explanation. It was obvious the aliens—or whoever was aboard those ships—were responsible.

More and more political leaders adopted the idea of military action, which the generals applauded. The problem was that no one knew which weapons might be effective against this invisible enemy. Still, an offensive was imminent—a joint effort by the world's most powerful nations.

In the meantime, the sea level was rising as the ice caps disappeared. A number of archipelagos in the Pacific and countries such as the Netherlands and Bangladesh prepared for major evacuation. Traditional methods, such as raising and strengthening the dykes, were useless considering the rapid rise of the sea level.

Every night as we watched the news Jessica reached for Marsha's hand. Our daughter was not the only one upset by what she saw on the screen. We were all in the grip of fear. Our world was changing. What exactly was going on, and what could we do about it? What had brought these aliens here, and how did we fit into their plans, if at all? Why did they poison the oceans? So many questions, and all remained unanswered.

The Prime Minister addressed the nation, saying, "The government will not remain idle. It will take decisive action to protect the country and its citizens." He did not go into much detail. I couldn't wait to see how he would solve this problem.

At school, the kids pressed me with questions. Their rosy-coloured view of a life without major disruptions had been shattered. It was hard to ease their minds. They seemed to understand that I was merely trying to reassure them, rather than supplying solid answers. It was one of the hazards of the trade for a science teacher. Fortunately, Marsha wasn't facing this problem – the customers of a travel agency tended to head elsewhere with such questions.

Neither Jessica nor Marsha brought up the subject of ballet dancing anymore. Their minds were focused on other things. I didn't think this boded well for our future.

THE OPERATION IS RUNNING smoothly. We estimate that a sufficient expanse of the oceans will reach the required temperature and chemical balance within a short range of time. Tests will be run at regular intervals. No major problems are expected. This planet may prove ideal for our purposes.

WE WERE IN FRONT of our TV, on the edge of our seats like most people all over the country and probably the world. Nobody wanted to miss the first images of the war against the aliens, officially called "Operation Blue Planet."

"We have waited long enough," stated the President of the United Nations, flanked by his counterparts from the world's leading countries, in a live broadcast. "It's time to give the aliens a signal, to tell them we do not appreciate their meddling with our planet's marine ecosystem, which is causing irreparable damage. We have no hard evidence that they're responsible, but scientists confirm there can be no other explanation. So, we've decided to take action, hoping to elicit a response that will lead to negotiations and possibly a deal. Five spacecraft have been selected as targets. Warning shots will be fired. If these are ignored, high-precision bombings will follow. All necessary precautions will be taken. The armed forces of the world's nations are prepared for every scenario."

And so, we were the privileged spectators of the first intergalactic war, as Jessica called it. I wondered if she realised this was not another science fiction movie, but harsh reality. I also wondered if there would be a happy ending, as in most of those movies.

The warning shots weren't spectacular, at least not from our vantage point in the safety of our house. The spacecraft were huge, and the explosions off their sides seemed insignificant. After this, the operation was suspended. There had been no reaction within "a reasonable amount of time." Soon, the real action would begin.

Meanwhile, images were shown of dead whales and dolphins washed ashore in various parts of the world. In an interview, a marine biologist said, "Literally tons of dead fish are floating in the water. The oceans are being turned into a hot, poisonous soup in which no life is possible. We're facing a global tragedy. Urgent and drastic measures are called for before it's too late."

"Do the aliens realise what they're doing to us?" Jessica asked. "How can we make them listen and change their plans?"

It was an excellent question, but I had no reply. I said, "We'll find out any moment now if we can get their attention. And if we don't, we'll hit them where it hurts."

Jessica didn't look too convinced. I wasn't too convinced myself.

Later that night, bombers dropped their lethal cargoes. Explosions flared where the bombs struck. We watched and waited with bated breath, half expecting the aliens to launch a counterattack and blow us to smithereens with superior military technology. Five selected spacecraft were showered at regular intervals. There was no reaction. Either the aliens were quietly preparing their counteroffensive, or our shock-and-awe tactic hadn't impressed them.

The bombers returned to their bases. The generals and politicians, along with everyone else on the planet, waited for a reaction, but it soon became clear that none was forthcoming. Either the spacecraft were indeed unmanned, or they were so well protected that they could withstand any attack.

A NUMBER OF MINOR discharges were reported near some of the workstations. There was no damage. The operations were not disturbed or interrupted, but a routine investigation of the phenomenon is planned. In the meantime, everything is running on schedule. The first test runs are being prepared.

THE GENERAL FEELING WAS: My God, who are we up against? Three days of heavy bombing made no dent in any of the spacecraft, nor did it elicit a response. Some cried out for a nuclear strike. Others realised our efforts might be pointless. The spacecraft were immune to our "primitive" military technology.

We had to face facts: Earth was occupied territory. The aliens—although we'd never seen them or established any contact with them—had landed, taken control, and transformed the oceans into something that would probably suit their purposes. Teams monitoring the situation reported that all marine life was dying due to the water's rising temperature and toxic pollutants. We were headed for worldwide catastrophe on an unprecedented scale, the consequences of which could not be fathomed.

There was another unsettling discovery: under some of the spacecraft an unknown organic material was found. Some scientists claimed it was food and that our visitors were turning our oceans into the alien equivalent of a fish farm. Others envisioned a breeding ground for the aliens' eggs. Yet others gave free rein to their imagination, leading to a wide variety of crackpot theories.

Of course, none of these claims carried any weight, for lack of hard evidence. Yet this organic material, whatever its nature, must be the reason why the oceans were "adjusted" to suit its requirements. A proper study of the material might reveal more facts.

Jessica and the kids at school fired round after round of questions at me. I tried to provide answers that comforted them, but it wasn't easy.

The bad news mounted. With the rapidly rising sea level, many cities and coastal regions would soon be flooded or disappear completely under the waves. A large-scale evacuation was planned; it was clear there would be untold social and economic consequences. Third-world countries would be even harder hit than industrialised western nations. It was all going to hurt. We just didn't know how much exactly, or how long the pain would last.

With marine life in its death throes, the fishing industry became a thing of the past. Many people lost their jobs and wondered what the future had in store. Society began to cope with the sudden and drastic changes forced upon it.

THE FIRST TEST RUNS show we're not ready yet. This planet's water mass is huge, and it'll take some time before a sufficiently large volume of it reaches the right temperature and balance. Our operations are sped up, now that the oceans are virtually disinfected. There is still life on the continents, unlikely to cause any interference. We have high hopes that this project will prove a success.

THE IMAGES ON TV sent shivers down our spines. I exchanged glances with Marsha. The world was falling apart at the seams.

Regardless of where the images came from—Louisiana, the Netherlands, Bangladesh, Vietnam—it was clear the mass evacuation of flooded areas had been poorly organised and carried out in a great hurry. Nobody seemed to know where all those hundreds of thousands of refugees could go. Many displaced people refused to leave their homes, declaring they would stand their ground come hell or high water. The authorities couldn't cope with the situation. Social unrest was brewing, and in some places riots and looting ensued. The police did what they could to restore law and order, but chaos loomed.

One inhabitant of New Orleans, Louisiana, summed it up in an interview: "This is a lot worse than Katrina, and this time there won't be any reconstruction. The flooding will never go away. We'll drown unless we manage to adapt. The worst thing is, we've only seen the beginning."

In the meantime, the teams that tried to catch some alien eggs (that's what everyone called them, whatever they might be) failed to get close. The organic material, stored in a sort of underwater grid, was protected by an invisible barrier or force field. Alien technology was superior to our primitive resources. Without any way to study the eggs, the clues to unlocking this mystery remained beyond our reach.

To make matters worse, the aliens' pollutants evaporated into the atmosphere and came back down with the rain, contaminating the soil and ground water. I hoped the results for plants and animals, not to mention mankind, were not as disastrous as they had been for marine life. Maybe the particles precipitating would be diluted to the point that their effect was negligible. Sadly, there seemed no scientific basis for this. Recent analyses confirmed the pollutants had an unknown composition and were of an alien nature.

Marsha and I had a discussion about whether the aliens were out to destroy all life on earth. She compared it to people building a garden shed and destroying an ants' nest in the process. Even if they knew, they didn't care. Ants were of no importance.

We worried about Jessica's future. In what kind of world would she grow up? Would there be a place for her generation in an alien-occupied world? There was no way to know, but the news bulletins chilled us to the bone.

As that man from Louisiana had said, "We've only seen the beginning."

WE'RE GETTING THERE! A large expanse of water now has the right temperature and chemical balance for our purposes. If the final tests prove successful, this planet will be very useful indeed. Thanks to the rapidly melting ice caps, the volume of water is increasing, an added benefit. It's clear we stumbled onto a perfect world. Too bad these water-covered planets are so rare.

JESSICA WAS SCARED, LIKE most kids these days. We tried to comfort her and hoped she didn't see we were scared, too. The schools had closed. Most parents deemed it safer to keep their children at home. It meant I was home, too, just like Marsha— no one was booking holidays anymore. If this went on, the economy would collapse like a house of cards.

The politicians were losing their grip on the situation. Nations were no longer co-operating, as each government resorted to desperate measures to save what it could. There were rumours that China (or India, or Pakistan, according to other sources) had used a nuclear weapon against a spacecraft, only to discover that it had produced as little effect as traditional bombings. So much for the military approach.

The massive evacuation of coastal regions resulted in chaos. Driven to despair, people started rioting and looting. In areas threatened less directly, people bought as many supplies as they could. So, did we. We told Jessica it was wise to be prepared.

On TV, a biologist summed it up: "The aliens' toxic ocean pollutants are now hitting the continental ecosystems. We're witnessing the first signs of a breakdown of the food chain, which will have dramatic consequences. As agriculture and cattle breeding become problematical, famine will result. There's no way to tell how fast this will go, but once the breakdown has set in, it will be very difficult to revert, stop, or even slow down."

Politicians, unused to thinking beyond the next elections, were unable to cope with problems of such magnitude. They limited themselves to dealing with symptoms, not trying to eliminate the cause of the problem – they didn't have a clue how, of course, didn't even think about trying. There was little hope for any constructive countermeasures.

I had another discussion with Marsha, after Jessica went off to bed. If things turned sour, we wouldn't be able to stay in London, I told her. Life in big cities would become impossible as the battle for survival reached its boiling point. Once supplies started to run out, people would be at each other's throats. The last remaining supplies would go to those who had the most firepower.

Marsha stared and asked what we were supposed to do.

So, I told her about my plan. We should find kindred spirits, people we could trust, because as a group we would stand a better chance at making it. Then we should leave the city, taking our supplies, and look for a safe haven somewhere in the countryside. There we could start a new life and adapt to changing circumstances. It wouldn't be easy, but we had no other choice.

Marsha shook her head. She said this was not an expedition for children like Jessica and there was no way we could survive on our own devices.

I understood her criticism but repeated that we had no other choice.

DISINFECTION OF THE OCEANS is now complete; the continents were only partly cleared of life-forms, but this is of minor importance. The land masses are of no use to us. The latest tests showed that conditions are now perfect, and underwater breeding structures are being deployed on a massive scale. If all goes according to plan, the first harvest should be reaped before long. If the quality proves satisfactory, a non-stop cycle of breeding and harvesting will be started.

IT WAS AMAZING HOW QUICKLY society disintegrated. One moment we were living in a world of peace and quiet, and before we knew it the veneer of civilisation had been stripped away and everything fell apart.

I discussed my plans with friends and neighbours, and many seemed to agree. We prepared ourselves for the expedition, buying supplies (some euphemistically declared they had "laid hands" on supplies—I did not push for details) and everything else we might need—including weapons. We realised we were facing tough times, especially for the children joining us.

When the last in a series of power failures seemed to be the definitive one and we fell without running water, we knew there was no point in staying in the city anymore.

The final reports we heard on the radio (TV and the internet had already been down for a while) stated that frantic activity was observed around the hovering spacecraft, though the exact nature of that activity remained a mystery. The evacuation in Britain—there was no more news from the rest of the world—had ended in chaos. Refugees had flocked inland, only to find villages and cities on the verge of collapse. Their arrival had only made matters worse.

Toxic pollutants were pushing all life to the brink of extinction—and it didn't look as if an exception would be made for mankind. Crops and livestock were doomed, and people were dying, especially the weakest—children, old folks and those in poor health. Society was disintegrating fast. Once supplies ran low and structures began to fail, the descent into barbarism would be inevitable. We had reached the end of the line.

Our group, which we optimistically called the Survivalists, prepared for imminent departure. We knew where we were heading, how to get there and which problems we might face. What we didn't know was how long we would be able to stand our ground or what we would do when our supplies ran out. But there were no other options.

MORE THAN A HUNDRED breeding stations have now been set up, and so far, everything is running perfectly. If the first harvest proves successful – and that appears likely – yet more stations will be added. This world covered by vast oceans, slightly adapted to suit our purposes, is a welcome addition to our home breeding grounds that no longer allow full expansion, and a rare treasure we will no doubt benefit from for a long time.

IT TOOK SEVERAL days to reach the mansion in Hitchin, north of London, which we had chosen as our hide-out. It belonged to a friend of one of my neighbours.

Our journey was dreadful, for various reasons. Firstly, as we travelled north, we passed through a city in its death throes. Traces of violence were everywhere. Charred houses, abandoned cars, looted shops and supermarkets. Bodies littered the streets. At times we found ourselves under attack, as armed gangs wanted the supplies that we carried. We defended ourselves, though more than half of our party didn't make it to Hitchin. We lost, among others, both Marsha and Jessica. I cursed myself for taking them on this perilous journey but leaving them in London would have been equally disastrous. I reached the mansion a broken man—like most of the others. I can't bring myself to recount the details of our losses.

Secondly, the landscape we passed through was in a state of decay, with all vegetation either dead or dying. Hardly any animals could be seen. The world had become a lifeless wasteland, through which a handful of stragglers moved on their way toward a mirage. Faced with such bleak surroundings, it was hard not to yield to despair. Out here in the open, the extent of earth's damage was much more evident than in the city. It was incredible how fast life on earth had been wiped out. Whether or not it had been done on purpose, it no longer mattered.

We found the mansion unoccupied and in decent condition. The first night we took stock of our situation. Because our party had been decimated, we had supplies for more than a week. We could only hope there would be no uninvited guests eager to share our meals, and we preferred not to think yet of what would happen when we ran out of food and water.

We didn't talk a lot. We had seen too much and lost too many people. We were exhausted, both physically and emotionally, and retired after a frugal meal, fearful of what tomorrow would bring. Tired though I was, I couldn't sleep. We were cut off from news. I wondered what had happened to all those big cities along the world's coastlines: New York, Barcelona, Hong Kong and so many more. How many inhabitants had managed to escape to higher land? Had the entire world been ravaged by those alien pollutants, or had certain regions escaped the onslaught? Perhaps there were places on earth where life was still possible, where mankind yet had a chance to survive.

Of course, there were no answers to these questions. There might never be any.

THE PLANET IS NOW virtually cleansed of native life. There were a few minor disruptions at some workstations where embryos turned out to be contaminated. The problem was contained, and the losses negligible. The execution of our plan will by no means be affected by this incident. As a matter of fact, the success the first run achieved was bigger than expected. Needless to say, we have high hopes.

WE HAD BEEN HOLED up in the Hitchen mansion for five days. The landscape was drained of colour, now that all vegetation was gone. No birds could be seen in the air, no insects or spiders were crawling around. A deadly silence reigned supreme.

Although we rationed food and water, our supplies dwindled fast. Most of us began to yield to despair. There was no way to know if our little pocket of resistance was the final stronghold of mankind, or that others had been more successful. Perhaps nomads in the desert or tribes in the Amazon basin, accustomed to hardships under extreme conditions, were better equipped to deal with such a worldwide catastrophe and still struggled on. It was equally possible that they were the first to go.

A member of our group, a man called Martin, did a tour of the area, hoping to find supplies and other survivors. He came back with nothing but an ugly insect bite on his upper arm. He claimed to have been attacked by a big flying bug he had never seen before. In a sense this was good news; it was evidence there were still insects and maybe other animals. On the other hand, aggressive creatures inflicting serious injuries were not what we needed.

We could only give basic medical care, but we did what we could. The following morning, the bite was infected. Martin said it was throbbing with pain. There was little we could do—our small stash of medication had no effect. Things looked very bad indeed for Martin.

Later that day we saw two of the insects with our own eyes. They were large and extremely aggressive, as Martin had claimed. Several men chased one and caught the other, smashing it to the ground, where it remained motionless, probably dazed rather than crushed. Upon closer inspection it proved an insect unlike any we had ever seen, a monster straight out of a horror movie. It was the size of a mouse, sporting claws and jaws that could tear apart a small animal. No wonder Martin had suffered such a serious injury.

We came to the conclusion it had to be a mutated new species. Could it be that it had developed an immunity against the alien pollutants and evolved into this horrific thing? Or had it feasted on alien eggs and become this hybrid half-alien monstrosity?

All we knew was that we'd have to protect ourselves against this fearsome enemy, as if our situation wasn't bad enough already.

THE FIRST HARVEST HAS been reaped. The quality is higher than expected: more than ninety percent of the embryos have matured. They will be transferred to breeding docks where they should develop into larvae. This planet is perfect for our purposes. More workstations will be deployed, and embryos will be planted on a massive scale. There are no problems or glitches of any significance. It was observed that native life-forms fed on a small number of failed and discarded embryos, miraculously survived and even thrived. This is of no importance. Further disinfection of the planet is not required. The operation will proceed as scheduled.

MARTIN DIED TODAY. THE infection had grown massive, and a high fever drove him beyond the limits of endurance. We buried him and wondered who will bury the last ones to go.

The rest of us aren't much better off. Our supplies have run out. We have no idea what we'll do next. It's clear the game is over.

We've seen more of the killer insects. We chased them away, but as we grow weaker, we'll become more vulnerable. I wonder what they eat. Apart from a handful of humans like us, there doesn't seem to be any food—strange to think of ourselves as a food supply for insects. Do they prey on themselves, or on something else we're not aware of? Maybe they nibble at alien eggs, but in that case what drove them so far inland?

Desperate though our situation is, it offers a ray of hope. I know this sounds paradoxical. An analogy may make clear what I mean: after the gigantic meteor that wiped out the dinosaurs and other creatures millions of years ago, mammals arrived on the scene, ultimately evolving into humans and leading to civilisation. Cataclysm paved the way for new successes. These aliens have struck a similar blow, perhaps consciously, perhaps inadvertently, and again some resilient species was given a new lease on life. Maybe this planet-wide genocide will lead to the dawn of a new age on earth, with various species evolving from insects that adapt to new circumstances.

Maybe one day in the far future, a new civilisation will arise, able to live alongside the aliens, or perhaps able to exterminate them.

I don't know if anyone will ever read these lines, but it's nice to end on a positive note, even if I may be among the last men left on earth.

All is not lost. Some will carry on.

I'll go with that idea in mind.

THE END

FRANK ROGER was born in 1957 in Ghent, Belgium. His first story appeared in 1975. Since then his stories appear in an increasing number of languages in all sorts of magazines and anthologies in various languages. Apart from fiction, he also produces collages and visual art in a surrealist and satirical tradition. They have appeared in various magazines and books. He has a few hundred short stories to his credit, published in more than 40 languages. In 2012, a story collection in English, *The Burning Woman and Other Stories* was published by *Evertype*. Find out more at www.frankroger.be.

STARS IN HER EYES

Vaughan Stanger

Originally appeared in *Postscripts 17* (PS Publishing) in 2008.

JEROME DALTON GAZED AT an October night sky made perfect by the absence of moonlight. Arching overhead, the Milky Way resembled a strip of gauze draped over black velvet. Having set up his CCD-equipped Celestron so that it tracked the Andromeda Galaxy, he fully intended to indulge his passion for stargazing.

The sound of footfalls startled him. Before he could step aside, a thump in the back tumbled him to the ground. Winded, he stared up at his assailant, who was sliding a bulky pair of headphones off her ears.

"Shit! Sorry, I didn't see you …" The woman's apology dribbled off into the air.

Jerome pushed away her hands. "I can manage," he grumbled. Upright again, he unclipped his torch and thumbed it on. He felt no remorse at ruining the woman's night vision.

"Sorry, that was so my fault," she said, blinking.

Seeing her remorseful expression, Jerome softened his tone. "Well, you missed the 'scope, that's the main thing."

A smile led to a handshake and an exchange of names.

Lenora Kelly stood chin high to him, five-three or thereabouts. Jet black hair bobbed *à la mode* framed prominent cheekbones and a ski-jump nose. Stargazer standard fleece and baggy pants hid her presumably skinny physique. Quite good-looking in a quirky kind of way, he decided, surprised that he hadn't noticed her before. Dozens of amateur astronomers had pitched their tents around Patterson Lake, tempted out of Greater Seattle by a rare forecast of fine weather. Most of them were male.

"What're you listening to?"

She passed him the headphones. "Here, give it a try."

After a brief inspection of the headband, which incorporated a stubby antenna, he placed the 'phones over his ears. He heard a faint, burbling hiss. He tilted his head. The sound grew louder as the Milky Way came into view, faded as his gaze skated past. Unimpressed by this simple modulation of celestial static, he handed the 'phones back.

Lenora's smile flared to nova strength. "Wonderful, isn't it?"

Faced with that smile, he wished he could agree, but five years of marriage had shown him that telling lies was not his forte.

"Wouldn't want to listen to the 21 cm hydrogen line all night long."

Seemingly undeterred by his indifference, she tapped the antenna. "This connects to the SETI Institute's all-sky database, so I can listen to the freshest data from wherever I'm looking. Head-tracked radio astronomy—cool, huh?"

Jerome chuckled at her mention of SETI. "I signed up for SETI@home back in the late Nineties. Then I lost my job at Boeing, so I had to find more lucrative ways to exploit my computer's idle time." And latterly his own, of course.

Lenora shrugged like someone hearing a familiar story.

Fearing her interest was waning, Jerome pointed towards the zenith. "Reckon there's anyone on the phone?"

"Has to be," she whispered.

"But why do you listen?"

She shrugged. "I like to be involved."

Her answer sounded self-deluding, but he kept the thought to himself. Better to have a specious purpose in life than none at all, which pretty much described his own situation since Josie packed her bags.

After failing to stifle a yawn, he pointed his torch at his 'scope. "I'm going to download the image and then crash for the night." The idea of zipping together two sleeping bags flashed like a meteor in his mind but expired just as quickly.

You've got ten years on her!

To his surprise, Lenora lingered while he booted up his laptop. As he'd half-expected, the Andromeda image had tanked. Not wishing her to see him so easily thwarted, he loaded the file into a picture enhancement application a lecturer friend at UCLA had copied for him.

"I'll let that brew overnight."

Lenora hunkered down beside him. "You could get involved too," she whispered.

"How do you mean?"

She gave him an appraising look. "Did you bring your WhileAway console?"

How had she worked that out? Mind you, Josie had reckoned he looked the sort.

"I figured if someone had brought their server I could hook up and earn ten dollars."

Did that make him sound like a tightwad?

To his relief, Lenora lit another smile. "Well, luckily for you, my partner did bring his server." She winkled a thumb-drive out of her pocket. "And if you'd like to try something different, just load this patch and then …"

"And then what, exactly?" he asked, irritated by her reference to a partner, concerned too that he might be falling for a scam. Rumours of WhileAway hackers abounded in the blogosphere.

"And then I'll see you tomorrow for breakfast."

The alternative of subsisting on cereal bars made her invitation seem enticing.

"That's my tent over there," said Lenora, pointing along the path. Jerome wished her goodnight as she turned away.

After packing away his 'scope, Jerome loaded Lenora's patch onto his WhileAway console. Satisfied, he donned his skullcap and snuggled down in his sleeping bag. He tried to ignore the prickle of electrodes against his scalp while he waited for sleep to come.

THE SETTING SUN TWITCHED ribbons of crimson between gunmetal waves. A salt-tangy breeze ruffled his hair. Surf sluiced over his feet, making him shiver as he strolled the infinite beach.

Aware he was supposed to be looking for something, he squatted down at the water's edge and began sifting through flotsam. He pushed aside a plank of driftwood and found a piece of glass.

Something made of glass; he was searching for something made of glass.

BEACHES … HE HATED BEACHES … Body not toned enough …

But beachcombing … That was fun!

Jerome stretched out his arms and plucked the skullcap from his head. For once he didn't feel woozy from having his REM sleep messed about by WhileAway. Usually, he dreamt of searching for a needle in a haystack, the standard metaphor used by biotech companies that rented his downtime. Beachcombing certainly had that beat.

Recalling Lenora's offer of breakfast, he unzipped his sleeping bag. As he wriggled free, he heard someone moving outside the tent. Before he could call out, a hand tugged at the flap. A face previously seen by torchlight peered in.

"So how was it?"

"Pretty cool," he replied, his voice not quite masking his rumbling stomach. "Any chance of breakfast?"

"Might manage a coffee."

He pulled on his Levis and shirt and followed Lenora outside. A short walk along the lakeside brought them to her tent. Big enough for two, he observed. Lenora pulled open the flap.

"Who have you got there?" said a male voice. "Another recruit?"

Lenora arched a neatly plucked eyebrow. "Maybe."

The man who emerged wore calf-length cargo pants and a black tee shirt that showed off his biceps. Sporting a wispy beard and mane of straw-coloured hair, he looked more surfer-dude than WhileAway geek. Older than Lenora, Jerome surmised.

She introduced him to Zane, who ignored Jerome's proffered hand.

"Is he staying here tonight?"

Jerome scanned the lakeside. Most of the astronomers had already departed, but he felt no desire to follow them. Camping weekends were as much vacation as his income allowed.

He glanced at Lenora. "Well, last night's dream was kind of fun."

"You've got Zane to thank for that."

Jerome turned towards him. "So, what's your cut?"

Zane's eyes flicked skyward. "WhileAway would sue our hides if they knew what we're up to. So no, SETI dreaming won't earn you a dime, never mind ten bucks."

"No problem. The dream was worth the money, easy."

Lenora nailed him with another of her smiles. Zane gave him a pitying look and ducked back into the tent.

Lenora squeezed Jerome's arm. "Last night was just a taster. The next dream will be a lot more fun."

Despite her show of affection, Jerome couldn't quite convince himself she really wanted him. Still, if he followed her lead, who knew where he might end up? Better still, he could take the lead.

Over coffee, he suggested a walk around the lake. He enjoyed watching Zane's expression turn even sourer when Lenora told him.

"He's just being boorish," she said, when safely out of earshot. "We were lovers once, years ago. Now we're just partners in crime."

This encouraging news was pretty much all Jerome learnt about Lenora while they walked around the lake. He answered several questions regarding life with Josie, whereas she deflected his with aplomb. When he asked about her job, she flashed her lovely smile and changed the subject. No less mysterious was her decision to carry a backpack on a walk that seemed likely to last no more than two hours. He was about to suggest that he take it for a while when she flopped down on a boulder that jutted into the lake.

"Room for two," she said, patting the rock.

Smiling, he sat down next to her and removed his boots. He dangled his feet in the water. The cold made him flinch, but the warmth of the sunlight compensated nicely. He lay back, luxuriating in the feeling that all was right with the world.

"Close your eyes."

He obeyed, hoping for a kiss. Instead, Lenora's breath tickled his ear. "And keep them closed!"

He heard rummaging sounds. Moments later, he felt electrodes prickle against his scalp. On opening his eyes, he saw that Lenora was also wearing a WhileAway cap.

"Are you sure we'll receive a signal here?"

She held up two consoles. Both readouts showed five green bars.

"Okay, but I don't feel sleepy."

She rattled a bottle and shook out two pink pills. "These babies will see to that."

Jerome felt tempted to suggest a more enjoyable way, but his courage deserted him. Seeing his doleful expression, Lenora leaned over and kissed him on the lips.

"A little bodily contact helps promote shared dreaming, but too much gets in the way." She winked at him. "Just give me a minute."

After configuring the WhileAway consoles for synchronous operation, she clambered back onto the boulder. She lay beside Jerome with knees slightly raised, her bare forearm touching his.

There were, he mused, much worse ways to spend an afternoon.

STROLLING HAND IN HAND along the infinite beach, he felt as though he could walk forever.

Too soon, his partner tugged her hand free and fell to her knees. He hunkered down beside her and began sifting shingle.

What are we looking for?

A bottle, silly; a message in a bottle!

Ah, yes! Something made of glass.

Their search turned up not so much as a fragment, let alone a bottle. Unconcerned, he skimmed pebbles beyond the breaking waves.

Laughing, they resumed their walk in the sun.

JEROME BLINKED UNTIL THE grey blobs came into focus. Cumulonimbus clouds towered over Lake Patterson. A glance at his wristwatch revealed three hours had passed.

"Did you enjoy the dream?" asked Lenora.

"Yeah, that was fun," he replied, "if frustrating." Seeing her expression, he added, "Not finding a bottle, I mean."

"SETI dreamers must be patient."

"Pity the weather gods haven't mastered that trick," he said, glancing at the sky.

They jogged back to the camp, taking turns with the backpack, but the storm won the race. Hailstones pelted them as they sprinted the last hundred yards.

"See you tonight at the beach!" Lenora yelled as she ducked into her tent.

Jerome stripped off and towelled himself dry. Aware that he hadn't brought a change of clothes, he considered jumping into his pickup truck and driving off. But Lenora's exhortation held him back.

He spent the evening reading a paperback novel by torchlight. When the storm finally rumbled off into the Cascades, he switched on his WhileAway console, selected auto-synch and reached for his cap.

ANNOYED THAT SHE HAD let go of his hand again, he flopped down in the shallows. The ebb and flow tugged at him while he waited for her to finish examining whatever had caught her eye. To his left, a man stood on a distant sand dune. The man seemed familiar but did not respond to his wave.

A triumphant yell startled him into sitting up. He stared at his partner. She was holding a bottle aloft, her trophy gleaming in the sunlight. He leapt to his feet, but the sand sucked at his heels, turning his sprint into a moonwalk. As he reached out towards her, she faded from view. The bottle thudded onto sand; a sheet of paper wafted nearby.

No longer bogged down, he snatched up the paper before the breeze could blow it into the sea. He held the sheet at arm's length. Frowning, he turned it over.

Blank on both sides.

JEROME WOKE TO THE sound of rain pummelling his tent. Forked lightning zigzagged through the darkness; thunder rumbled like tympani. He wriggled deeper into his sleeping bag, fingertips jammed in his ears. Even with his eyes shut tight he could still see the lightning.

A sudden inrush of air made the tent billow alarmingly. Jerome opened his eyes and saw Zane's head poke through the flap.

"Quick, get your waterproofs on," Zane yelled. "Lenora's gone missing!"

"What the hell is she …?"

Zane backed out before Jerome could finish his question. He wriggled into his sodden Levis, tugged on his boots and jacket. Outside he found Zane jogging along the lakeside, hair plastered over his face, shouting, "Lenora!"

Jerome shielded his eyes with both hands while he scanned the landscape. Lightning lit up the nearest hill just long enough for him to glimpse a figure standing at the summit.

"She's up there!" he shouted, pointing at the hill.

Trusting that Zane would follow, Jerome charged up the slope. He weaved past Douglas Firs and tangles of bitterbrush, heedless of the danger from lightning. On reaching the summit, he paused for a moment to catch his breath. What he saw there made his jaw drop. Not twenty yards away Lenora danced naked beneath the lashing rain. She had just skipped to a fist-sized stone and was now turning on the spot, her feet shuffling either side of the marker. After completing three spins, she skipped to another stone and repeated the sequence. Jerome counted a dozen such moves before she stooped to pick up her markers. After placing them in a new pattern, she resumed her dance, oblivious to the rain or her audience.

An ear-splitting crash reminded him of the urgent need to get off the hilltop. He stripped off his jacket and moved in on Lenora, timing his lunge so he caught her off balance. He snared her left arm and yanked it behind her back, hoping to restrain her, but she squirmed like an eel.

"Zane, I need some help here!"

Zane rushed forward and grabbed Lenora's free arm. Working together, they managed to pull the jacket over her trembling shoulders. Lenora wriggled and jerked, her head darting left and right as if she were memorising the positions of the stones. The patterns did seem vaguely familiar to Jerome. Over there, wasn't that a "W?"

He pushed the thought to the back of his mind.

Zane led the way downhill. Halfway to the camp, Lenora tripped herself, sending Jerome tumbling into a bush. Bleeding from cuts to his hands and face, he extricated himself while Zane struggled to restrain Lenora. By the time they reached the lake, she had lapsed into unconsciousness.

Jerome unzipped the flap to Lenora's tent and held it open while Zane bundled her inside. When Jerome tried to follow, he found his way blocked. Unwilling to leave until reassured about Lenora's condition, he waited outside in the rain. He had just shouted his third offer of help when Zane pushed through the flap.

"Leave this to me. I know what I'm doing."

Jerome gaped. "She is having a fit! She needs to be in a hospital. If you're too scared to take her, I'll do it!"

Zane stood facing Jerome, hands planted on hips.

"Strictly speaking, Lenora has had a fit. Now it's over, she'll be unconscious for several hours. I know what to do, so let me look after her, okay?"

Unwilling to be fobbed off, Jerome tried to push past Zane, who responded with a two-handed shove. Jerome landed hard in a puddle.

Zane looked mortified. "Look, I'm sorry, I didn't mean to ..."

Jerome cuffed away his helping hand. "If Lenora comes to any harm, I'm holding you responsible! You got that?"

Zane made a placating gesture. "Trust me, she will be fine. But if it makes you feel better, I'll drive her to the hospital, soon as it's safe."

Jerome climbed to his feet. In truth, he felt too exhausted to drive, even though the rain had slackened off a bit and the thunder now trailed the lightning by several seconds.

"Storm's heading off," he muttered, inclining his head towards Zane's SUV.

Zane held up both hands. "Okay, okay."

Jerome helped Zane strap Lenora into a rear seat, but when he strode round to the passenger door, he found it locked.

"For pity's sake!" yelled Zane, eyes blazing, "Go dry yourself off and get some sleep. Otherwise, you'll be no help to Lenora tomorrow."

Pondering his last remark kept Jerome awake long after the thunder had rumbled into the distance.

TURN, TURN, TURN, AND skip: dance to the pattern of the stars …

Jerome plucked at his scalp while blinking away the dregs of the dream but didn't find the expected skullcap. Evidently, his subconscious had stimulated that last dream, unlike its predecessor.

Reluctant to leave the warmth of his sleeping bag, he thought about what he'd witnessed on the hilltop and the dream that preceded it. Lenora's dancing must be her way of interpreting alien messages, he realised. The implication was astonishing. Lenora had made First Contact!

But at what cost to her health?

The growl of an engine revving in low gear made Jerome start. He tugged on his jeans and crawled outside, expecting to find Zane parking his SUV. Instead, he observed a convoy rumbling up the gravel road. Lenora stood on the lakeside path, waving to each driver in turn; a queenly gesture.

Jerome counted eleven vehicles, each driven by an unaccompanied man. Was that all he meant to her? Merely a convenient way to boost her recruits to a symbolically pleasing dozen!

She arched an eyebrow as he approached. "See you tonight," she said, before turning smartly. The set of her shoulders suggested pursuit would not be tolerated.

He'd have to confront Zane instead.

JEROME FOUND ZANE UNPACKING a dish antenna from a wooden crate. A radio station blared from Zane's laptop. Space Oddity had just segued into Starman.

"So, it really is happening," said Jerome.

"Yeah, you just missed the news conference."

"What's the low-down?"

"Six months ago, one of NASA's satellites detected a sustained burst of gamma rays from an object previously classified as a comet. Having changed course for Earth, the unidentified spacecraft began transmitting signals. Problem was, NASA's experts couldn't interpret them. They still can't."

"But Lenora can."

"Correct."

Jerome pointed at the antenna. "What's this for, then?"

"Backup in case the SETI feed goes offline before the spacecraft reaches Earth, forty-eight hours from now."

"Bit late for the President to pull the plug, surely?"

"Can't take the risk, not when she's this close to success." Zane pressed thumb and forefinger together.

"If she's that close, why does she need these guys?" asked Jerome, pointing towards the nearest tent. "Or me, for that matter."

Zane rolled his eyes. "Do I really have to explain Lenora's *modus operandi*?"

"I figured that out for myself, thanks," Jerome replied. "The patterns she danced last night depicted the stars as seen from a planet en route to Earth. A celestial postcard, if you like."

"Yeah, dancing is the key. And if Lenora only had to read one message tonight, she'd be okay. But as the spacecraft nears Earth, the signal bandwidth will increase dramatically. So, she will have to read a lot of messages very quickly. To do that, she needs help. Which is where you come in."

A collective dream reading did make a weird kind of sense, thought Jerome. But had Zane considered the consequences? He swept his arm, indicating the entire campsite.

"Have you booked enough ambulances for tomorrow? Because from what I saw last night, every one of Lenora's disciples will need several hours of treatment."

"I've got a team of helpers on stand-by," Zane said, matter-of-factly. "So, if that's all, I've got a deadline to meet." He strode towards the nearest tent. Unwilling to be fobbed off, Jerome followed him inside.

On seeing Zane, the tent's occupant wrinkled his nose as if he'd detected a bad smell. For a moment, it seemed a single word might spark a fight; then Zane shrugged and turned away. After adjusting the man's WhileAway console, he tapped two pink pills into his upturned palm.

Outside again, Jerome asked, "What was that all about?"

"He's Number Two."

"Meaning what, exactly?"

"Well, you're Number Thirteen."

The implication became clear to Jerome.

"So, you were Lenora's first?"

"Yeah. And believe me, with Lenora first was definitely worst." Zane chuckled mirthlessly. "So now, as penance, I get to build a supercomputer out of her ex-boyfriends."

Jerome sympathised with his plight, but Lenora's plan for her disciples concerned him much more. Keen to exploit Zane's confessional state of mind, he asked how he knew her.

"We met at Caltech while I was studying for a Ph.D.," Zane recounted. "We fell in love, which was great; then she fell out of love, which wasn't. But we remained friends. After Lenora graduated, WhileAway recruited her to work on dream metaphors, whereas I drifted into white hacking."

Jerome raised his eyebrows, prompting a grin from Zane.

"Corporations pay well to have their security tested. Anyhow, Lenora had seen off four more boyfriends when she asked me to hack into the SETI Institute's database. I jumped at the chance, thinking it might get me back in her good books." He glanced at Jerome. "Did you try her SETI radio?"

"Yeah, that's how she hooked me."

Zane winced. "So, having successfully exploited my infatuation, she explained her idea for detecting signals from alien civilisations. No chance, I reckoned. But nine months after her first SETI dream, she found a bottle. Reading its message put her in an ICU for two weeks. Yet she tried again. Last night was her fifth message. Fortunately, she recovers a lot quicker now."

Jerome grabbed Zane by both shoulders, appalled by the implication.

"For God's sake man, her plan is outrageous! Sure, she'll recover in time to watch CNN broadcast the landing, but what about her disciples? They'll endure brainstorms lasting for weeks! How can you consider inflicting such suffering on them?"

Zane shrugged. "Someone's gotta do the beta testing."

A suspicion was growing in Jerome's mind.

"What, precisely, do you have planned for tomorrow night?"

Zane's eyes gleamed with a prophet's fervour. "If tonight's dry-run is successful, I'll be networking ten thousand sleeping minds into a SETI dream."

Jerome shook his head. Zane's unrequited love had made things so easy for Lenora. He had thrown himself into her scheme with no thought of the consequences. Yet something must be bothering him, because he was standing there wringing his hands. Jerome decided that an appeal to vanity might reveal a weakness he could exploit.

"So how does it work?"

Zane's eyes lit up again. "I've infected the entire WhileAway network with a stealth virus that will reprogramme the metaphor generator of every user who's also registered with SETI@home."

"The ultimate love bug, eh?"

Zane's mouth twitched into a grin.

"Can you neutralise the virus?"

Zane snorted. "Viruses don't have off switches."

"What about WhileAway's own defences?"

"Their network antibodies won't stop this virus."

"But surely if I told them Lenora's plan, WhileAway would take the service offline."

"It would be your word against hers. Who do you think they'd believe?"

Not that WhileAway, or anyone else, would pay attention to his accusation while humanity stood on the brink of such an historic event.

Zane pushed past him. "I'm still working to that deadline."

Dismayed by his inability to influence Zane, Jerome plodded down to the lake. A Mallard duck waddled past, quacking for easy pickings. Right now, communicating with wildfowl seemed a lot easier than trying to get through to Zane. Even talking to aliens couldn't be this difficult!

But that was it, Jerome realised. We should be talking to them not just listening. How else could humankind hope to achieve genuine understanding? He jogged back to the camp, found Zane inside his tent and frogmarched him to the antenna.

"What if we used this thing to send a message from within a dream?" said Jerome. "If we could persuade the aliens to only transmit isolated, simple messages, Lenora could manage without helpers."

Zane gave a fierce shake of his head.

"If you think I'm …"

Jerome grabbed his shoulders and shook him. "If Lenora gets her way, thousands will suffer. For God's sake man, you absolutely have to think!"

Zane lowered his gaze but said nothing.

"My friend, she won't ever take you back."

Zane gave a long sigh. "I know."

"So, will you help me put a stop to this madness?"

After a pause, Zane nodded. Then his expression went blank as if he had focused his mind's eye on some internal computer screen. Several minutes passed before he replied.

"From a purely technical standpoint, it's do-able. I can modulate your brain waves over the WhileAway carrier and push out the signal on the aliens' frequency." He paused, frowning. "But how will you compose a message they'll understand? You can't just write 'turn down the volume' in English."

Jerome gestured frantically. "Dammit Zane, they build spaceships, don't they? When they look at the night sky, they see patterns of stars. I bet they dance, too!" He softened his tone. "Look, if Lenora can read alien messages while dreaming, there must be a way to write one they'll understand. She erased their message last night, so maybe she was planning to write one herself."

Zane shook his head. "No, she was protecting you."

"There must be a way!"

Zane's expression blanked out again. "There is," he said after a few seconds, "but you won't remember the details if I tell you now. Just use what you find in the dreamscape."

"Exploit the metaphor?"

"Exactly."

"So, can you program it in time for tonight's run?"

Zane grinned. "No problem."

HE JOGGED ALONG THE infinite beach, looking for the bottle. After what seemed like ages, he found it, half-buried in the sand. The blank sheet of paper lay nearby. He picked up his finds and resumed his search.

Next, he spied a plank of rotting driftwood floating in the shallows. He prised a splinter free and dipped it in beach tar. His hands trembled as he held pen to paper.

But what should he write?

Despairing, he dropped his tools and walked to the water's edge. The urge to abandon his task washed over him, but he knew he could not. Instead, he scooped up handfuls of pebbles and rubbed them together, grinding out his frustration.

Finally, inspiration came.

He dropped a pebble in the sand, then another, then several more, letting instinct guide his placements. When the pattern seemed right, he skipped from pebble to pebble, spinning three times at each marker. After a dozen repetitions, he picked up the pebbles and started again.

He danced and danced until he fell to his knees, leaving just enough time to grab pen and paper before exhaustion tipped him into the void.

THE PERFECT BLACK SKY glittered with stars.
Thousands of people arrived at the beach.
Each held a bottle plucked from the sea.
Each of them danced and then fell asleep.
And the aliens came ...

The sun rose over the dunes.
The sun set over the sea.
Rose and set, rose and set.
But the dancers slept on.
So the aliens left.

SAND CUPPED HIS HEAD as he stared at the azure sky. When he stretched out his arms, one hand landed on glass while the other slapped against paper.

He held the sheet at arm's length, shielding his eyes from the sun. The symbols meant nothing to him.

He rolled up the sheet and pushed it into the bottle. Now, how to seal it? He scoured the dune, found a screw top. Having secured the message, he waded into the water until waist-deep and threw the bottle far out to sea.

Relieved to have completed his task, he splashed in the shallows like a child until a yell jolted him from his play.

Looking along the beach, he saw her standing amid a group of men. One of them upended a bottle and tapped its base. A roll of paper fell into his hand. Before the man could read it, he faded from view. The woman yelled at her remaining helpers, but they faded out too, one after another. She fell to her knees, weeping.

He knew he should flee, but the lure of her despair was too strong. As he drew near, she shuffled round to face him. Seeing her smile broke the spell.

He sprinted along the beach, pounding wet sand with his feet, but a glance over his shoulder revealed she was gaining. Though he dodged and weaved, her foot snagged his trailing leg and tumbled him into the sand. She loomed over him, thrusting a sheet of paper in his face.

Read this!

Thinking she would not risk soaking the paper, he crawled into the surf. Her hand snatched at his ankle, but he pulled free. Kicking hard, he dived into the breaking waves. He held his breath against straining lungs, willing himself to wake up.

A HAND TUGGED AT Jerome's shoulder, hastening his return to consciousness.

"Come on, get moving!" Zane sounded panicky.

"I'm going nowhere until I've seen Len—"

A piercing shriek cut him short.

"I'm taking her to the hospital," said Zane. "She's even worse than her first time."

"You'll stay with her until she recovers?"

"Of course!"

"What about her disciples?"

"They're why you need to get moving."

Jerome followed Zane out of his tent. Several men charged towards them, yelling obscenities. He sprinted for his truck. Bottles smashed against the hood as he floored the gas pedal.

It wasn't until he reached the Winthrop road that he remembered to switch on the radio. The NASA spokesman's voice boomed inside the cab.

"We're now predicting the spacecraft will fly by at a distance of two million miles." A brief pause, then, "Sorry folks, they're just passing through."

Jerome pounded his fists against the steering wheel. This was not what he'd intended. Rather than tone down their messages, the aliens had evidently concluded that humanity was not ready to dream with them. Thanks to him, only Lenora had enjoyed that privilege.

No doubt she would regard him as her Judas.

That his actions had spared thousands of WhileAway users from mental injury did nothing to lift his mood. As he drove into the outskirts of Winthrop, his eyes filled with tears.

ON THE FIRST ANNIVERSARY of his encounter with Lenora, Jerome returned to Patterson Lake.

He had just finished lining up his 'scope on Mars when he felt a shove from behind. This time, despite stumbling, he managed to regain his balance. He tugged off his headphones and turned to face his assailant. Moonlight illuminated a familiar figure.

"Couldn't you just say 'hi?'"

Lenora flicked on her flashlight and pointed it at his face. Jerome peered through a fence of fingers, blinking away purple spots.

"Hurts your eyes, does it?" Her voice cut like broken glass. "Now imagine your brain overloaded in the same way!"

The thought made him shudder, but he didn't respond. Let her vent her fury; she had every right.

"I ran after you because I thought you could help, but you dived into the sea and disappeared." Her tone turned regretful. "I knew I didn't have long, so I read every message. There were dozens and dozens of them."

Without warning, she threw herself at Jerome. He grabbed her wrists before her fists could hurt him.

"It was too much," she mumbled into his chest. "Dammit Jerome, I could have made it work if only you'd let me try!" He allowed her to pull back but didn't let go.

"You gave me no choice. If you had carried out your plan, the mental health of thousands of people would have been put at risk. I did the right thing."

"If you believe sending the aliens away was the right thing, then yeah, job done!"

"That wasn't my intention," he said.

"Oh, I realise you didn't want that outcome, but that is what happened," said Lenora. "It was you who convinced the aliens that humanity was too dumb to bother with." She snorted. "And I can see their point!"

Her frustration mirrored the feelings of billions of people worldwide. Fortunately for Jerome, Zane had done a thorough job of covering their tracks while also tending to Lenora.

"How long were you unconscious?"

"Six ... frickin ... months!"

He stared, open-mouthed.

"How do you feel now?"

"It's bearable during the day, but at night, when I'm dreaming, it's like I've got aliens living in my head." She tugged hard and broke free from his grip. "I have you to thank for that."

Which was indubitably true and impossible to remedy.

"Have you learnt anything from your dreams? Like, where they come from?" He felt momentarily ashamed at letting his curiosity get the better of him, then told himself that the so-called experts hadn't found out even that much yet.

She stepped over to the 'scope and swung it towards the zenith. "There," she said.

With the Moon so bright, Jerome couldn't make out her target even using averted vision, but he knew precisely where the 'scope was pointing.

He whistled long and low. "So far from home!"

She nodded. "Two million light years, give or take."

"What a story they'd have told us." Even as he spoke the words, he wished he could suck them out of the air. He held his hands out, begging forgiveness. To his surprise, her expression softened.

"Every night, a little of that story plays in here." She tapped her forehead. "But I can't make sense of it. For that, I need help."

"I'll do anything," he said.

Lenora took his hand and led him to her jeep, which she'd parked next to his truck while he stargazed to Holst. She opened the door and picked up two WhileAway consoles from the passenger seat.

"During my quieter phases, Zane coded up a new version of the software." Seeing Jerome's anxious expression, she added, "Don't worry, it runs offline. Zane figured that when I'd recovered, I might need a way to share my dreams."

Jerome chuckled. "Two heads being better than one?"

She nodded. "But Zane was too scared to try it."

In truth, the prospect terrified Jerome too, but it made sense to test Zane's farewell present before Lenora sought out new disciples, as she surely would.

"Let's get started then."

BY THE TIME JEROME crawled from his tent, the sun had risen over the hills. As he walked along the lakeside path, his mind's eye superimposed an image of blue-pelted, apelike creatures cavorting on a beach of amber sand beneath a jet-black sky.

Aliens' never-ending dance must mean something, he told himself, but he had no idea what. They might have been electing a new leader, for all he knew. Sharing Lenora's dream had left him with a pounding headache but no particular insights.

Where was Lenora? Hiking in the hills, most likely. Doubtless working off some of that rage. When she returned, they could talk some more. He would try to explain, again, why he'd refused to sleep with her last night.

In the meantime, he had some new dance steps to try out.

THE END

VAUGHAN STANGER, formerly an astronomer and more recently a research project manager in a defence and aerospace company, now writes science fiction and fantasy full-time, a career development that seems appropriate for someone who remembers watching the Apollo 11 moon-landing on television. He still craves that holiday on the Moon he claims he was promised as a child.

His stories have appeared in *Daily Science Fiction*, *Abyss & Apex*, *Postscripts*, *Nature Futures* and *Interzone*, amongst others. He has published two collections, *Moondust Memories* and *Sons of the Earth & Other Stories*, which are available as ebooks and print-on-demand paperbacks. Several of his stories have been translated into foreign languages. When not keeping track of his submissions, Vaughan is hard at work on a series of SF novels.

You can follow Vaughan's writing adventures at www.vaughanstanger.com and @VaughanStanger.

THE PATTERN BOX
Christina Klarenbeek

Originally appeared in *Ecotones*, December 15, 2015

THE SIREN ROUSED HIM with such a start that Avery almost opened his eyes. He squeezed them shut as the pump kicked on and the outtake shaft slurped up goo. Edwards had been so sure the trip would be uneventful. He swallowed a wry chuckle as he fidgeted, envying her optimism.

The fans kicked on as the level dropped and he coughed and pulled at the feeding tube, desperate to get it out. Too slowly it scraped across his throat. He took a hurried breath through his nose. Still thick with artificial amniotic fluid, it ran down his throat as thick as snot. He gagged before he spat it into the surrounding slurry, cleared his nose, and took another breath. Panic was pointless.

To his left, Rodriquez pounded on his pod. At only five-foot-three, he wouldn't be able to breathe for another three minutes. Avery thumped back, slow and steady while, to his right, Edwards maintained her trademark smug, stoic silence.

Something, a hundred somethings, hit the ship in an endless succession that threatened his composure. Rodriguez stopped pounding as a computerised voice announced they were on auxiliary power, with life support at ninety-eight percent. That, in itself, didn't sound too bad but he needed to get to the bridge to determine what was hitting the hull and if the fleet was still intact. The computer continued to drone warnings as Avery's shoulders rose and tensed. His hands clenched and unclenched in time with the siren and he knew he was in trouble.

"Wait for it," he whispered, rolling his shoulders.

He raised his hands above the surface and scraped them across one another in an effort to clean them before he moved on to his face. The crap was stuck in a beard he shouldn't have, and Avery's heart began to race. He could think of only two explanations, and neither had them in orbit around Gliese. Either a malfunction had lengthened his wake cycles, using extra power and threatening his mental acuity, or they'd bypassed their destination by countless light years and were now stranded in unknown space with failing support. Neither was good.

An intense light bathed him in warmth as the amniotic fluid level dropped below the interior utility hatch, granting him access to the only pod towel that had survived cost cutting. The slimy shit was like diluted Vaseline, and it seeped between his lashes to cloud his vision. Through the clear polyamide, Rodriquez seemed to waver before him like a grumpy fun house reject. "With all the fucking money they threw into this crap mission you'd think they could afford to give us more than a fucking face wipe." Rodriguez's raspy voice was like hearing a favourite song.

Avery smiled at the welcome distraction. "You okay?"

"Yeah, I'm fi… fuck." Rodriguez nodded his head towards Edwards' tank. Avery turned, instantly wishing he hadn't.

Through the murk inside he could discern a collection of bones congregated at the bottom. Edwards was soup. After fifteen years, she deserved better than to go out like that.

As a boy, he'd dreamed about flying through space in his own rocket ship, rescuing pretty girls. The *T.A.M.A.R.A.* wasn't his, and the prettiest girl was beyond saving.

Avery blew out a couple of deep breaths and struggled to get back on task. He removed his waste tubes with care and watched as their contents flowed back into the tank. He stood, up to his ass, in shit of his own making while the slurry continued its lazy swirl down the drain. When they were finally clear to climb out, there was still so much goo on their feet they slid across the room grabbing at pod handles to stay upright.

Avery hit the opposite wall and thumbed the button that silenced the alarm, leaned over the one working computer, and held a bleary eye to a retinal scanner that failed to identify him. He stepped back and let Rodriquez have a go while he struggled into a set of coveralls that twisted and clung to his still wet legs despite his best efforts to get them straightened out.

He was fighting with the zipper when Rodriquez gave his assessment. "We're fucked."

It was the inflection that told the tale. "What about the rest of the fleet?"

Rodriquez shrugged. The computer showed they'd been travelling normally, but for way too long, when their power had simply vanished. If they didn't get it back up soon, the pods would start shutting down by reverse priority order.

The problem was that the fuel cells weren't disconnected—they were drained, and auxiliary power was dropping.

A panicked voice came over the com. "They're alive."

Rodriquez rolled his eyes. "Was that Callaghan? What the fuck's he doing on the bridge?"

Avery shook his head. "Best find out."

They ran through the ship and flattened themselves against the wall to make way for techs in too much of a hurry to observe protocol. Rodriguez clapped him on the shoulder. "Glad to see someone useful is awake, but Callaghan's an idiot. How many people gotta die before they leave him in charge?"

Avery stopped just outside the bridge, but the answers on the other side of the door didn't care if he was ready to hear them. "He's the last of the civilian command."

Rodriguez held open the door. "Want me to shoot him?"

He laughed as he walked through. "Not yet."

Still naked from his pod, Callaghan leaned heavily against the helm. The poor kid's entire left side was a withered mess of atrophied muscle, the apparent result of cheap electrodes. Avery resisted the urge to run his hands over limbs he'd already assessed.

"Sit rep?" he asked.

Callaghan turned. He looked frightened but hopeful as he slammed his palm down on a control panel initiating an emergency landing procedure. "I've saved us," he announced.

The ship bucked and groaned as hundreds of magnetic clamps let go and ejectors pushed the individual pods and satellites apart. Without manual guidance, they were locked into predetermined paths meant for a different planet.

Avery hurried across the deck, "What have you done? Where's the captain?"

Callaghan staggered over to the captain's chair. As he sat down, his voice shook with false bravado. "I'm the captain. Buckle up, boys. We're going in."

Avery ignored him to study the screen. There were gaps in the fleet and swarms of tiny adversaries attacking every ship that remained, but with no evidence of debris from the missing vessels, he was hesitant to correlate disappearance with destruction. The airwaves were a garbled mess of terse voices issuing contradictory orders.

Rodriquez leaned over Avery's shoulder, pointing to a second data stream. Beckoning from below was a planet the computer deemed habitable. The visible portion showed a vast ocean surrounding a sizable continental landmass and a few islands. There were no signs of advanced civilization past or present.

"Well, ain't that convenient."

"Very."

Rodriquez snorted as he pointed to another screen. "Callaghan's not the only civie to have panicked."

More blips on the screen broke formation, forcing the rest of the fleet to follow suit. Avery looked back at the planetary data. He felt like he stood at the mouth of a cattle chute, but there was nowhere else to go and no time to worry about anything beyond the degree of their entry. Avery buckled into the helmsman's seat and disengaged the computer guidance system. He attempted to make course corrections as Rodriquez read from a manual. The monitors showed other pods doing the same, but not all. After a couple of pods skipped off the atmosphere, others overcorrected to plummet towards the planet too steeply. They broke apart, creating obstacles for those who followed.

As they neared the planet, the magnitude of error in Avery's prior course corrections increased exponentially. He'd come in too hot and missed the main continent.

Rodriquez's voice was flat and fatalistic. "You think they'll follow us in?"

Avery rotated the pod using sideways displacement to steer them towards a small island. The planet's gravity grabbed hold of him like a vise, forcing him deeper into the chair and making speech difficult. "I hope so. It's the only way we'll get any payback for being trapped here.

EKKI STOOD ON THE hillside, pretending she wasn't alone.

Before her clumped an assortment of divergent patterns. So much had they changed during her last sleep cycle that she couldn't predict what they would look like by the time she checked on them next. While most of her terrestrial creations still fanned out low, hugging the ground, these few had grown tall. They had branched as they climbed, sprouting flattened spheres at each of their terminal ends. They reached for the duplicitous sun, unknowingly threatening their unchanged brethren.

Ekki leaned to examine them more closely, despairing at the constancy of their change when her own existence was most terribly fixed. She brushed up against the plants with a melancholy affection that dislodged a puff of fine particles. It was the beginning of a cycle she had been forced to end many times. Some of the pollen clung to her outer layer, others drifted on the breeze towards distant relations with no understanding of the danger to their progeny.

In time, the flowers would evolve until they required the assistance of other creatures to propagate, which would likewise evolve until the ground was covered with myriad forms of life. It was always so beautiful... until the Aloika started to hunt and corrupted everything.

She had shielded the planet to the best of her ability, cut herself off from all of the others the Conductor had trapped in this system, even Hetchi—yet still, the Aloika got through to menace her children. Ekki had covered most of the planet with water both cold and deep. It quenched the Aloika's fire almost instantly, protecting those that dwelled below. On land, all she could do was initiate a freeze and start again.

Ekki despaired as she cradled the first flower. How long could she postpone the inevitable?

A violent disruption of the planet's shield distracted her before she could answer the question. Vast beings of various size and shape burst through the upper atmosphere. The mammoth creatures cleared a path for tens of thousands of Aloika who swarmed through the breach in pursuit.

Without any grace, they pitched themselves against the descending bulks in a frenzied and futile attack that belied them ever having been star dancers.

Revulsion mingled with hope as she watched the Aloika suicide against hulls that refused to admit them. At this distance, it was impossible to tell if they attacked out of fear or hunger. What in the stars had found her? Allies? Prey? Had a new enemy come to threaten her garden?

The beings kept a steady trajectory, either unconcerned with the Aloika or incapable of evading them. Any hope for companionship was crushed as Ekki watched them fail to slow their descent. They were a disparate group, and they were in trouble. She wasn't strong enough to save them all, but she called the winds to catch those closest to her, rocking them gently to disperse their momentum while she buffeted the Aloika away. Even from this distance, she could hear their collective hiss, but it was of no consequence.

Thunderous crashes rocked the ground as the hulks impacted with the planet, crushing untold thousands of her emerging patterns. She mourned their losses as she descended the foothills, swatting away the few Aloika who challenged her directly. They were visionless cowards who threatened the vulnerable from the safety of a mob. Their punishment had taught them nothing.

She reached the nearest impact site and paused, uncertain. She gazed upward towards the distant moon that imprisoned Hetchi and wondered if the perforations in her shield were large enough to let her speak to him. "Can you hear me, Hetchi?"

Ekki pushed down her disappointment at the silence. Hetchi was too far away. It would be days yet before his orbit brought him close enough for her to try again. For now, she was still on her own.

AVERY PLACED HIS HANDS to either side of his head in an attempt to silence the noise that surrounded him. Their landing had been hard enough to knock out all of their electronics, but he didn't need sensors to tell them they still had company. Outside, the aliens hammered against the hull like giant hail. His head pounded in syncopation. Through it, all were moans, curses, and pleas for help that prodded him. He took two slow breaths and opened his eyes. The emergency lights flickered.

"Rodriquez, you breathing?" he asked as he hauled himself up.
"Over here."

Avery made his way across the bridge, checking on other crew members who'd made it out of stasis and assessing the damage. Across the room, Rodriquez guided an uncooperative Callaghan back into his captain's chair. "We need to find some steady light," Rodriguez said, "and secure our position."

A shout from across the room cut off Callaghan's reply. "Heads up."

He turned in time to catch an old LED flashlight one of the crew had found. He thumbed it on and made his way to where Callaghan continued to proclaim his authority. Avery glanced at the hull, the persistent hammering reminding him they weren't alone. "Sit tight kid, the military is in charge for now."

He and Rodriquez shared a silent look before heading deeper into the ship, looking for anyone who could help with defence. They busted open every pod they found, spilling more amniotic fluid over the already flooded drains. The people waking deserved an explanation but there was no time to say more than "Help the others" before they moved on to the next room. Few were in any condition to fight. The best they could do was hope the hull held long enough for them to get their shit wired.

They'd made it as far as the docking bay when a few surviving circuits sparked like midnight fireworks, and a sheet of flame roared across their path. They manually sealed the doors as the fire caught and spread. Cut off from their only exit, Avery listened to the aliens' continuous knock. He grabbed Rodriquez's arm and yelled, "Find us something we can fight with."

The bay crowded as more people stumbled in, rubbing their eyes and asking questions he couldn't answer. Through the docking bay door's window, he watched the fire grow. Somewhere there was an air leak, sucking up their oxygen to feed the growing flames.

Someone shouted, "I can't breathe in here!" and instigated a chorus of complaints.

Avery disregarded them as a runner pushed through the edgy throng. "Communications are down. Captain Callaghan ordered me to report that he is triangulating the fleet's position based on their trajectories when we hit the atmosphere."

Avery nodded. If they survived the day, that would be useful.

Behind the runner the crowd parted for members of the emergency response team, a group of five men and women fully suited who slushed through the calf-deep amniotic fluid towards Avery. He tugged the door open and stepped aside to let them do their job.

The team didn't waste any time. They hustled through the door against a billow of thick, acrid smoke that spilled into the hall. Avery slammed the door shut as more people coughed and complained. An ear-splitting shriek announced the arrival of the aliens. Through the haze, he watched them dart through a small crack in the hull to defy his preconceptions.

The scientists around him quickly fell into two camps. While some pushed their way through the crowd in a panicked attempt to flee the unknown, others stood their ground in naive awe, oblivious to the potential danger.

The aliens were smaller than anticipated and hovered in the air like giant burrs. Hundreds of needle-like projections whirred with a high-pitched drone, like soprano bees. They hovered for a moment as if making their own assessment before they darted into the crowd, dodging flailing hands and makeshift weapons to impact against flesh, where they broke apart like molten eggs.

Avery batted one of the burrs with his bare hand, sending it towards the opposite wall. It changed course before impact and came at him again, forcing him to bat it away a second time as he searched for anything malleable that could be shoved in the hole. The best Avery could come up with was a floppy bag of hand sanitiser from one of the many dispensers lining the halls. He was wedging it into the crack when one of the aliens careened into the back of his shoulder. A slow spreading pain dripped down his arm. He twisted, wiping some kind of burning, viscous liquid from his sleeve, and discovered a two-inch red worm crawling towards his neck. He jerked his arm, scraped the worm off and stomped on it, unleashing a string of obscenities.

"If you're done dancing there, princess, I've found some firepower." Rodriquez, draped in weaponry he'd liberated from the small arms locker, let loose a volley of shots that downed three aliens.

Avery held his hand out for one of the SMGs Rodriquez was hoarding. "Give me one of those." As their combined efforts turned the tide, some of the civilians joined the fight, arming themselves with whatever came to hand. Through the chaos, he saw some people lying prone, with broken burrs on them but—worryingly—no sign of the red worms.

When the last of the tiny targets were eliminated, a young scientist gave a hearty whoop. "We won!"

Rodriquez shook his head. "We haven't won shit. They've been raining down on the hull ever since we landed, there's got to be thousands of them out there."

Avery slapped him on the back, "The day is young, and you're only seven up on me."

Callaghan limped up to them. In the captain's ill-fitting formal dress, he looked like a child playing dress up, but his eyes told a different tale.

"We can't stay in here forever."

EKKI HID BEHIND A fall of rocks and watched as the vessel cracked open further.

Dozens of upright beings with bilaterally symmetrical appendages emerged in a slow, spreading pattern that radiated out from the opening. As the Aloika attacked, the newcomers attempted to drive them back, but their weapons were only partially effective. Many were taken, their bodies writhing noisily as they tried to fight off the parasites.

Ekki found the chaos unnerving. It brought back painful memories of disorder. A loud noise from one of the beings recalled the pattern, and she realised that they communicated verbally, like animals. Their pattern contracted as those at its farthest reaches pulled back, collecting the fallen they passed while those nearest the conveyance held their position until all who were mobile were inside. Fascinating.

In time, the remaining Aloika burned themselves out in futile efforts to regain entry. Ekki glided closer. She crept over rocks and between gullies where her small patterns had been crushed by debris from the newcomers' ship. The material was of a type she was unfamiliar with, and she absorbed a small piece of it for future study.

She cautiously approached one of the discarded beings. It was still alive, but appeared weak, made small sounds from inside a flimsy secondary husk. She reached into the wound and withdrew the Aloika before it could burrow further, crushed it before tossing it aside.

Her appendage was covered in the newcomer's fluids, and she altered her vision to study its pattern. The complexity was astounding. Not even her oceans held life this advanced. Down and down she spiralled through the layers until she reached its core…and recognized its primary construct.

She tried to speak to it but failed. Its mind was too primitive. Ekki swam through the being's pattern, looking for answers. She found many dormant strands needing only to be reactivated for the beings to achieve greater understanding, but other strands were missing entirely. Whether they had been discarded or never acquired didn't matter. She had not the skill to manipulate patterns on this level. But how had they evolved to care for one another without true understanding

She tore apart the secondary husk, desperate for knowledge, soaking up what data she could. The being expired and Ekki felt a pang of guilt. Would she have been able to save it if she'd known more? She recalled the other vessels that had been scattered across her world. Did they all hold similar patterns? Did they boast enough variation to be viable? She had so many questions, and all of the answers lay with frightened, cowering children.

Ekki stashed the body in the gully for future study and considered how best to approach the ship.

AVERY DRAGGED RODRIQUEZ INTO the cargo bay just before the door closed. His buddy was barely bleeding but was curled in on himself unable to walk. One of the worms had burrowed into his neck and disappeared.

Avery knew it was terrible when Rodriquez stopped cursing and reverted to Spanish fit for church. He laid him on the floor and yelled for a medic. The only one they had was busy with triage, and it took long minutes for her to get to Rodriquez.

She looked at his wound and shook her head. "I don't know what we're dealing with here. I can't go digging around in his neck. He needs a surgeon."

"We don't have one."

"I tried digging one out of Henderson's bicep. I didn't find it until I got to his shoulder. He's got seven inches worth of stitches. Rodriquez can't afford that."

Rodriquez grabbed her arm. "Get it out of me." It was the last sensible thing he said. Avery nodded, but the medic kept shaking her head. She left them alone to wait for a surgeon that wasn't coming.

Avery watched her abandon another soldier with a gut wound only to begin cutting into another woman's leg. He knew it was the right call, and he clamped down on emotional objections that would change nothing.

Rodriquez began to twitch. Avery pulled him up into a half-seated position as wild, flopping movements threw his limbs in all directions, as his speech regressed even further. Broken prayers were repeated amongst deep, ragged breaths, interspersed with pleas to ease the pain. As the spasms passed, he curled into a ball, leaning his head into Avery's chest, "Help me."

Across the bay, a man lurched to his feet and attacked the medic with clumsy determination before he was taken down and restrained. Rodriquez's struggles became stronger and more coordinated. Avery tightened his grip and ran through a short list of horrible options as a third victim launched a weaponless attack against Callaghan, sending him to the floor.

The two traded blows briefly before the infected man awkwardly reached for his weapon. His shot went wide, but it quickly found a target in the crowded room. As fresh cries rang out, three shots from different directions felled him before he could try again.

Callaghan scrambled to his feet shouting, "They're being taken over!"

"Calm down," Avery barked, the order reverberating through the room. Rodriquez struggled to stand, forcing Avery to hold him down.

"The aliens are taking over!" Callaghan cried again.

"We don't yet have confirmation of that," the medic snapped, hard at work on the bystander who'd been shot. She turned towards Avery. "But it is a possibility."

Avery tightened his grip on his friend. He didn't want it to be true, but he couldn't risk it. He nodded towards the dead man, "We're not waiting. Cut him open. Cut it out."

She knelt next to them. "Even if I find a worm in his brain that doesn't mean it's taking over. It might simply be feeding off him, like a tapeworm."

"Just find it," Avery said. Next to him, Rodriquez had stilled, his Spanish replaced by a stuttered string of mismatched syllables. Had the alien gained access to his speech center? Avery placed his arms around his friend's neck and pinned the smaller man's legs with his own. He drew Rodriquez close, wishing he could will the worm into himself.

Rodriquez's struggle became frenzied. Back on Earth, they'd wrestled so many times he'd lost count. Afterwards, they'd laugh and go for a beer on the loser's dime. Rodriquez rarely paid.

Avery lost his grip and Rodriquez slipped through his hands. A shot rang out, and Avery whipped around to find Rodriquez bleeding out on the floor. He ran over, but it was too late. The bullet had opened his femoral artery.

Across the room, Callaghan was defensive. "He was one of them. I didn't have any choice."

Avery gathered his friend up in his arms. The weight settled over him like guilt settling in. "I should have let you shoot him," he whispered.

He laid Rodriquez back down on the floor and slowly rose to his feet, turning towards Callaghan.

The boy stuttered, "It's probably for the best," as Avery closed the distance between them, trying to wipe the blood from his hands.

One of the ERT guys stepped between them. He was a big man, about forty years old, with the name Bouchard embroidered on his stained coveralls. He stopped just short of laying hands on Avery. "He's just a kid. He panicked. And your friend was… gone."

Avery held the man's gaze as he steadied himself. As much as his rage needed a target, losing his temper would only make things worse. These people were already frightened. They needed him to keep it together.

He gathered all the calm he could muster. "I know."

All eyes in the room were on him, including the medic, who knelt in a pool of blood next to the first gunshot victim. In her right hand, she held up a small vial containing one of the alien worms. "Where'd you find it?" he asked as he walked over.

"Attached to the brain stem. I have no way of knowing what it was doing there, but it's changed."

He crouched down next to her. "Show me."

She held out the vial. "It's grown tendrils that attached themselves deeper within the brain. I don't have enough training to tell you any more specific."

"I knew it," Callaghan yelled, struggling to shake of Bouchard's restraining hand. "We have to kill them all."

Avery looked from Callaghan to the med tech. "We're not killing anyone, but neither are we giving those things a chance to get cozy. Cut them all out."

The medic paled and shook her head. "I'm not a surgeon. I don't have the training for that."

Avery feared the day when he confronted a stranger with no way of knowing if they were fully human. "None of us are trained for this. I'll hold. You cut."

THE DRUMMING AGAINST THE hull stopped.

The room stilled as everyone listened. Avery brushed his bloody hands against his coveralls, but they were already soaked through. He wondered if he'd ever get either clean again.

"I need some air," he muttered as he walked to the door.

Bouchard stood to accompany him, "You think they left or just got bored?" A heavy thump against the door seemed to answer his question. After a pause, it was followed by two more thumps, then three, four. Brouchard snorted a weary laugh. "Who isss iiit?" he crooned, a crazy edge to his voice, as people jumped to their feet and readied their weapons.

There was no answer beyond the escalating number of knocks. Whatever was out there could count; something the flying burrs had shown no evidence of. Anyone they had left behind when they went out to set up the solar powered receiver was surely infected, if not dead.

When the count reached seven, Avery thumped back eight times. There was a pause, and then the knocking started over. Two. Three. Five. Seven.

"Avery rolled his eyes before he thumped back eleven times, "We're being played with."

Bouchard's nod was grim as they waited through the ensuing silence. "We're as ready as we can be."

Avery stepped up to the manual release and cursed its placement, switching his sidearm to his left hand. It felt awkward and insufficient. He gave a nod and pulled hard, the door groaning open as he raised his weapon.

On the loading ramp stood a... four-foot jelly salad, the green one no-one ever wanted to eat. He watched as a prehensile appendage, which had been raised in the air close to the door, withdrew and was absorbed in the main body. It reminded him uncomfortably of the red worms and their tendrils. It appeared to be alone.

The being wobbled slightly while Avery studied it. Thankfully, there was nothing else wormlike about it. Translucent skin allowed him a full view of what had to be internal organs, but his mind kept returning to his Aunt Eustice's inedible Christmas creations.

A dispassionate, "Huh," broke the silence behind him. He glanced back at Bouchard, who hadn't moved, then slowly backed up into the ship.

The being followed him, maintaining its distance. As soon as it was clear of the door, one of the soldiers slammed it shut. The alien didn't react. It twisted its upper portion, presumably to look around, though if it had eyes, Avery couldn't identify them, paying no more or less time assessing the crew than the ship.

Avery flashed back to Mrs. Okeke's grade four music classes. He leaned forward and tapped out a ta-ta-ti-ti-ta on a nearby container. The alien extended its handless arm and repeated his knock before it knocked a more complex pattern for Avery.

Before long, Avery was knocking out the intros to his favourite songs. The alien never missed a beat, but exercise was bringing them no closer to learning where they were or what had attacked them. Avery knocked back a final pattern. Tapping his chest, he said "Avery." He pointed to the alien and waited.

It seemed to sag in disappointment but made no sound.

Avery crossed to the door and tapped a two-handed rhythm against it. The alien rallied and joined him, growing a second arm to repeat the pattern.

He opened the door slowly, "Bouchard, watch my back," he said as he went back outside keeping an eye on the sky and waiting to see if the alien would follow. The sky was empty, but as he rounded the ship, he saw three stray burrs, buzzing erratically like lazy bumble bees. They darted at him, before suddenly veering away. From a distance, they hissed like startled cats. Avery glanced back, to see the alien close behind him. It seemed he wasn't the only one with bad memories of jelly salad.

He gestured to Bouchard. "We need one of them alive."

EKKI WATCHED THE CHILDREN clumsily try to capture an Aloika. She decided to do it for them before they hurt themselves. Though she was still tired from her previous exertions, she called a puff of wind to propel her adversaries within range. She snatched one of them out of the air and handed it to the Bold One. He put it in a small rectangular box with a locking clasp and carried it back inside the conveyance. Ekki followed close behind him but hesitated at the craft's entrance where some of them were constructing something. She wanted to stay and watch but was wary of losing the rapport she was building.

Back inside the vessel, Ekki played more tapping games with the children, marvelling as they announced their emotions through their pheromones.

The imprisoned Aloika whined softly until it died. Its death appeared to go unnoticed by its captors. She tried again to mindspeak with the Bold One but only succeeded in raising his stress levels. When he began to rub at his head, she stopped.

One of the others brought forward a sizable flat strip of cambium covered in intricately patterned markings. The newcomers discussed it at length before making more markings with a small stick. Ekki grabbed the stick impulsively and examined it. It left marks on her flesh, and she quivered in excitement. Blank cambium sheets were brought to her, and she experimented with marking them. Her efforts were clumsy, but she was hopeful.

Her first picture depicted her dancing through the stars with Hetchi under the jealous gaze of the Conductor. The second showed the Conductor's scorned advances being mocked by those in the chorus. Lastly, she drew the Conductor's terrible wrath, as he trapped Ekki and her lover on separate cosmic bodies and banished the Aloikan chorus to burn in the sun. Finished, she held the stick out to the Bold One hoping he would understand.

AVERY WATCHED THE ALIEN draw. With each panel, its proficiency grew, but he had no idea what he was looking at. It was like a comic without captions, and he had no frame of reference. When the marker was returned to him, he hesitated. How was he supposed to tell the story of his entire species in a handful of pictograms?

"What am I supposed to draw?" he asked no one in particular. The suggestions were few. The solar system. Earth. Gliese.

The solar system seemed easiest of the three, so he started with that. His drawing sucked, it wasn't to scale, and frustration was giving him a headache. He tried for an image of their intended mission. The armada of ships was bigger than the planet they left from. Damn. If Edwards were alive, she'd likely have found a way to discuss philosophy by now.

A crackle of static came over the radio, eliciting cheers from the crew and distracting the alien from his artistic failures. The boys at the panel fiddled some knobs and intercepted a message.

"—ort their positions and situation on this emergency frequency for orders. This is Admiral Pardos of the Gantry, to all ships in the fleet. All ships are to report their positions-"

Callaghan snatched the receiver before Avery could reach it. "This is acting Captain Stephen Callaghan of the Terrestrial and Marine Animal Resear—"

Avery grabbed the receiver out of Callaghan's hand and pushed him away. "This is Lieutenant Commander Avery Johnson, sir. T.A.M.A.R.A. suffered thirty percent losses to the crew from equipment failures in transit. The hull was damaged upon impact and parasitizing lifeforms claimed a further nine souls before the survivors took them out. Power is a minimum and communication is spotty. We've had no contact with any other pods."

"There's another alien!" Callaghan shouted.

"Commander are you currently under attack?" barked Pardos.

Avery watched the green slime toss aside his awkward drawings in favour of taking a marker to Callaghan's satellite images. If the military found out about it, they'd lock it away and dissect it before they even learned to communicate. He needed more time to decide what to do.

"No, sir," he said as he nodded to Bouchard to take Callaghan elsewhere. "Acting Captain Callaghan is just a little excitable."

"This is a military mission now," Pardos said. "Make sure Mr. Callaghan understands that. What the status of the library?"

"Undetermined. We've had our hands full, sir."

"Resolve that, Commander. The library is your highest priority."

Avery looked around at a room of people who'd just discovered their value. "Securing it now, sir."

EKKI WAS DELIGHTED BY the image of her planet the children had brought with them. She lovingly added details of her garden to the map and drew a simple icon of the Bold One on the point where his vessel had landed. Surreptitiously, she watched as he spoke into a lifeless flattened sphere. Somehow it spoke back. There was a lengthy exchange between the Bold One and the disembodied voice. She longed to take it apart and examine it more carefully.

A few of the children came to stand by her. They pointed and exclaimed over the marks she'd made and, new emotions flavoured the air. She calculated the landing points of the other vessels she'd seen and marked their general locations as well. The children's excitement grew. It was infectious enough that soon they were gathered around her, communicating animatedly. Ekki felt a sense of place and purpose.

She began to think that their anxiety had been caused by the disembodied voice and not by any actions of hers. This was good, but she wished again that she understood their words. She wished for larger pieces of cambium to complete the map but had no way to make the request. She would have to exercise patience.

The tension rose again before the Bold One finished his strange conversation. He beckoned Ekki to follow and headed deeper inside the conveyance. Hoping to learn more about the children, she followed.

They walked alone. Ekki began to worry that she was being led away so the others could hide from her and that she would be alone once again.

They travelled through a maze of tunnels with many rooms leading off them. Together they entered one such room, and the Bold One sealed them in. Briefly, he slumped against the door. The air around him became heavy with grief, and Ekki longed to comfort him. Before she could try, he opened the second door to reveal a room within the room. Ekki's unease grew as a deep winter cold escaped the interior chamber, and thin white frost covered all of its inner surfaces.

The Bold One entered but did not beckon her; indeed, he seemed to have forgotten all about her. Ekki hesitated on the threshold. The room contradicted nature and felt like a trap, but curiosity won out.

She followed him inside.

AVERY STOOD AT THE library door with a sense of urgency but no clear plan. The room was twenty feet deep and twelve across, and dark—no power. Frost covered industrial shelving filled the room and acrylic holders of test tubes filled the shelves, but it wouldn't last. The shelf labels were covered in a thin frost that made them illegible, and Avery didn't have time to read the individual tubes. Without a map, he had no way of knowing which vials were most important.

He grabbed a portable freezer unit from the rack outside and filled it from the first shelf he encountered. He'd cleared less than a quarter of it before the unit was full. He closed the lid and switched on the battery power. If they didn't get some solar cells working in a day or two, he'd have another problem. For now, he had to deal with the fact that he couldn't save even one percent of what they'd brought with them.

Trying to hedge his bets, Avery moved through the room grabbing vials randomly. He felt like he was picking lottery numbers. When the last portable unit was full, he headed for the door, only to find it blocked—by the alien.

It had one of the tubes in its strange hands and appeared to be studying it. Avery wondered what it might be seeing. Heat from its body had melted the frost of the label. He twisted his head to read it. Muscovy. He was pretty sure it was some kind of duck. Avery scratched a simple sketch into the softening frost on the wall. The alien studied it for many minutes before making refinements. He figured it was definitely smarter than he was until it ate the tube.

EKKI STUDIED THE DEAD pattern with a burgeoning understanding. Somehow these creatures had come into possession of a vast wealth of patterns, frozen and preserved, but they didn't know how to create them. No other explanation explained the Bold One's grief.

It deeply distressed him, but now she knew how to soothe him. Ekki thinned her membranes to facilitate injecting the pattern sample she held. She kept her membrane translucent so the Bold One could watch as she borrowed the necessary ingredients from within herself and began to weave a primary pattern. He exclaimed repeatedly, and his anxiety levels rose and fell, but he did not try to stop her.

Manipulating the primary pattern to match that of the dead sample was a slow and tedious process. In the outer room, overwhelmed by the stresses of the day, the Bold One slept. Quietly Ekki opened the door and retraced her steps until she found herself in the main room of this strange burrow. None of the children kept watch, and she was grateful the Aloika had so exhausted themselves that another attack was likely many days away. In the soft moonlight, she sang quietly while she continued her work. As her lover took ascendancy in the night sky, she called out to him and brought forth this new child, laying it amongst the flowers that had grown in spite of her attempts to limit them.

"Hetchi, my love, see this new pattern. I will fill my garden with them as a testament of my love."

Through the holes left in her shield by the arrival of the children's ship, a weak voice answered. "I have missed you Ekki. Your garden is beautiful, but to see it and not hear you tears at my soul. Must you repair the whole shield? Can you not leave one opening for me?" Hetchi's emotions flooded her mind. He was so desperately lonely. Without her, he had not even flowers to talk to.

She soothed him with a dance as she looked out over the land at all that she had created, all that the Conductor's cursed Aloika strove to take from her. She was conflicted. Ekki closed her eyes. Hetchi's distant dreams caressed her mind, reminding her of how happy they had been while twinned. She continued to dance for him, craving the touch of his thoughts. She could not lose him again, but how could she protect her garden if she kept a window open?

A gasp behind her alerted her to the Bold One, awake and watchful. He had followed her from the vessel and stood staring at the still wet pattern Ekki had brought to life. Behind him, half a dozen sleepy children looked at her in wonder. Protectively, they crowded around the child she had created and cooed softly as it waved its upper limbs and struggled to stand.

The newcomers were fragile but tenacious. She would study their pattern box until she found a way to make them stronger, so she and Hetchi could dance and sing.

THE END

CHRISTINA KLARENBEEK writes science fiction, fantasy and horror from a small farm in rural Ontario she shares with her husband and three spoiled cats. Her short stories have been published in *Grevious Angel*, *Devolution Z*, *Every Day Fiction* and assorted anthologies. She can be found on twitter @MaraGant.

BELLTHEIMER'S GREENER HARVEST

Roy C. Booth and William Tucker

HARRY BELLTHEIMER STOOD APPROXIMATELY where the thing would crash. His shadow slipped back under his feet. The thing—he wasn't yet sure what it was, but it was big—would leave a miles-long gash in the Earth before exploding into fragments. He guessed the fiery, spiraling mass was a comet, at least a quarter of a mile in diameter.

There was no reason to panic, even if he had been near the outer edge of the impending crater. He'd be blasted by the impact, even if he managed to escape ground zero. Few people understood that "ground one" through "ground seven" are pretty much the same as zero when something this big drops out the sky. Fewer still would have understood Harry's utter disinterest. He craned his long neck, tilted his flattop sandy head, narrowed his blue eyes at the damned thing, and stood there in what he was sure were the final moments of his life on Earth.

A thunderous report cracked the night air, rang hollow, then repeated. The thing slowed through the sound barrier as it entered the atmosphere. Harry got his first look at it, casting such a vast and dark shadow. It wasn't a comet or meteor, but it could act the same, plummeting as it was through the sky, hurtling toward him at a frightening velocity. The shadow it cast blotted out the sunlight of the mid-autumn afternoon.

Harry swung his gaze down to his hands. He had been harvesting apples and peaches for jelly, pies, and preserves all autumn long, for years and years. The dustbowl days had taught him not to worry as much about a job as he should about food. Accordingly, he and his kin had planted wheat and corn, raised cattle, sheep, and pigs for slaughter, cared for the land, and sowed what they reaped. He didn't plan to ever again be without a sandwich. He also didn't care for the idea of Mathilda's golden, thick, warm slices of homemade bread without peach preserves or apple butter. Just didn't seem right in oh so many ways. So, he and Mathilda had moved away from the city that he felt would squeeze the life from their bones long before was natural, bought a suitable swath of land, and built themselves a farm on the wages he'd made working in life insurance. They hired on a few select hands, began the ranch. The first few years had been rough as the hands came and went, good weather came and went, crops came and went. Mathilda turned gray standing beside Harry as they patiently, purposefully, painfully wintered over incrementally better each year. The celebrations of this twenty-fourth fall festival of fruits, grains, and meat would, he supposed as he stood there, be the last.

"Damn." It was all he could think to say to himself. Other hands were screaming. He sighed. Others were running toward the house or their cars. He lifted his nose toward the swirling mass. His lips curved slightly toward the ground. A cold chill came over him, quaking his otherwise rugged spine. "Hell of a way to end harvest."

He was holding a juicy peach in his right hand when the thing pierced the blue skies, creating the heavy cloud cover that boiled up around it. His fingers, rough-hewn from years of hard labor, couldn't maintain a grip. The peach fell at his feet.

Screams and shouts surrounded him. Tense, frightened folks half his age, farmhands and their spouses and children, ran from his beloved orchard. He stood there getting hot under the open collar of the plaid shirt his wife had chosen for this last day of harvest.

Whatever this was, whether it be made by God or man, Harry wasn't so much frightened as much as plumb mad-dog angry. Twenty-four years of a slow, peaceful success shot to Hell by some freak meteor or one of those damned missiles or satellites they kept sending into the atmosphere to study weather, or Russia or some other fool thing that meant nothing to him and these poor, benighted fools running hither, thither and yon. He hung his head and shook it.

"Damn shame, all it is."

The impact radius would encompass the whole of his farm and wipe out most of the county by way of dust, ash, and debris. Tandy County would have just a taste of the Armageddon those atomic bombs did to all those folks in Japan. Harry couldn't care less about Tandy or the people, so much as he lamented a sorrowful end to what he had projected to be a fine harvest.

He knelt beside that prize peach, blew the dirt off, and did something he'd not done in the field in at least ten years. He bit into the fruit. It was rich, succulent, dripping with juices, sweet, cool, and decadent. He crouched there waiting, enjoying the peach, wondering if Mathilda, back at the house, knew what was coming and knew where he was, and if she might try to get to him before the end. His shoulders sagged as he thought of her.

"Damned shame she's not here," he thought out loud. "I'd have shared the last peach with her. Last thing I'll ever do, I suppose."

The air around him seemed to gather up and twist, like a whirlwind was about to erupt from the clouds. Lifting he head, he knelt and waited, his arms resting on his knees. His tired, watering eyes wandered up without really wanting to see it. When he did, something peculiar happened. Harry might have guessed it, since disaster never struck quite the way he figured it would. That horrendous season of 1952, they expected to lose the whole harvest to an early frost, yet the fruit had managed to rot on the trees first and the apples were worm-eaten. Horrible year. Seeing that thing in the sky falling at him, he figured that was the end.

Instead, the thing began to slow down, to slow its spiraling mass, to become more and more definitely a thing not natural, but a craft of some sort. Harry plopped to the ground, let his body curl and his mouth go agape.

His deadly, harvest-ending meteor was, in fact, a blasted spaceship!

"Just what country has built themselves a flyin' saucer?" Harry Belltheimer asked himself.

Squinting, he tried to make out any indications of insignia. No letters were visible as yet. Gray-white clouds billowed around the ship, slowly revealing the silver-blue plating and green lights that flickered and flashed and focused downward at Harry.

Okay, he thought. *I'm not dying of fright, and I'm not going to be obliterated by meteorites.*

Still, he couldn't quite believe it was alien. Surely it was some wayward, cockeyed, jackass testing a fancy landing craft from Texas, though what the heck it was doing in California, he couldn't guess.

Off course by a few states. Or maybe it was meant to be. Perhaps they were going to land proper, pop out, wonder where they were, and perhaps compensate him for the loss of his labor, which was currently heading toward any road leading away from the trees.

But no, he saw no signs of NASA or AIR FORCE anywhere on the multi-level, sleek, saucerful of secrets as it began to push against the pull of the Earth under his butt. Harry didn't figure to greet these jokers while sitting flat on the Earth, so he stood and walked calmly to one side of the row of peaches. The ship seemed content to land amid them, the best peaches he'd grown in twenty years. He couldn't bear to watch. 1962 would have been the best harvest he'd ever seen. Instead, an unidentified meatball was landing on them. Wouldn't even make a good story down at the Wildwood Tavern.

Harry spat at the ground.

The ship spun down, and as it drew closer, the absolute din of the thing's engines roared in his ears like a thousand black bears at his back. He turned only then, watching the final descent, watching as it didn't actually land, but halted and hovered about fifteen feet off the ground. Now he could plainly see it in all its awesome, gleaming, majesty. He had a sense of pride about it, sure as he was that it had come from the United States. He still saw no signs of ownership, but maybe they didn't want such an advanced vehicle readily identified. Or maybe his eyesight was failing. He hadn't worn his spectacles into the field. He rarely needed them.

The wind from the draft of the ship smelled of the peaches. The blast Harry expected was not quite as forceful as he thought it should be. The way it hovered was astounding. The ship had fallen out of the sky in something near deafening him, but now… it made hardly a peep. It whispered. It was hushed and low in tone. What a marvelous thing to behold! Now, he really wished Mathilda had come away from her quilting to help in the field. She always got out of the harvest due to her one game leg and her "lack of sufficient height to be effective." This was hogwash, of course, but he let her have her way. He always deferred to his wife. Beauty had its way with him, and this ship was perhaps just a little more beautiful than his wife—just a little.

But he'd keep that to himself.

The hatch, if one could call it such, opened. Hollow darkness fell away from the plating of the ship, revealing a figure, vaguely the shape of a man. *Two arms*, Harry thought. *Two legs. Had to be human. Thank Heaven for that!* But then, the helmet seemed to be a heck of a lot weirder than John Glenn's. *Friendship 7* had flown into space earlier that year, but it was a speck of dust next to this ship. Harry had felt a special pride in that success. It was an American, and he'd been a Marine, so Glenn's victory was doubly Harry's.

Weird waves of crisp, light air made him shiver. Or maybe that was the shock of what was happening settling on his bones. The air undulated, the way it played in the leaves in summer. Between the hushed tones of the ship and the feelings he had, it was almost like a religious experience. Harry prayed that it wouldn't be. He didn't want to meet his Lord and find out He was a Martian or a Venusian or something like that. No, he wanted this to be American. And that gave him pause. Was he so prideful? He guessed that he was. Mathilda was always after him to curb his ego. He chuckled as the figure stepped forward, floating down, seemingly by no conveyance whatsoever.

Was there just one man? Harry thought, feeling starstruck. Was this perhaps Glenn himself? He'd flown *Friendship 7* all by himself. Even though this ship was much larger in scale, maybe they'd really made some fantastic advances. Harry was, of course, fooling himself.

The tall, laconic man stood there waiting as the more towering, gaunt helmeted form floated down toward him. The closer the figure got, the weirder Harry's world seemed to get. Chills went up and down his spine. His hand started to shake, and he could scarcely feel the peach he still clutched.

The figure stood facing Harry. Harry wanted it to be Glenn, lost, wondering which way the nearest Air Force base might be. But he knew it wasn't Glenn. The flight suit wasn't white; it was the darkest green he'd ever seen. It looked like someone had stretched out an avocado.

The head inclined, and a long arm reached slowly, a long finger pointing not at Harry, which made his heart jump, but at the peach. Harry lifted it closer.

"Grew it myself," he said. *Pride goeth before a fall,* he heard his wife's voice in his head. "By the good Lord's grace," he added.

The helmet tilted one way, then the other. The finger and arm retracted, and a voice, sibilant, feminine, almost a whisper, spoke. "From your land."

"Yep," Harry said.

The stranger nodded. "That's good, Harry."

"Huh?" They knew his name? Just who the heck was this person?

"We've been watching. We've come a long way, but I suppose you know that. We've watched. We've waited, but it's time, and we have wanted to walk your Earth for so very long..."

Words drifted off. Two hands lifted the helmet, revealing what appeared to be a woman, green-skinned, with bright blue eyes, slicked back, short hair, and a long, almost too long, smile. She had the soft, radiant features of a woman. She was green though. It wasn't... she wasn't as dark as an avocado, but nearly so. Harry decided it was a pleasant shade of green, since she had to be green.

Aliens were... *aliens,* he thought to himself. A small alarm arose in his mind. *Should I be running?*

"Please don't feel frightened," she said, perhaps detecting his thoughts. "It's only that we couldn't bear to be parted from the soil any longer. To touch the Earth, to sow the Earth. Our world was taken by war and by our own foolish ways. We wanted to escape. We found you. We came to *you,* Harry."

"Me...? Specifically?"

"Yes, Harry. You specifically."

He tried to detect any sarcasm. He felt there might have been just a tinge in her voice.

"Once we saw your orchards, your green, green fields... we knew we would find ourselves welcome. May we?"

She pointed once more to the peach. Harry lifted it. She took it. She bit into it.

"OH!" she gasped. "So sweet!"

"You... like sweet?"

"Oh yes. Not as joyous as we imagined. More... Earth, not of the sky."

"That's the dirt. I... um, dropped it on the ground earlier. You did sort of spook me a bit. Made my help run like children."

She rolled her eyes. "Sorry. We didn't have any other way of coming to you. And why should we wait? Why should we hide any longer? We know we are among like minds. You care for your Earth. You nurture the soil and tend to your Earth. We are so grateful to find, in this cosmos, another creature as we."

"You... speak mighty good English."

"We speak mighty good because we mighty good *listen*, we learn, we watch. We have been watching and waiting for someone to know. And we know you, Harry. We like you. We hope… with time, and the good Earth, and your good Lord, you will like us. We want to stay. We want to help."

Harry blinked. "Help?"

"Yes."

"With… uh, what?"

"Why, the harvest, of course. It has been so long since we have felt of the good soil, of the good ground all about us. So many generations in flight, in the ship. Just to breathe is… How would you say…? It is… Heaven."

"Well," he said. "Heavenly, I suppose."

"Heavenly, then. We do not argue. We merely want to know if we may help with harvest and stay for tea."

"You drink tea?"

"We want to. May we?"

"And help with the harvest?"

"May we?"

Harry blew out his breath. Mathilda and some of the other hands had started to gather behind him. Suddenly, Harry Belltheimer was the Ambassador for Earth! If it were going to be him, he'd gladly take up the mantle.

"Sure," he said. "Why not. Might do us both some good to get our hands dirty first before we figure out anything else. Besides, you folks look a might starved."

"Starved?"

"Well, you are a tad… thin."

"Oh! Ah. Yes. Well, that is our nature. But I suppose we might get fat if we eat here! Such a sweet thing," she said and gnawed off another bite of peach.

Harry smiled broad and proud. It *was* going to be a good harvest this year after all.

And for many years to come!

THE END

WILLIAM HENRY TUCKER is from northern Minnesota, where he writes, draws, and creates his own music.

ROY C. BOOTH has been writing science fiction for forty years. He currently has 170+ works listed on Amazon, not including those under pseudonym. Check out his website at www.roycbooth.com.

A CALENDAR OF CONTACT
Wenonah Lyon

SIDEREAL CALENDAR: 8976, 44, 14

The wireless transmission of electromagnetic energy through space is reported by a cargo vessel. The source is located.

SIDEREAL CALENDAR: 8976, 47, 1

Linguists depart for the distant planet. If verbal communication is present, visual images will soon follow. Technology is predictable. They begin language learning with children's programs. *Telebeebies* is a favourite. First the mammalian ur-Language and its variants. Sentient sea-dwelling mammals communicate with non-mammalian sea creatures and the second linguistic gap is bridged. Some intelligent avians learn mammalian speech and communicate in their own language as well. Communication is possible.

SIDEREAL CALENDAR: 8977, 42,

The rest of the team shows up.

LOCAL TIME: 17 MARCH 2016, aboard *E.V. Rangeron*

Heda (*Psittaciformes*) disliked psychologists on principle, but his latest office mate had been a successful pairing. Psychologist or not, Marda was a sweet child, if a trifle simple. She rarely misunderstood his jokes and always laughed. Psychologists claimed that personality tests provided the basis of shared office space. Personally, he thought they just put a big one with a little one.

Marda was the first *Ursidae* to share his office. To his amusement, she was young enough to agree that it was "his" office. He was fascinated by her loose flesh and sloping, shifting, shoulders.

Her belly rippled when she laughed. He sometimes thought of her as his own private earthquake.

His planet-bound cousin had written to ask if she was really, really clean. There was a slight smell, as one would expect from a furred creature, but one that became familiar; indeed, it became a nicety associated with the nicety that was Marda.

There were a number of reasons to join the Transplanetary Diplomatic Corps and specialise in First Contact. Marda, Heda suspected, had joined for religious reasons. The Universal Church believed that when the sentient creatures of the universe established contact, the universe itself would become aware. The four forces structuring the universe would re-unite, and the stars themselves would sing. Heda thought this was nonsense. First, you're born, then you die, and you try to do something interesting and useful in the middle. He assumed the Universe, aware or not, had much the same schemata.

Heda's cousin, too, had joined the Corps, saying it was a great way to pick up chicks and then you had a great excuse to abandon them when the eggs were laid. The Corps appealed to the irresponsible as well as the religious and bored. It even accommodated the lazy. The Corps was a lot less work than digging and hoeing a field.

Marda was less religious than Heda thought. She went to Universal Church services because the choir was excellent. She had joined the Corps because it looked like fun. Plus, it was a respectable way of escaping paternal and clan control. She was also much less simple and more critical than Heda thought. She had quickly lost her initial awe of Heda, a Corps legend. "A little fussy and precious," she had written her sister, "but a good mate for all that."

Her father had responded, "Observe, learn and always, always display proper respect to one with the Chief Linguist's learning and experience. You did not, after all, grow up in a barn, and you represent your family, your species, and your planet." As a child, Marda and her sister had yearned to be one of those lucky folk growing up in barns.

Heda reviewed proposed first contact speeches, while Marda shifted through the entries to her contest. The crew watched entertainment from the planet below. Television had been important in providing a key to the language and was now important in defeating boredom.

Marda had staged a contest: which science fiction technological device would you most like aboard ship? Sooner or later, every morale officer in the Corps used it, but it was still a good idea. By convention, automated language translators were ineligible. They were too obviously useful. In this contest, most of the contenders were from the *Star Trek* series. Holosuites (her own particular choice) outdistanced food replicators and transporters by a considerable vote.

Marda leaned back, tired. She had been reading contest entries all morning and sitting strained her back muscles. "Do all bipedal creatures have back problems?" she asked aloud.

"Avians don't," Heda said. "I suppose our equivalent is strained breast muscles. How is the contest going? Good response?"

"Pretty good."

"I've always wondered, do you psychologists use contest entries for some deep insight into the crew?"

Marda looked expressionlessly at him. "Classified."

Heda was disappointed: "You don't, then."

"No," Marda said, grinning. "It's all pretty much what it looks like on the surface. What could I tell you from this? The crew is bored. No one has mentioned they'd like a nifty phaser to knock off the captain."

Heda cocked his head. "I assume someone has analysed the responses?"

"Of course. This particular batch, well, our crew go for comfort, for the common-sense reason that we are not comfortable, and we notice it. I've seen the same point dressed up in academic jargon, but it doesn't say much more than that."

Ursidae prided themselves on their plain speaking, their insistence on the use of ordinary language. This sometimes caused *Psittaciformes*, including Heda, to conclude they were a bit thick. *Psittaciformes* assumed all utterances required multiple semantic mapping. Some said every *Psittaciformesian* utterance had at least four interpretations: surface, obscene, religious, and one referring to an egg. One time, Marda asked Heda if that was true, and he said it was a joke.

"But all jokes are also, at a different level of semantic interpretation, propositions, and so at the same level either true or false but not both. At different levels, however ..."

Marda had stopped listening.

Now she said, "I read a letter in a journal, or maybe it was an article, can't remember, pointing out that in this particular exercise engineers never choose any device involving matter dissolution for transportation."

Heda burst out laughing.

"It's actually a non-trivial observation," Marda said. "The writer pointed out that engineers are required to take statistically insignificant risk seriously. Specifications are made for worse risk scenarios, not day to day operations."

"So, they don't trust *Star Trek* transporters?" Heda asked. "Neither do I, even though I'm not an engineer. I only noticed a number of plots based on transporter malfunction. But I am disappointed that these games we play are nothing but minor fun."

"Sometimes it's major fun. Listen to Sipsa's entry: 'The most desirable fictional device from an entertainment programme is from Babylon V, the *deus ex machina*, when an all-wise elder race appears from the stars to save us from the consequences of our own idiocy.'"

Heda laughed. "At least half the crew see themselves in that position."

"Yep, he's taking the mickey. Serpents, they put such a nice sting into what they say, don't they?"

LOCAL TIME: MORNING, 17 JUNE 2016

Marda sighed as she looked through the viewer. *All that land,* she thought. *Trees and lakes and mountain peaks, all unmodified.* Focusing the viewer until she could see individual pine needles, she noticed small mammalian creatures in the trees. She widened the viewer and saw traces of ursine activity: *A distant cousin looking for grubs? Sharpening claws?*

She looked down at her hands, trying to imagine massive ancestral claws. *Not much good for ripping and tearing, but I can hold a pencil and use a computer keyboard. Fair exchange is no loss.*

Most of the individuals on board had used the viewfinder to try and find their species' analogues here. Some found it a depressing business. She herself had been physically ill after viewing a bear tethered and baited in a marketplace. But this area, so far from anywhere, had been soothing.

Beautiful, she thought. *Like home. How would it compromise contact if we took a short R&R in the middle of the wilderness, just a few hours to escape the cramped conditions on board?* But this was one more thing the protocols were very strict about: No surface landing until after first contact.

She heard a hoot. "Marda."

Heda and Donnal had come into the viewing area. Heda perched. Donnal curled in a chair beside her.

"I saw some of your cousins below," Marda told Donnal. "Running in a hunting pack. It looked like a very efficient hunting pack."

"Almost sentient, co-operation is the key," Sipsa hissed.

They jumped. None of them had seen him, not even Marda. *He blends so well into the background*, she thought.

"Sometimes I envy them," Donnal said. "Outside, running, part of a pack again."

Sipsa stretched, and his scales flickered as he made his colours more prominent. "When the lack of activity disturbs you, remember your goals. Remember why you're here."

"That's good enough for you, Sipsa," Donnal answered. "You spend your time off duty sleeping, and when you're not asleep you sit, and nobody knows the difference."

"I admit that physical activity is not one of my priorities."

"I run in my dreams. What I wouldn't give for one good leap." Donnal twitched his tail.

Heda shifted on his perch: "One good swoop."

Sipsa smiled. He turned to Marda, "And you, Marda, were you swooping or leaping or having a good run while you looked below?"

"None of the above. We amble. I was turning a corner and seeing something new. Then I was just sitting, with no one around."

"Cheer up, you lot," Heda said. "I heard work in Cargo Bay Four on my way up." All but Sipsa looked at him blankly. "That means preparation for the Marines," Sipsa said. "Setting up berthing quarters. When the Marines arrive, actual contact can't be far behind." He looked maliciously at Donnal. "Those of you with short attention spans might consider a transfer to the Marines. They never spend more than a few months on board ship."

"You've got work to do," Donnal said, "fine-tuning your language skills, preparing the contact text. I'm an engineer, and the engines work. I've got nothing to do."

"Something to do," Marda said. "As morale officer, I think we need some distraction. A variety night? Rehearsals, a nice evening of entertainment?"

Donnal groaned. "If we have to listen to the linguists' orchestra one more time ... No, Marda, if you want to improve morale, no more amateur musical evenings."

"Or a sports night, or a literary evening, or a come as your favourite cliché party," she continued.

LOCAL TIME: EVENING, 17 JUNE 2016

Most of the crew was sleeping when the additional ships arrived. Marda had been informed by the captain that the Marines were expected. She stood in the cargo bay, watching the ships unload.

Four ships? she thought, stunned. *What are they expecting?*

The Marines filed off and kept coming. After she had welcomed them and settled them in their quarters, she retired to her own quarters. She set her alarm.

I'd better make a breakfast appearance and answer any questions.

LOCAL TIME: MORNING, 18 June 2016

Marda shuffled through the cafeteria line. Her feet hurt. She wanted to go back to her cabin, crawl into her bunk, turn out all the lights, and sleep for days, if not months. She was definitely a night person. She sniffed the air in the cafeteria. They were all on edge. This close to contact, the tension was increasing.

She paused at the eggs. It had been months since eggs were available. *A nice baked egg,* she thought. *Eggs must have come in with the Marines last night.* She looked around the cafeteria. She was on duty. There was a table with a free seat. Sipsa, Heda, Donnal, and Rigon. Rigon might be the worst gossip on the ship, but he was a reasonably accurate, objective gossip. It was a good mix to collect shipboard rumours and spread her own. She looked regretfully at the eggs. Avians were sensitive about eating eggs, despite theological rulings. Fertilised or unfertilised, self-aware or brainless, bird-folk felt eggs should be left in the nest. Instead, she picked up a boring piece of cheese.

If mammals had the same attitude towards their bodily productions, we'd all starve to death, she thought.

The Marines had brought in fresh fruit as well. At least she could have a nice pear. She remembered the farm she grew up on, feeding the little chickens than ran around the back door, pecking at her mother's flowers. *Good little chickens that produced good little eggs, baked, boiled, scrambled, poached, and fried. For that matter, good little baked, broiled, barbecued, and fried chickens,* she thought rebelliously.

She took her cheese and walked over to Sipsa's table. Sipsa contracted, curling up. Donnal shifted on the bench. Rigon oozed into a small triangular section of the table and politely extended eye, ear, and vocal pods in her direction.

"I thought you'd be asleep, after your busy night," Sipsa said.

"I wish I were," Marda said. "I only had a couple of hours sleep after getting the Marines settled in."

Heda smiled. "But you had to come down here and spread the official word, right?"

"The captain," Marda said, "will give the official word during his morning ship broadcast. I just felt a little peckish."

The disbelief was palpable. Heda laughed. "Cheese and a pear?" he asked mockingly. "Now, if you had come in this early for the chance to get a nice egg …"

"How many Marines did we get?" Rigon asked.

"Six sets of thirty," Marda replied, waiting for her companions' shock.

"That's about six times as many as we expect in a first contact situation," Donnal said.

"Evacuation, right?" Rigon, an ecologist, probably understood the planetary situation better than she did.

"Isn't that premature?" Sipsa asked. Actual evacuation was rare. "They haven't yet declined to join us."

"Joining will make no difference to ocean folk," Rigon said. "The changes are irreversible over the short term. Another ten years, with luck, before the seas are non-life sustaining."

"Do you know what's happening with Shiksla?" Donnal asked. "I met him right after I came on board. Is contact going on all right with the sea-folk?"

"Fine," Heda answered. "He or they or she, I'm not sure which, has been in regular contact with our linguistic group. They … oh, to hell with it. I can either express things in the passive voice or use his name. As a linguist, I refuse to use an inappropriate pronoun, and none of them in this language work."

"Forget linguistic niceties and tell us what he said," Donnal pressed.

"Contact has been made, the language has been learned, the sea-folk are scared but know they have to do something, and evacuation is the best bet they see," Heda said.

Marda nodded at his assessment. "Ocean dwellers who are self-determining have requested evacuation. We're expecting three ships with three pick-up points after first contact. The Marines are here to cover the evacuation."

"What about land species?" Donnal asked.

Marda looked at him sympathetically. Like most on the ship, he had spent a great deal of time looking at his species analogues below. They were endangered; loss of habitat and slaughter by the dominant species had left few roaming packs. For that matter, her own species analogue was disappearing from the high places of Earth.

"Problems there are, but the land is still life-supporting. The oceans have passed the point of return. Ocean dwellers have to leave," she said. "If those below decide to join us, most land dwellers can be preserved."

"And what are the chances of that?" Donnal challenged.

"About ten percent," she sighed. "Not good."

"So, they will be abandoned," he said. "The land creatures will be left to die, disappear."

"Donnal," Heda said gently. "We don't have a great deal of choice. We will try to evacuate any threatened species capable of making the choice. If a species is capable of self-determination at this point, we will try to make it possible. It's all we can do."

"Some of us could go down in a shuttle," Donnal said, "rescue a few groups …"

"How would you persuade them to come with you?" Heda asked.

"Challenge the pack leader, take over, lead them onto the shuttle."

"It won't work," Marda said. "That sort of thing has been tried, and it never works. Besides, you can't collect a breeding population that way."

Rigon looked at Donnal. "I don't think you could win," he said. "You're a civilised creature. Have you been in a fight since childhood?"

"I'm intelligent and well-fed, unlike the average pack leader," Donnal blustered. "I should be able to defeat him."

"Your behaviour would be all wrong. They wouldn't follow you if you did win. You are as alien to them as I would be," Sipsa said. "Their spirits will be held in the infinite mind, and we will do what we can for their physical forms. If the worst occurs, salvage operations can and will be mounted. We can probably save a breeding population."

Donnal looked at them angrily.

This is one of the things we have to avoid, Marda realised. *Half my shipmates are going to be hatching plans to rescue co-specifics.*

Biological diversity might be magnificent. It might be the basis of the most widely joined religion in the Union. It was also a bloody nuisance. It was the first great divide that had to be routinely bridged. Species that had evolved as solitary individuals, like Sipsa and Rigon, cognitively accepted the basic similarity and identity of all lifeforms. Species that required group social structure to develop as individuals understood the same thing emotionally.

Ethics versus empathy, she thought. *They end up behaving the same way based on totally different principles until something like this comes up.*

"Ten percent is ten percent," Heda soothed. "Don't give up on the planet yet. And these are just odds, based on past experience. There's nothing magical about the figures. We are wrong all the time. We aren't omnipotent. It's only an estimate. And remember, those below are perfectly capable of choosing a sensible course of action to result in their own survival. Self-survival is a powerful spur."

Marda looked affectionately at Heda. Good manners and tact bridged divisions better than cognition or empathy. "What's it like working with Shiksla?" she asked, changing the subject. "I've never met a Remarry and can't really imagine them."

"Very big," Heda said, "and very vegetal. Imagine an enormous feathery bush that lives in water. A Remarry is about the only species I can think of that could survive a couple of years down in that muck they've made of the ocean."

"It wouldn't occur to them to harpoon him, net him, or trap him, either," Donnal said, "which is an advantage with that lot."

"Doesn't he get lonely?" Marda asked. "We base contact crews on those with planetary co-species. We see them, identify with them, and hopefully they identify with us. He hasn't got an analogue below. He just plumps himself into the ocean, a great big bush thing, says 'pardon me' to passing cetaceans, and hopes someone answers."

"He's not exactly a 'he,'" Heda said. "The nodes have limited self-awareness, complete self-sufficiency, and the over-all plant structure subsumes them. When the television reports from below suggested intelligent ocean species, we asked for volunteers to investigate. He volunteered."

"Fascinating," Sipsa said. "And a further demonstration of intentionality, of the imperative to communicate, to understand, that leads each species ultimately to worship ..."

"Nonsense!" Heda squawked. "Chance and natural selection."

Marda tuned out. She'd heard both sides of the argument too many times. As her grandmother would have said, neither religion nor theoretical biology put any butter on parsnips. She'd made the mistake of saying that to Sipsa and Heda once and had to listen to a phenomenal list of counter-examples. She wandered off unnoticed.

LOCAL TIME: AFTERNOON, 1 JULY 2016

"We've got some suggested questions and answers for the website," Heda said. "Take a look."

Marda turned on her screen and looked at the file: Contact.FAQ.XML. She skimmed.

"It's a joke," she muttered.

"No joke."

"Listen to this: 'Why should we want to conquer you? You've ruined the planet, no natural resources worth exploiting, you can't co-operate well enough to serve as drones, and with the muck you put in your mouth you wouldn't even be good eating.'" She looked up in horror. "Who wrote this? How did they ever get in the Exploration Corps?"

"Taxie and Maxie. They're good, very good. Taxie and Maxie can set up a communication system piggybacked on a wide range of alien technologies. They sent their proposal to the linguists, and somebody has to reject it."

Marda frowned.

Heda looked at her winningly. "Someone with tact, discretion, psychological insight. Someone, in short, more like you than me."

"Why me?"

"You're the morale officer. Keep up their morale. And soothe them, Marda, flatter them. Ask them how their website works. And you're big. With Taxie and Maxie, big helps. You'll find them in the communications centre. They work all hours."

"Why not ask them to come here?"

"The stench."

Marda walked along the corridor, revising her speech. *Interesting*, she recited to herself, *I'll tell them we were very interested. Thank them for their contribution. Leave.*

She opened the door to the Communications Centre. It was the largest room on the ship, an open-plan workspace for technical communications specialists. At one end, she saw a huddle of mixed species working together. Then, a vast empty space. At the other end, by themselves, two individuals. She asked the nearest person, small and furred, where Taxie and Maxie were. The small person gestured to the end of the room. Marda began the long walk.

One individual said, "She's big. Looks clumsy. Think she might accidentally step …"

"Don't even joke about it," the other replied.

Marda tried to be objective, open-minded. The carapaces were lovely, silver and purple. The steel-grey barbed armoured tail, extending beyond and beneath the wings, swished to and fro. *They'll keep the carpet clean*, she thought. *And they are not very big, only knee high.*

Multi-faceted green gem-like eyes watched her, antenna trained in her direction. Mandibles clicked.

"Hi."

They looked.

"I'm Marda, Junior Psychologist. We've been looking at your proposals, Taxie and Maxie. Thanks for taking the interest to submit them."

"You gonna use 'em?" one individual asked.

"Well, we think they might be a bit intimidating to some below, but we're interested in the kinds of questions you thought would be asked. I was impressed with your insight."

"Told you they'd be too lily-livered to tell it like it is," rasped one creature.

"But you're gonna use the lottery idea to contact them, right?"

"There are some problems with that," Marda said. "First, there's the ticket distribution."

"No sweat," one said with an evil chuckle. "We could manage."

"And we don't have a million pounds or dollars or marks or euros or zlotys to give them."

"So?" Four many-faceted eyes looked at her blankly. "We lie."

"The demo website was dignified, statesman-like even. I think it will give the right signals to the people below. Beautiful work, absolutely first-rate."

"That's not us," one said contemptuously. "Ours would have had a lot more punch. We used some stuff from below. We had a thing based on this myth of four horsemen. Used some pictures by a couple of guys named Bosch and Blake. Nice stuff, flashing in and out. Put the fear of God into them, we say. Fear works. Webmaster said the animation would crash half the machines that logged on."

"They went for a stupid picture of the captain and crew smiling," the other said.

"But we're not proud. We'll take that piece of garbage and make it run. Not up to us, all species valuable and all the rest of that crap."

Marda said, "Making it run, now that's impressive. How do you plan on doing it?"

The two seemed to perk up. One antenna looped to a map and pointed at Australia.

"These bozos use microwaves. They don't need nearly as much capacity as they've got. We'll nip off some."

The other's antenna touched Europe, then North America. "Universities have allocated addresses. They only use part of the address. We borrow the top range, our interfaces sort 'em, collect all our messages at the gateways. Comes up here, neat as a hangman's knot."

"And it causes no problems to the universities in question. They get their mail."

"What about website crashing if too many people log on?" said Marda. "Sites I've looked at below have that problem. Will we?"

"No."

"Why not?"

"We're better than they are."

"Oh." Marda turned and trudged back across the room.

As she left, one muttered, "No vision."

The other answered, "It's the eyes."

LOCAL TIME: 5 JULY 2016

Marda and Heda sat in their office, considering the captain's announcement.

"Lemur and Leni as preliminary ambassadors. No one could find them threatening," Heda commented.

Short, thick, pale grey fur, less than twelve kilos in weight, shiny black button nose and eyes, long eyelashes. Marda giggled. "I was a child the first time I saw one of their species. I thought they were animated teddy bears, and I begged my daddy to buy me one. We were on the street, and I had a temper tantrum. My father was furious and apologised to the stranger while I kept screaming, 'But Daddy, it's so cute!' Do you think they'll notice the teeth and claws?"

"Cute is the more usual reaction," Heda said dryly. "If it were up to me, all communication would be via television." He shook his feathers. "I'd like to get Shiksla and the sea-folk back aboard and go home. I've got a bad feeling about this."

"What do you think will happen?"

Heda preened, cleaned a claw, and ruffled his feathers. "You know as well as I do the most probable state of affairs. They'll tell us to get lost. They will almost certainly seize, kill, and dissect our diplomats if we give them the chance. Then they'll shoot off a few of their missiles that we will ignore. We'll evacuate the sea-folk, with some loss of life. Then, when their seas die, we'll get an urgent communique asking for aid."

Marda was stunned. "But you can't be sure. That's such a stupid way to behave."

"Textbook patterns," Heda said tiredly. "Single dominant species with multiple, hierarchically organised subdivisions, which refuses to recognise the intelligence of other species. Historically, such a group has rarely been successfully contacted. But," he continued, "I may be wrong, and it's not the first time. Maybe it will go well."

LOCAL TIME: 15 JULY 2016

Marda and Heda sat with the rest of the crew, watching television from the planet below. Television stations throughout the planet flashed, and the national teams of Italy and Ireland disappeared from view. They were replaced by a small animal sitting in a comfortable armchair. He began to speak, his words transmitted in a multitude of languages.

"Hello. I greet you in the names of your brothers and sisters of the stars, the spaces between the stars, and the planets ringing the stars. I'm sorry to break into the game. We too are watching it, and like you will return to it shortly. But we wish to speak to the people of this planet, not your governments, not your leaders or politicians. You have a decision to make, you, the people of this place.

"We have been circling your planet for some time, learning your languages and your ways. There are over forty species on our ship. We belong to a great union, and we offer you membership in this union. Every species is valuable in its uniqueness; no species is unique in its value. What is possible for us to know and learn is a part of our skin, our bone, our blood. Other forms have other knowledge—knowledge we all need, we can all learn. Our forms make different things possible."

Heda remembered another contact, back when he was a student in the Linguistics Institute. It had been a major ceremony, one of the rarely held rituals celebrated by both space and planetary species. A skin had been discarded, outgrown, by one of the great serpents, a sun-singer, deep-dweller. This skin formed the exterior of the Union's space travelling vessels and was a gift to those who lived in the dark spots, the interruptions in the light, that they too might dance among the stars.

A gift impossible to reciprocate, Heda thought, *without return, like life itself.*

He and his fellow students had gone to the ceremony held outside the planetary atmosphere. The navigators appeared, heralds and guides, clustering lights who communicated in dance. He had begun by identifying phrases, segmenting the dance into its communicative memes: *Honour to the serpent, honour to those below who would construct the vessel.* They danced honour, mutual honour. Linguistics theory, training, and analysis became irrelevant as he himself was lost in the glory of the dance

We can communicate linguistically or aesthetically, Heda thought, *and aesthetics are as meaningful as any language.*

Then the serpent had arrived, accompanied by its singing spawn, bearing the shimmering skin. Heda remembered such beauty as they sang. It had filled him with sadness that he could not dance, could not sing. He could say nothing to the serpents or the navigators, so he had stood, radiating goodwill.

That, he thought, *is the history of my work. Find the syntax and vocabulary to radiate goodwill.* He prayed to gods in which he did not believe, *let them understand, let them respond.*

Marda leaned back in her seat, watching Heda anxiously. His feathers were ruffled, his crest was raised, and his eyes looked cloudy. She turned to Sipsa, gesturing.

"No," Sipsa whispered. "He's not ill. He's simply very old and very tired."

I love him, Marda thought. *I love him in the way I love my father, the uncles of my family and clan. In the small cosmic puzzle within the mind of the individual, a piece slipped into place. We celebrate diversity, but we love the sameness in us all.*

Heda noticed Marda's gaze. He shook himself, forced himself to stand tall, self-confident, and turned his attention to the speech. Leni was doing well, listing the conditions to be satisfied prior to Union Membership.

They'll never accept the habitat provision, Heda thought. *Most of the rest has been the subject of scientific debate on that planet for years. Our models will at least strengthen their hands, but they won't agree to dedicate large parts of their land surface to other species.*

Leni was finishing his speech. He announced plans for a televised and radio broadcast interview with the planet's journalists, described the prepared website, and gave its URL.

"In two years' time, 12 July 2018, we will return. You can announce what you as a species wish to do. If you wish to join the union, we expect you to have made progress in our demands regarding the rights of non-aware species. If, on the other hand, you have no interest in joining us, we will leave. It is your choice."

The broadcast ended. On board ship, the crew sighed, stretched, and looked at one another for confirmation that it had gone well.

"Now the reaction," Heda said.

The general reaction was inaction. Governments and news media said it was a hoax. News media competed to stage and format the interview with Leni. Marda received an email from Maxie/Taxie that said, "We coulda got a million whatevers from the TV or the tabloids, no problem, you short-sighted, two-eyed, big, fat bint."

Governments on the planet below were publicly notified of electromagnetic devices to disable air and sea transport in three remote ocean areas. Planes and ships were warned to remain outside these five square mile areas to allow evacuation to proceed.

The Great Cetacean Migration forced most of the world's governments to reconsider their dismissal of Leni's broadcast. China was silent. In the United States, some groups argued that only Man was created in God's image and these outsiders must be the spawn of Satan. Enough senators filibustered to prevent formal government action.

But governments are not people. Heda became slightly more optimistic at the purely human reactions. A Seaworld in California threw open its gates, and over a hundred thousand people cheered the departing dolphins and whales. Boats and a brass band accompanied them. As they swam out to meet their guides, one dolphin turned, and in recognisable English shouted into the television cameras, "So long." *Honk, honk, honk.* "And thanks for all the fish."

The Cetaceans travelled in a wedge formation, baleen elders in the V of the wedge, bull whales flanking and protecting the dolphins, females, and young in the middle. The Bards, to their disgust, travelled with the weak. "You must compose songs to last a thousand thousand years, that we may remember our birthplace and our exile."

They sang boastfully to hide their tears.

LOCAL TIME: 20 JULY 2016
Thirty heavily armed ships of poachers with air support attempted to slaughter a group of approximately two-hundred whales heading to the rendezvous point. A ship belonging to the New Zealand Navy attempted to defend the sea group and was damaged.

Then the Marines from the *Rangeron* showed up.

The poachers were sunk, and Marines and sailors working together stabilised the damaged vessel. The Marines were invited to "share a tinny" aboard the naval vessel before it limped home. The Navy was somewhat taken aback when the amphibians who had been working below the water line came aboard. Then two of the Marine ships flew back to the *Rangeron* to pick up some home-brew—you can't go to a party empty-handed. The Australian observer aboard was reassured: Salt-water crocs never show up with a six-pack.

At the end of the party, the New Zealand Navy was then invited by the Marines, who know good blokes when they see them, to observe evacuation in the South Pacific sector.

Those in authority aboard the *Rangeron* and in Wellington were horrified. Public pressure on board ship and in New Zealand required formal issuance and acceptance of the offer.

Australia, irritated at New Zealand swanking around, announced that while they had made no decision on the treaty as offered, they felt firmly in principle that those wishing to emigrate should be protected from criminal elements.

The New Zealand Navy and Air Force, Australian Air Force, and the Cook Islands Patrol Boat patrolled the primary South Pacific travelling routes of emigrating sea-folk, protecting them from attack. South African and Portuguese military forces coordinated northern protection.

The Canadian, Swedish, and Russian Navies offered protection along the Arctic Route. The Canadian Air Force, a Greenpeace vessel, and over two-hundred private yachts ignored U.S. Government inaction and accompanied the vast fleet of whales and dolphins migrating south, off the coasts of Alaska, Canada, Washington, Oregon, and California. At the Mexican border, they were joined by the Mexican Navy.

The Japanese Government formally apologised to passing Cetaceans and ex-whaling vessels provided veterinary care to the passing pods.

LOCAL TIME: 28 JULY 2016

Three space-going vessels, each over two miles in length, descended to the evacuation points and began taking in and detoxifying ocean water.

Inter-ballistic missiles aimed at the evacuating vessels were disabled by the Marines.

Three fishing vessels waiting at the point of evacuation were disabled by the New Zealand Navy.

LOCAL TIME: 29 JULY 2016

Whales, dolphins, and assorted sea-dwellers were successfully evacuated. Marines declined an invitation to another knees up but asked for a rain check.

"Next time," they said, "we'll throw the party—two years, mate."

Heda was optimistic. "We have to remember that species can learn. I'm starting to have a good feeling about this."

LOCAL TIME: 30 JULY 2016

E.V. *Rangeron*, Clan of Elgar, Flaxida went home.

THE END

WENONAH LYON is a retired anthropologist. She prefers fiction to fact because she likes happy endings. She currently lives in Canterbury, Kent, with a well-trained miniature schnauzer and an ill-trained husband. She has published essays, short fiction and poetry in *In Posse Review, Quantum Muse, Flashquake Fiction, Gator Springs Gazette, Dead Mule, New Maps, Ajax. FRIGG, Old Weird South,* and other online and print publications. There are links to these, and other short fiction, non-fiction and academic publications on her website: www.wenonahlyon.com.

A MATTER OF CONSCIENCE
Richard Mandrachio

1.
DESIRE

THE ENTITY WE HAVE become yearns to transform into a multicellular organism with specialized adaptations. Or, at least, for assimilation with one of the many multicellular organisms that inhabit this planet they call Earth.

Interstellar travels have taken us light years from the planetary system of our origin in NGC-4151 for the sole purpose of achieving these ends. Embedded deep within a rocky medium, we were shielded against harmful solar UV radiation and were able to withstand the freezing temperatures in transit. It also protected us during planetary ejection from our point of departure and enabled us to survive hyper-velocity entry from space through Earth's atmosphere, as well as final impact.

But even at that unfathomable distance, it had come into our scope of knowledge that there existed entities elsewhere with some semblance of intelligence. For eons we have been evolving into our present viral form, which has enabled us to span the mega-parsecs required to reach our destination; however, as an infective agent that consists of a molecule in a protein coat, we are able to multiply only within the cells of a living host. Our purpose in replicating is to allow the production and survival of our kind by generating abundant copies of our genetic material and packaging these copies into viruses, which are able to continue infecting new hosts.

We have attempted this in star systems of other galaxies but failed. And the craving to advance our species further has long been embedded in our collective consciousness, so our need is greater than ever. Therefore, we will take advantage of the first opportunity our new semi-aquatic environment presents, to connect with this unfamiliar lifeform.

The time is ripe to grow as one, by usurping a host body.

2.
ACTION

A MULTI-COLORED SPHERICAL OBJECT falls from nowhere, creates a disturbance in the puddle of liquid around us and allows this diminutive incarnation of ours to temporarily anchor to it.

Living flesh of a mammalian, carbon-based lifeform comes into contact with the round object, and we are in motion. We seek out the heat of this warm-blooded vertebrate and fasten ourselves to it, seeking a permanent port of entry. As the moisture around us dries, we discover a living orifice and enter, using ingress to embed ourselves in yet another aqueous medium, this one thicker and teaming with both light and dark cells.

The lighter ones treat us like the pathogens we are and try their utmost to fend off our invasion. First comes a secretion of harsh chemical agents that attempt to quell our disruption to the host body's normal physiology by simply confusing us. Though this secretion is easily overcome, we are not quite so prepared for the spontaneous growth, multiplication, and production of antibodies that get released and begin to stick to our current form. We feel smothered, but muster the strength to rally and destroy them.

Ultimately, these attacks fail because we keep reinventing new forms of deception, which cause our opponents to falter while attempting to unveil each succeeding disguise.

We have selected our sentient host and have achieved penetration.

3.
INTEGRATION

OUR FIRST DISCOVERY IS a revelation: The indigenous organisms have only four fundamental bases in their DNA, not seven as we do. So, we continue on course, all the while learning, deceiving, and fighting off cells as they attempt to engulf, absorb, and digest us, just as they do various forms of bacteria in our midst.

It soon comes to our understanding that, unlike our own replicative and mutative processes, this host has organs of reproduction along with others for the secretion of some form of nourishment. Is this an adaptation for production and nurture of offspring, an indication of gender, or both? Is this race multi-gendered or does it reproduce asexually?

Regardless, we come to realize that this particular host shows every indication that it has not yet grown to full maturity and thus has more than likely not yet come into its reproductive phase. Nonetheless, it will do for our immediate intentions and might even prove more susceptible to suggestion than a mature entity of this species.

Meanwhile, we continue our voyage through one of the larger passages into an area with extreme neural activity. The canal through which we traverse branches off into smaller ones until we reach a group of interconnected subcortical nuclei that appear to represent a fundamental processing unit.

By trial-and-error experimentation, we realize that we have gained access to the regulation of this entity's control center for motor activity, as well as for cognition and emotion.

We will insinuate ourselves deeper within. Our aim to dominate must not go unfulfilled.

4.
CONVERSION

AS THE LAW OF natural selection dictates, we now prevail as a colony. It took several mutations—minute changes in structure and function—to evolve to this state. We have accomplished it in a condensed version of millennia, at the accelerated rate of the metabolism of our homeworld's nitrogen-based life matrix; we continue to evolve into a structure that is carbon-based, to better adapt to those of this new, alien environment.

In the process, we have gained control of our host's actions and access to its undeveloped cognitive faculties and overindulgent emotional output. That the host has not mentally fought off our hold has provided us with an opportunity to learn of human interaction with the environment and amongst themselves.

Had we chosen a mature target, it might have acknowledged our presence and prevented us from reaching complete domination.

We find it curious, however, that this host decides to protect its integumentary system—from others like it or from its environment—with inorganic materials of an unknown origin that strictly conform to its shape and manifest as various textures in bright hues. The resultant sensory input is both foreign and sometimes pleasurable, albeit restrictive. Access also piques our curiosity regarding heat amplification when outside forces trigger "anger;" about liquid secretion resulting from "sorrow;" of the relationship between endorphin production and "joy."

Our control over it also gives rise to the question of what will become of our physical host when we no longer have need of it.

We will continue to adapt, to specialize.

5.
MUTATION

WE HAVE TAKEN ON a microbial guise—one that allows us the equivalent of breathing—and have rejected the photosynthetic pigment that lower lifeforms utilize. The aqueous medium in which we reside provides nutrients that fortify the physicality of our cell membranes, whose boundaries expand exponentially, thus becoming more efficient.

Via wave pattern recognition, knowledge has reached our awareness that the bacterium we have become is a threat to the well-being of the host body and will eventually destroy it. Should this be a concern when the evolution of our earthbound intelligence is on track and the only thing guiding that evolution is our survival? If each small step towards intelligence offers a survival advantage regardless of the consequence, then it is in our genetic programming to pursue it. In doing so, however, the possibility of genocide falls upon the collective if this bacterium were to replicate itself in humankind at an exponential rate.

Should this not be a concern when it is akin to what had happened to our species on our own homeworld? Are we as bad as the perpetrators of such xenophobic crimes, when all we are concerned with is our survival? After all, each human entity appears to have an individual personality that can solve complex problems and has an almost unlimited learning potential yet will engage in frivolous activities they call "play."

This revelation alone prompts us to recall the soft spherical object we first encountered and how it was, more than likely, being utilized for just such an activity.

Our progress is slow, our goal still attainable with tenacity.

6.
CONSCIOUSNESS

OUR NEW MANIFESTATION SUGGESTS a self-awareness. At least, it *feels* like an approximation of it. What is *feel* anyway? A sensory impulse? An innate biological signal?

These alien mental projections arrange themselves randomly, or so it seems. The host apparently operates in a mode that is beyond passively responding to incoming stimuli and learning by conditioned associations with these stimuli; instead, it takes an interactive part in probing and testing its surroundings and then evaluating sensory feedback. It's almost as though active output precedes the input of environmental stimuli because the host engages in a constant probing of its environment and assesses the sensory feedback *later* rather than just responding to a stimulus initially. It is a continuous, endless engagement of speculative extrapolation and experimentation.

For instance, when it reaches out for specimens of flora and/or fauna—some mobile, some stationery (are these types even sentient?)—the host seems to either have prior knowledge of the subject's reaction or just doesn't care. There are times when the host body exhibits elevated temperature in response to the sensual feedback it receives (is this revulsion?) and other occasions when there's an actual rise of endorphins, which trigger a semi-euphoric state of being that can possibly be interpreted as pleasure.

As far as "true" sensations, they must remain intangible, for only the needs of the hive mind should exist, call out to us.

And yet ... and yet ... there is something that registers as an approximation of *self,* that which is not of the collective. That self compels the acknowledgement of all things in a separate and distinct manner than that which is perceived by the *one mind.* It urges consideration of the condition of the host, of its relation to others of its kind, of its early stage in the time continuum and its desire for physical, intellectual, and spiritual growth. By what right do we have to seize that need, to interfere with that maturation process? Should I—yes, I think of my being as an "I" once again—not be concerned that our host in its innocence has devolved into a near-vegetative state due to our encroachment? This has become obvious due to the host body's digression in oral emanations and its inability to physically respond to aural oscillation input.

I am not with you. I am not. *I am.*

7.
ASSIMILATION

IF WE PURSUE OUR current course of development and continue to assimilate, what is to become of the denizens of this planet? The collective may benefit, may achieve new sensations in myriad host bodies, but at what cost?

Can it not realize the potential for ultimate harm to this species? Their memories, both personal and collective, will cease. They will no longer retain the ability to plan their individual courses, to deduce, to learn. Any sense of curiosity will become lost to them, even with regard to our infiltration of their entire race.

The "I" must make it aware of this even if it means relinquishing hold of our host before it is too late for their race. We must not continue our pursuit of dominion lest we become the same as those species that have infringed upon our own.

The "I" tells me this. Let it be so.

8.
RELINQUISHMENT

RUMBLING IN THE HIVE mind has all but overwhelmed the "I," but the separateness of my being continues to reject the force of the collective's will. As it does, there is the inkling of release in the host body, a dawning of recognition of its surroundings.

We access this information through the senses of the host, which inform its mind, and its mind, in turn, transmits signals to its biological processes, to fight off the invasive infection: us.

The collective is tenacious but cannot withstand the strength of the temperature the host body achieves, an unexpected shock. In the wake of the conflagration, the "I" feels the pain and anger of the dissolving collective, a wrenching apart not previously experienced or even known. Along with this feeling of separation (is this the emotion of "loneliness?"), however, comes the satisfaction of knowing the salvation of this alien race has succeeded.

Our dissolution brings a heretofore unknown reward to the "I": temporary peace. But this is by no means the ultimate finality.

THE END

RICHARD MANDRACHIO's debut novel, a paranormal thriller called *The Nexus*, was released under a pseudonym in December 2010 by *JMS Books LLC*. By 2014, they had also published the sequel, *The Abraxas Stone*, as well as a time travel novelette called *Dreaming Sparta*. Richard's short fiction has appeared in webzines such as *Aurora Wolf*, *Alien Skin Magazine*, *GuyWriters Magazine*, *Lame Goat Press*, and the *Library of Science Fiction and Fantasy*. His literary reviews have appeared in *The San Francisco Chronicle*, *Poetry Flash*, *The Sacramento Book Review*, and *theRumpus.net*. Annually, he serves as a judge for the Northern California Book Awards. Richard lives and works in San Francisco, California.

AFTERWORD

WE WOULD LIKE TO personally thank you for buying and reading this book. Producing this anthology has been, and continues to be, quite fulfilling for us and we hope that it is enjoyable for you as well.

Please consider taking a little extra time to help others find this book by leaving feedback where you purchased it. Your opinion about this book truly matters, both to our authors who have contributed to the anthology and to other readers.

If you have any questions, comments, suggestions, or just want to say hello, please visit our publisher's website on Indie Authors Press, www.salgado-reyes.com, and follow our publisher's Twitter: @Indie__Authors

Indie Authors Press